ON ACCOUNT OF BECAUSE

[BY]

KEITH B. HOWARD

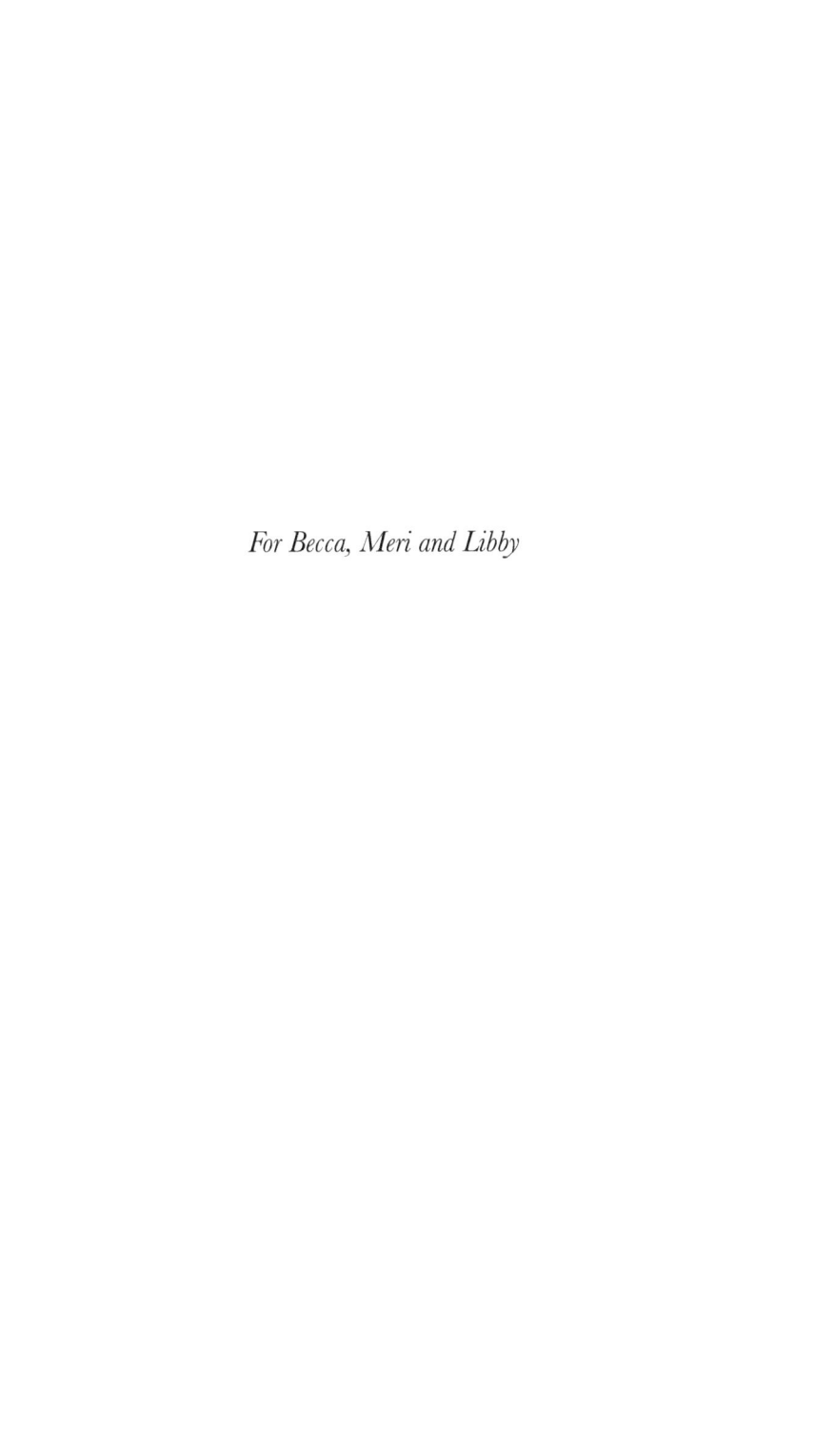

For Becca, Meri and Libby

" *It's not that you lied that has shaken my core.*
It's that I can't trust your word anymore. "

—Fred Nietzsche, German philologist
and Tom Sawyer fan

TABLE OF CONTENTS

In Sunday newspaper magazines, you'll see advertisements for family crests and mottoes. You know, a lion with crossed swords and a Latin phrase translated as "Faith with Honor," that kind of thing.

Up until six months ago, if I were going to order a family crest, it would have shown two crossed bottles of cheap fruit-flavored brandy, with a man passed out behind them, X's for eyes. A scroll would display a Latin phrase meaning "Used to It." I'd grown used to a lot of things—a drunk for a father, a runaway mother, moving from place to place every three or four months.

Things started changing about a year ago, though, when Rota Fortuna (and you'll learn a lot more about her) started spinning for me. My family crest and motto changed, too. Even my name was shortened, from Clayton to Clay Clevinger, which is a dud of a name either way, I know, but I didn't choose it. Before I tell you about my new life, though, you'll need to know about my old one, starting just about a year ago now.

* * *

It was the morning of my eighth-grade graduation, and Pops and I were staying, for the umpteenth time, with my grandparents, Gramper and Cookie, at their house in Mastricola, New Hampshire, a town without even a 7-eleven. I was excited about the ceremony, although I couldn't have told you why.

I had lived in Mastricola off and on for years, so I kind of knew some of the kids who were graduating, although I couldn't call any of them friends. Just knowing I had completed something made me happy, even if the something was only eighth grade.

I had learned at birth that nobody really cared if I were miserable, so I might as well be happy. I generally kept any happiness to myself, being afraid that Pops or fate would yank it away from me and smash it on the street like a pumpkin. I buried good feelings along with the bushels of bad feelings I'd been handed over the years. Maybe I was an emotional minefield, but it didn't really matter. I was used to it.

Pops drifted from job to job and I drifted with him from town-to-town, mainly because of his drinking, which came in binges. Guys who drink every day live under some pretty gray skies, but

Pops saved up his thirst and unleashed it like a hurricane. The forecast with Pops was ninety percent chance of sun, with a ten percent chance of gale-force winds, torrential rains and devastation.

I straightened my tie in the boys' room. I'd borrowed it from Gramper and he'd tied it twenty minutes before. He laid it around my neck like a ribbon or an award. Pops had promised to teach me how to tie a tie one of these days, but it was just one of many "one of these days" that never came. If I were going to learn, Gramper would have to teach me.

Usually, I tried to keep a blank expression. Some people probably thought I was wicked smart but keeping my opinion to myself. Other folks might have thought I was borderline retarded. Neither smiling nor frowning, my mouth remained the world's simplest horizontal connect-the-dots puzzle. One. Two. Done.

"Don't ever get too high or too low," I wanted my face to say. "You never know what's going to happen next."

I liked my eyes when I looked in a mirror, but I was the only one who saw them most days. I spent a lot of time staring holes in people's shoes.

Even though I'm a little short, I am muscular, because of a near-obsession with lifting a pair of twenty-pound dumbbells, found in a Boston dumpster. I didn't know anything about weightlifting, so I lifted and saw what worked. First, I made the exercise a habit, and then, after a while, the habit made me.

My name was not going to be called for any award. I wasn't in the program for sports or other extracurricular stuff. It didn't matter. I might still be a nobody from nowhere, but I would be a bona fide, genuine eighth-grade graduate.

Adjusting my tie one more time and thankful for the new khakis Cookie had bought me, I walked out to join the sixty-seven other graduates, milling around the cafeteria until we were called to line up for the march into the auditorium. None of the other kids looked for me. Not more than a handful even knew my full name. To most, I was just "that kid who moved back again," better than being "that fat, smelly kid" or "that slutty girl," but still not much.

I had been paired up with Kelsey Cahoon, known as "the girl with big boobs." Not "the girl whose uncle was a veterinarian who specialized in turtles." Not "the girl who can sign her signature equally well with either hand." Not even "the girl who can whistle 'Hello,

Dolly' like nobody's business." No, Kelsey, the first girl in our grade to develop breasts, bra straps apparent under her shirt by the end of third grade, would always be "the girl with big boobs."

To be fair, Kelsey did have huge breasts sitting guard over her equally large belly. Unfortunately for Kelsey, her breasts were more freak show than peep show. They scared me. I was no expert on big boobs, of course, or even small ones. I could barely talk to guys, much less hope to get inside some girl's shirt.

Kelsey's face was like a cow's, serene and blank. I couldn't imagine what anyone would say about Kelsey if she were to die today except, maybe, "for a girl with large breasts she was not very popular."

Not once in my years of wandering the planet had I walked into a room and had someone call out my name to join them. So I did what I always did, and searched the room for a few kids standing in a sort of group, not too close together, maybe one of them talking a little bit more and a little bit louder than the others. I found my target and walked over, not exactly to join the group, but close enough that someone looking over might think I belonged. Now, I would stand half-in, half-out, until we were called to graduation.

"I'll tell you what I'm going to do this summer," said the designated loudest, Frank something-or-other, who could burp both the alphabet and various swears. "My parents have a place on the lake and a speedboat. Every day I'll be out there waterskiing with the cutest girls on the lake."

Frank looked around at the faces, searching for jealousy I guess. I was pleased Frank looked at me too, making me, in my own mind at least, a member.

"That's nothing," said Rico LaPlenza, a pinch-faced boy wearing a three-piece suit. Most everyone else wore blazers and khakis. I just had my tie. Rico had a reputation as a lady's man. I'd overheard him tell about girls he'd done stuff with.

"I'm going off to Camp Mi-Te-Na for eight weeks. They've got archery, riflery, baseball and, best of all, weekly dances at Camp Foss with some of the hottest girls I've ever seen."

I tried to picture my summer, but all I could get was a haze and all I could feel was dizziness. When other kids talked about the future, they seemed so sure it would hold good things. All I knew was it would be different, and yet the same. When it came to uncertainty, though, I was used to it.

Mrs. Andrews, the assistant principal, came into the cafeteria and clapped her hands three times, like she was some preschool teacher. She cleared her throat. It was time to line up for graduation. Kelsey and I were near the front and I tried to think of something to say, but all I could come up with was, "So, how are your breasts on this fine June day?" which didn't sound quite right.

Even without anything to say, being paired with Kelsey was way better than marching in with a popular kid, who would have about twenty-five friends and relations cheering them when they walked in. Kelsey was unlikely to have more than a mother or father out there.

We'd walk out of the cafeteria, onto the back of the stage, then march double-file to the front, split up, boys to right and girls to left.

I knew Cookie and Gramper would be there, and figured Pops would be too. He'd been going to Alcoholics Anonymous meetings again, a good sign.

We walked onto the stage. I was wicked surprised at how nice the room looked, with congratulations posters on the walls and balloons everywhere. I saw Cookie, in a flower-print dress, and Gramper, in a black suit with his hat perched above his face. They smiled at me.

When I got to the front of the stage, I heard the voice I dreaded most, thick and slurred, and washed out.

"Would you look at the jugs on that girl," Pops shout- ed from the back, weaving back and forth in front of his seat. "Way to go, Clayton. Those puppies are huge!" Pops oozed himself into his seat, oblivious to the disapproving looks thrown at him by other kids' parents. Throwing himself back into the auditorium chair, he passed out, his head dropping over the back. Too far away to hear or smell, I still knew Pops was snoring and reeking of booze.

I guess I could have gotten angry.

I guess I could have cried.

Instead, I just accepted the obvious. Pops was drinking again.

After all, I was used to it.

The ceremony itself was as much a blur to me as it was to Pops. When it was over I blinked hard walking into the sunshine looking for Gramper and Cookie. They didn't say word one about Pops. It was weird, but the more noticeable Pops acted, the less we mentioned him.

We climbed into their old black Buick Park Avenue, a huge beast of a car without even looking back for a minute to see if Pops might need a ride. I sank back into the deep burgundy seat as if it were a recliner.

"That was a real nice graduation," said Cookie. "And you looked very handsome. You were easily the handsomest boy in the room."

"Thanks, Cookie," I said. "I'm mainly just glad it's over. Finally, I'm out of middle school and now I can spend the summer looking forward to high school. Pops was talking about looking for a job over in Oxford, so I guess we might be moving there."

"That's something we'll need to talk about when the time comes," said Gramper stiffly, although he kept a smile on his face. "Now, let's figure out what you might like for your graduation dinner. Lobster, steak, shrimp, whatever you say."

"I guess I'd like some hamburgers on the grill and maybe some of your potato salad, Cookie."

Cookie's potato salad was legendary in the neighborhood. She used two kinds of potatoes and three kinds of mustard, even making her own mayonnaise instead of using the bottled stuff.

"Potato salad, yes. But today calls for steak, not hamburgers. We'll also grill some corn and make that asparagus with Hollandaise sauce you like so much. And that's not something we're going to talk about. Period."

When Grammy Cookie spoke that way, I knew she was serious. I hadn't had any say in my own name, but I had named Cookie myself. "Cookie" had been my first word. I said it when I was one, reaching for one of her home-baked cookies. Even neighbors called her Cookie.

Now that we were back with Gramper and Cookie, things like dinner and clean clothes could be taken for granted. Sometimes I wondered how they could have raised Pops. For him, things like paying the rent and buying groceries were optional. Pops had been making noises about finding another job, but he made even talking about it a day's work in itself.

We were back with Cookie and Gramper because Pops was trying to get back on his feet again, having been fired in April from the horse track in Salem. As a joke, Pops had tried to feed one of the horses a bowl of dog food. Even though the horse hadn't eaten anything, any race horse was worth more than Pops. The owner demanded Pops be fired, which didn't bother Pops much at all.

"It just struck me as funny to turn a horse into a cannibal," said Pops when he came home from work. "No matter how fine a horse that might be alive, it's going to end up dog food eventually. I was just giving it a preview of its future, doing it a favor, really.

"They're all too uptight over there, anyway," Pops continued. "Just my luck to get mixed up with them. Bunch of morons. Anyway, getting fired is just nature's way of telling you that you had the wrong job in the first place."

From the dizzying smell of booze on Pops' breath, I doubted it was just showing that horse its destiny that got Pops fired. The job gone, Pops sat around our rented trailer, complaining about his bad luck and drinking until our money was gone. We called Gramper and Cookie to rescue us in the middle of the night, because the trailer's owner was threatening to take the back rent out of Pops' hide.

When Pops was sober, he was a quiet mouse of a man, with gray-speckled brown hair that hung down to his shoulders. His beard, which pretty much grew up to just under his eyes, was long. Together, all the hair gave him a Rip Van Winkle kind of look, like he'd just been awakened and didn't quite know what was going on. Even Pops himself probably couldn't remember what his chin looked like. On some men, all that hair could have looked tough or rebellious. Pops just looked like a man who didn't take care of himself.

Other than drinking buddies, who went away as soon as the booze was gone, or AA buddies, who disappeared as soon as the liquor came out, I never knew Pops to have any friends, or to even have acquaintances, really. I remember reading once that Willy Loman, was "liked, but not well-liked." It seemed like Pops was "tolerated, but barely tolerated."

He wore oversized brown tortoise-shell glasses, and hadn't had the prescription updated in years. Those glasses were always filthy, not just with grease, but with real dirt and eyebrow hair and stuff that I didn't even want to think about. I always wondered how Pops could possibly see anything through those things, but I figured there wasn't much that Pops wanted to see anyway.

He almost always wore the same blue overalls with one button unbuttoned and the bib folding itself into a triangle. He thought that showers were overrated, and he always had a distinctive odor, which I thought of as the smell of death. What with his dried sweat, dirty clothes and the three packs of cigarettes he smoked every day, many people thought he was homeless.

If Pops sat on a bench, kind-hearted strangers sometimes offered him spare change and he would always take it. A funny thing about Pops, though, was that if a man gave him a quarter, he'd thank him like crazy, but if the guy gave him a dollar, Pops would curse him out for not giving up everything in his wallet.

When Pops drank, he was an obnoxious back-slapper, calling all men "buddy" and all women "babe." People often talk of happy drunks and angry drunks. I always thought it was more like likeable and unlikable drunks. Pops was the undisputed king of the second group. The best thing I could ever see about Pops drunk was that he always passed out pretty quickly.

I was used to the fact that Pops could only hold a job for so long before either the boss man, his co-workers or the work itself became impossible. Either he would quit or he'd be fired. Then he'd stay at home drinking until a week or so after the last paycheck was gone.

During these times, Pops would look back over his life, spotting time after time when luck had failed him. No matter how long he searched, he'd always find a sign of luck's unfairness, but never see any of his own mistakes. Pops had an almost religious faith in his bad luck and he liked nothing better than showing me times he had been a victim of life's circumstances.

"If only I could find a boss who would understand me and my problems," Pops would say, "instead of always harping on me. If I could get just one shot of luck in my life, the way other folks do, things could be different. It's not like I want my luck buttered. I'll take a hard, dry piece of good luck and be thankful."

I had my own theory on luck, but I never bothered to tell Pops about it. It seemed to me luck just kind of flowed to people who took care of their responsibilities first and let pleasure find them later. Pops liked to drink first and then hide out from responsibility. He would chart out his bad luck, being a cartographer of failure. Once

Pops had fully reviewed his ill fortune, we usually ended up back at Cookie and Gramper's.

A local beauty as a girl, Cookie, now more than seventy, still carried herself like a woman accustomed to having a full dance card, as they used to say. From the pictures on her walls, you could see Cookie's different stages of beauty. Cookie's high school graduation picture shows her looking away from the camera, her face telling you that if you could look into those eyes you'd probably be in heaven. When she got married, ten years later, she looks up into the sky as if God Himself was begging to get a look at her. In a portrait taken on her seventieth birthday, even though she was a lot heavier than she'd been in the earlier pictures, she still carries herself like a queen. Each time I look at her, staring into the camera, she seems to be saying "life has not been easy for me, but, look, I have maintained my dignity."

I'd once read that the mark of a genius was the ability to simultaneously hold contradictory beliefs. If that was true, then Cookie was right up there with Einstein.

As a grandmother, Cookie had been great; she was always available emotionally and physically. She had nursed me when I was sick as a very little boy. She played games with me. She had tried to teach me right from wrong; there, unfortunately, was the rub.

While Cookie was a good and decent woman, she had tried to instill in me her core belief: Ted Kennedy was evil, stupid and deluded. In fact, anyone who didn't look down and spit on the ground when his name came up was suspect in Cookie's eyes. While World War Two might have ended for the rest of the world in nineteen-forty-five, for Cookie it still raged on in the convoluted form of her hatred of Catholics in general, who were the linchpin behind every evil act in history, from natural disasters to the Holocaust to Pops' drinking, and Ted Kennedy in particular.

Cookie had developed the seed of her hatred for Catholics growing up as a Protestant in a New Hampshire mill town filled with Catholic immigrants. The only daughter of a schoolteacher and his wife, Cookie had been shy as a girl. She told me many times how the immigrants stuck to themselves and how alone she had felt until Marie Goldstein moved to town.

Marie was the only Jewish child in town, her family having escaped Nazi Germany, when Marie was an infant, on the heels of the opening of both the Dachau and Buchenwald concentration camps. Her father had worked in a mill in Germany, so he found work easily in Cookie's hometown.

Cookie regularly told me how she and Marie became best friends, with Marie learning English through their play. The girls formed a universe of two, keeping even their other family members out. The two of them made elaborate plays together, which they performed for only themselves.

As it happened, Marie died of consumption, or tuberculosis, a year later, probably contracted because of poor nutrition and living conditions as a younger child. The death, of course, struck Cookie deeply. In her grief and despair, she somehow combined the evils of Nazism with Marie's death with the fact that believers surrounded her; out of this cauldron came deep and vicious hatred of Catholicism.

"They say it was consumption that took Marie, Joseph," Cookie had said on her first date with the man she would eventually marry, "but you know who really killed that sainted girl, don't you?"

"Why no," Joseph responded.

"It was the Catholics. They're evil and dumb as dirt. Take the so-called 'Immaculate Conception.' You ask your typical Catholic about it and they think it's about the virgin birth of Jesus. That's a crock. That evil church tries to keep it a secret, but it really means that Mary herself was born without sin.

"Now, it's hard for a reasonable woman to swallow that there was *one* sinless baby born two-thousand years ago, but the Catholics want us to believe that Jesus was just a follow-up act to his own mother

"That's how stupid and evil they are."

Over time, Cookie's hatred had deepened and refined itself with a laser-like intensity, so that while she disliked all Catholics, she had homed in first on Catholic politicians at which to direct her ire. From among the many senators and congressman who were Catholic, she had focused on the Kennedy family. When even this was too broad a brush, she chose as her target Edward Moore Kennedy. Teddy Kennedy was, to Cookie, evil personified. By the time I was born, all of Cookie's anger had been focused on Teddy Kennedy for long enough that she not only connected him with the death of that poor Pennsylvania girl he had drowned, she also pictured him at Marie Goldstein's death bed, strangling her and laughing while

guzzling from a bottle of expensive scotch.

Although a sensitive woman in general, Cookie can tell the coarsest stories imaginable if they involved the senior senator from Massachusetts.

"Why did Ted Kennedy spend three hours in the voting booth, Clayton?"

"I don't know, Cookie."

"Because he thought it was a confessional. He knew that he had more sin and blood on his hands than any hundred other men combined, and he was so stupid he thought some priest could forgive his sins."

Once she got started, she could go on for hours, always followed by a lengthy sermon on the evil of the family. It was the closest to catechism I ever received.

"Clayton, how many Kennedys does it take to screw in a light bulb?"

"I don't know Cookie."

"Two. One to hold the light bulb, and one to drink until the room spins. You see, Clayton, Ted Kennedy was an alcoholic, just like your father, although your father has never murdered some poor Pennsylvania girl by driving off a bridge drunk. That's the way the Kennedys do it, you know."

Gramper still believed Cookie the most beautiful woman in the world. He had pulled off a great victory in getting her to marry him. She was his first and only love.

Retired from the post office now, Gramper did odd jobs around the neighborhood.

During World War II, while the fighting and dying went on in Europe, Asia and North Africa, Gramper served his country at the Oakland Army Terminal, making dentures for soldiers shipping out to the Pacific Theater. Personally, Gramper said, he thought it would have made more sense to fix teeth when a soldier was mustering out, sort of a going-away present. Instead, Gramper toiled away to fix the smiles of men who might have nothing to smile about ever again. Leaving good-looking corpses throughout the Pacific seemed an odd way to do his part. Still, it got him a veterans' preference, which got him into the post office, which got him a chance to marry Cookie.

* * *

I remember when I was six, and we lived with my grandparents for six months. Cookie took me to the Well Child Clinic for free immunizations, check ups and all that stuff. Each time, we played games there.

Sometimes it was "Hide the Penny," where one of us closed our eyes and the other hid a penny in the waiting room. The finder followed "warmer" and "colder" to find the coin.

We also told jokes. My all-time favorite joke at the time:

"Cookie, I bet you don't even know how to spell your own name."

"Sure I do."

"Okay, spell it."

"C-o-o-k-i-e."

"Nope. You spelled 'cookie,' and I told you to spell 'it.' I-t."

In the waiting room were copies of "Ranger Rick" and "Children's Digest" and "Highlights for Children," with their rip-out subscription cards. I knew only rich people got those magazines. No kid at the free clinic thought about ripping one of those cards out.

It was "Highlights" I liked, looking at snapshots of normal. I'd thumb through "The Bear Family," look at the pictures kids my own age had drawn, realizing even at six I had already fallen behind. My favorite feature, though, was "Goofus and Gallant."

It wasn't clear whether Goofus and Gallant were brothers or classmates or complete strangers. They divided every moral or ethical decision into two possibilities. You could do the right thing like Gallant, the happy kid who loved to please authority, or the wrong thing, like Goofus, who was angry except when he was laughing at bad things happening to other people.

I knew Gallant was who I should follow, and I tried to. Still, I also knew, deep down, expecting life to treat you well because you are a good person is like expecting a wild bear not to kill you because you are a vegetarian.

I thought of Gramper as a grown-up Gallant. Gramper said all it takes to be happy is to have something to do, someone to love, and something to hope for. He kept busy, he loved Cookie and me, and he walked with a hopeful bounce.

My life didn't have a whole lot of other Gallants. It was overrun with Goofuses, from my mother when she had been around to Pops

to the kids who teased at school.

"Gallant sees a new student and invites him to sit down in the lunch room" but "Goofus sees a new student and makes fun of the boy's accent and clothing."

"Gallant notices his elderly neighbor's lawn covered with leaves and rakes them for her, not accepting any money" but "Goofus notices his elderly neighbor's lawn covered with leaves and tells her the yard is an eyesore, but he will clean it up for twenty dollars."

"Gallant plays nicely with his younger sister, helping her build block castles and praising her for good work" but "Goofus kicks his younger sister's block castle apart and teases her when she cries."

I felt like my life was one big example of Goofusness run wild and I wished I could meet just a few more Gallants.

* * *

Overall, the latest stay had gone well, but with Pops' getting drunk at graduation, I figured this visit would be ending, giving Pops another site to visit when he strolled down Hard Luck Lane.

When we got home, I helped Gramper start the fire in the grill, and we waited for the coals to turn from black to white.

"Clayton, there's something I want to talk to you about," said Gramper, poking at the briquettes with a stick. "And it's not easy for me to say."

"What is it, Gramper?"

I was terrified that Gramper was going to try to tell me about the birds and the bees. I'd heard the outline on the back of a school bus in third grade, and had done some book and magazine research into the subject later on.

"It's about the future. Your future," Gramper said. "You're a smart boy and a good boy and you deserve to have some stability during your high school years.

"And, much as I love my son, your father, he is no more stable than a Golden Delicious in an apple-bobbing contest. Life is a grindstone. Your father has chosen to let it grind him down instead of polishing him up. You deserve better."

I'd never really thought of myself as "deserving" anything. I tried to accept life as it got served up. I tried to be like Gallant, Goofuses surrounded me, and that, pretty much, was that.

"So, your grandmother and I have talked about this for a long time. We are both getting older and don't need this big house any longer. We are placing the house for sale soon and moving to a two-bedroom apartment in Plattsfield, probably by Christmas. While we can't promise to take care of you forever, we'd like you to live with us for the next four years, until you finish high school."

"I don't know, Gramper," I said. "Pops and I have barely ever lived in one place four months, much less four years. I'm not sure Pops would be able to stay put that long. And a two-bedroom apartment might be a little too small for the four of us."

"This is not an offer to your father, Clayton. It is strictly an invitation to you. Your father has, quite honestly, been a disappointment to me since he was your age. I learned a long time ago you don't drown by falling in the water, you drown by staying in the water. Your father is drowning, but he has no reason to drag you with him."

"He dropped out of school in tenth grade and ran off. He got your mother pregnant, but he couldn't hold on to her, not that she was such a prize package. He has gotten no further training and he is now incapable of providing for you properly.

"Without wanting to betray any confidences, Clayton, I can tell you throughout your childhood your grandmother and I have tried to *guide*, shall we say, your father in his raising of you. He has chosen not to take our advice, nor, except monetarily, accept our help. In addition to his other shortcomings, he is a very proud man. But pride without portfolio is empty. Still, he is your father, and I do not wish to speak ill of him any further.

"Unfortunately,' Gramper continued, unable to stop himself, there is also the problem of his drinking. You don't have to give me an answer now to the question of moving in with us. Just think about it."

"Sure, Gramper."

The size of this offer grew in my chest. The idea of life without Pops was hard to fathom. He wasn't the greatest father—when you came down to it, he was pretty lousy—still, life with Pops was all I'd known. I was used to it.

As we tended the fire, I drew on the only moral compass I had.

"Goofus betrays his father, who loves him, and goes to live with his grandparents, just because they've got a home and money and don't drink."

"Gallant moves in with his grandparents, to help them and perhaps to set an example for his own dear father."

"Gallant recognizes his father truly needs him and, despite his personal loss, sticks by him no matter what."

"Goofus ditches his father, a drunken loser who can't hold the jobs he doesn't like and can't find a job he likes."

This last piece, liking work, had always bothered me. It just seemed so unnecessary. I mean, if you're going to change jobs every few months, shouldn't you go to a job you liked not trade one dead-end boring position for another?

Pops was only happy about work for eight weeks every year, from mid-August until mid-October, when, in addition to working whatever laborer job he might or might not have, he worked the New Hampshire county fair circuit.

He'd start with the tiny North Haverhill Fair at the beginning of fair season to the big Sandwich Fair that closed the season. Pops would sign up as a casual worker, and the fair organizers would direct him to someone who was driving from where he lived. Pops would make a phone call or two to arrange for a ride to come by on Friday afternoons and Saturday and Sunday mornings to take him to the week's fairgrounds.

Before I was born, Pops had been a traveling carnival worker, a carny, for seven or eight years and he would sometimes tell me what it was like in the old days, about life on the road in small-town America. Most of these stories starred people named "Oklahoma Red" or "Fertilizer Phil" and the funny things they had done when they were drunk in a tiny burg in Arkansas or Pennsylvania.

"Clayton," Pops had once said, during the tiny window between his first drink and his being drunk. "The carnival life is no life for a child. That's why your mother and I quit when you were born. Children aren't made for the constant moving, the hard work and the long hours.

"Time gets turned on its head in a carnival. You're constantly going from ten in the morning until midnight or later and there's no such thing as a day off. When I was a First of May myself, I once asked an older carny, 'When do we get to sleep?' and he said to me, 'Not until the season's over.'

"Nope, that's no life for a little child. Still and all, life on the road with a carnival can be a little taste of heaven for a young man, a little taste of heaven. It's a chance for a man to see the world, meet people you wouldn't otherwise meet. I wouldn't have met your mother if it weren't for the carny life."

Here, dreaminess came into Pops' voice. Whenever Pops talked about my mother, I hated the affection in his voice. When I was three I had given her all my love; now that she was gone, all I had left was hate. I'd heard this story a bunch of times, and was tired of the way it made this woman I didn't have much use for sound like some kind of saint. Still, I knew he was going to tell it anyway, so I just sat back to let it roll over me.

"I remember one morning in August we'd just pulled into this tiny little town in Ohio, Duncan Falls, population no one, hardly. It was in Muskingum County, just southeast of Zanesville," Pops said.

To me, whose traveling had consisted of moving around Boston and various small New Hampshire towns, Pops might just as easily have been saying, "It was the little village of Elysium, right northeast of Xanadu."

Still, other than the story of how Pops had met Lucinda Watkins, I always really liked to hear Pops talk about his carnival days. His eyes got a certain brightness that I wasn't used to and his voice carried some excitement for once.

"I was, what, twenty-five or twenty-six, just rolling in alfalfa, because there wasn't much to spend your money on. Hell, we wouldn't leave the carnival for days on end. You'd get a buddy to buy carton of smokes and maybe a couple bottles of blackberry brandy and you were all set. Food we'd just get from a friend working a cart. Nothing like a sausage sandwich with onions and peppers and brown mustard for dinner, followed by fried dough and cinnamon sugar for dessert. That's living, I tell you.

"I remember the carnival owner said we could burn the lot, just take the town for what it was worth, because we'd never be back there again. I was working a jenny at the time, one of those real old-fashioned merry-go-rounds, and I needed to get it set up before the marks poured in.

"Anyway, there we are in this one-horse town, when I look up from the greasy underbelly of the jenny. I must have been a sight, covered with oil and dirt, but there, Clayton, right in front of me I saw the most beautiful girl in the entire world standing there, waiting to take a ride as soon as I had the contraption put together.

"She was only seventeen, and wearing a black R.E.O Speedwagon t-shirt and cut-off jeans, cut off way up her thighs. She had huge red hair and the most beautiful blue eyes, with blue eye shadow to set them off. I told her she was so beautiful, she didn't have to pay, that if she'd give me five minutes to finish up, I'd let her ride free. She just smiled the prettiest smile.

"The minute she climbed onto that chipped red horse and I got the jenny going, I turned to my buddy, Michigan Slim was his name, and said, 'No more dirty magazines for me. I'm going to get that girl.

"Well, that pretty little girl was dying to get out of her hometown, and she became a carny herself. It took some time, a couple of years, and I wasn't the first man she'd been with, not by a long shot, but eventually I made her into your mother, Lucinda Watkins."

Here, Pops would wave around the walls of whatever apartment we were living in. On them were always four needlepoint creations, one for each season, in dime-store quality black frames. Winter, for example, was a needlepoint of snowmen and children sledding down a hill with "Merry Christmas" in red and green letters. Spring was a collection of flowers of no particular type, waving in a field with a sun shining down on them.

I guess the pictures were nice enough, but I couldn't see the difference between the craft of needlepoint and the art of painting by numbers.

"Each and every one of those was done by your mother," Pops would say with pride. "She has always been quite an artist, could have gone pro if she'd wanted, and needlepoint was what she liked doing best. I suspect she could have put those in a museum."

These days, Pops got his carnival fix for eight weekends running at each of the New Hampshire fairs. Sometimes he would run into carnys he had known back in the day, and almost always there was a friend of a friend to catch Pops up on carnival news and gossip.

Like some baseball player called back for an Old-Timers' Game, Pops would go to the fairgrounds and rub shoulders with the same kind of men he had traveled with when he was younger and a genuine carny. He would relive his youth by cleaning manure out of livestock areas or tearing tickets at a front gate or running ride.

Even during the years we lived in Boston, Pops had always found some way to work the fairs, even if it meant quitting the job he was currently holding, or honestly, especially if it meant quitting a job.

While Pops had no real marketable skills, he did have a number of talents that a fair could use. He could spot a pickpocket with accuracy. He could prepare a ring for horse riding. He could keep on eye on drunken teenagers on the midway to make sure they didn't try to steal anything or pass out in a public place.

Pops could even fix rides, because when he'd been a carny, everyone had been a jack-of-all-trades. If a ride broke down in Orangeburg, South Carolina, you couldn't just go to the Yellow Pages and look under carnival ride repair. You had to be able to fix whatever ride you were working.

Yep, at a fair Pops was useful. At a fair, he was somebody who mattered. At a fair, Pops looked men in the eye instead of staring a hole in the ground. Throughout the year, I looked forward to fair season, so that for once I could look with pride on Pops, instead of averting my eyes in shame.

* * *

My thoughts were disrupted when Pops stumbled up the driveway, having walked from the school. He had the embarrassed grin he got when drunk, a look that seemed to say, "I know I've made a big mistake, but what choice did I have?"

"Where's my boy? Where's my scholar?" Pops asked, weaving slightly on the grass, waves of alcohol drifting off him. "Sorry about this afternoon. I guess I was pretty tired and all the emotion must have gotten to me. Just my luck to take a nap at your graduation. Really sorry."

In some families "please" is the magic word; in ours, the magic word was "sorry."

"C'mon Clayton, give your old man a hug. What, now that you've graduated eighth grade you're too big to hug your father?"

Pops' lit cigarette fell out when he spoke. With the deliberateness of a man trying to convince others he is sober, he bent to look for it. Once he spotted it, though, the booze in his system attacked his fine motor skills. He picked up the burning end of the butt, immediately dropped it and stood up, keeping his back falsely stiff. He tried to be invisible as he stepped on the cigarette and ground it out.

"Damn thing bit me," he said, laughing and pulling another ciga-

rette out of a mostly empty pack in the pouch pocket on his overalls. Appearing to recognize that lighting a cigarette might be even more challenging than picking one up, he tried to put it back in the pack, breaking off the filter.

He held his arms out, apparently expecting that I would ignore his drunkenness and hug him.

"C'mere, Clayton," he slurred. "I said I was sorry. How 'bout little love for your old man, huh?"

I was torn. On the one hand, I wanted to hold Pops, if only to keep him from begging again. On the other hand, Gramper's words were in my head. I imagined making a floating apple into a lifeboat.

"That was fine graduation, Clayton," Pops said, hands back at his side, "Real fine, and you looked good, real good and that little filly you were walking with sure had a nice pair . . ."

"Enough, David!" Gramper's voice boomed. "That will do! You've been drinking and you're behaving like a horses' ass!"

"Aw, Dad, I'm just playing around. Don't be so serious all the time. Just lighten up for once. I had couple drinks is all."

Pops voice sounded hurt, with a sense of injustice that people would think he had been drinking when he had been drinking.

"Dad, I can still talk a straight line. I mean, I can walk in complete sentences. Aw, heck. Well, one good thing about having a couple drinks is can't fall off the floor. Now Clayton, how about that hug?"

Pops again held his arms out, closing his eyes slowly. I looked at Pop, then at Gramper, then at the ground.

Most fathers must inspire either fear or love with their actions. Pops, however, chose a third route: humiliating embarrassment.

"Gallant sees his father's desperate need for love. Although Gallant disapproves of the man's actions, he holds him closely and lovingly."

"Goofus is disgusted by his father's existence and pushes him to the ground, easy to do because his father is drunk."

"Gallant holds his father tightly, and guides him to bed."

"Goofus puts his father to bed roughly, then goes through his wallet, swearing at him when he finds the old man has spent all his money"

Luckily, I didn't have to decide anything, because Pops decided for me. Without a nod, Pops buckled, dropped to his knees and threw up on the grass. He passed out, face down in his own vomit.

"Just think about our offer," Gramper said.

Together, the two of us rolled Pops over and cleaned him up the best we could. Gramper dragged his body into a flowerbed. I looked onto Pops' face, and then up into Gramper's. I guess evolution doesn't mean things get better, just that they survive.

After Gramper and Cookie went to bed, I brought a light blanket outside, tucking one end under Pops' feet and pulling the other end up to cover his head. After a moment, I folded the blanket back down, revealing his face. I realized then if I'd had two coins, I would have happily used them.

Pops never really gave me any kind of religious instruction or training. Besides cursing his own bad luck, and the good luck of others, Pops didn't appear to believe in much of anything himself. Still, I found a way to learn from the flotsam and jetsam that the universe sent my way.

From when I was seven until near my tenth birthday, we lived in Boston, where Pops had found occasional, but sometimes lucrative, work on the so-called "Big Dig," the building of a tunnel under Boston Harbor. Pops had no real trade or skills; he was a lifelong laborer who would show up where a lot of tradesman worked, and try to find something that needed to be done.

When in Boston, I found the warmth and dryness of neighborhood public libraries a better place to be than whatever semi-furnished apartment we were living in, particularly when Pops was drinking. To earn my keep in the libraries, I had read widely, deeply and until my eyes dried out, reading without a filter beginning when I was seven. I didn't have anyone to tell me what was good or bad or why. I just learned to trust my gut. The stuff I liked was good and the stuff I didn't like I didn't read.

I remember loving Dr. Doolittle, the veterinarian who could talk with animals, and Chitty, Chitty, Bang, Bang, the talking car who could fly, and Wilbur, the pig who was "some pig."

I also enjoyed reading about Homer Price and his donut machine, and Henry Huggins and his dog, Ribsy, and even Ramona and Beezus, the sisters who fought on Klikitat Street, although their lives seemed to have less connection to mine than straightforward fantasy did

For a two-year period, though, during second and third grade, I loved stories, self-contained ones that lasted only three to five pages. Bre'er Rabbit and Aesop's fables and fairy tales had made up most of reading for that time.

In the middle of third grade, I had completed the obvious children's stories, so I asked Miss Fauth, the librarian at the neighborhood library, where I could find some more stories to help fill my afternoons.

"I'm not sure what stories we've got left that you haven't read," the attractive young brunette said. She smiled down at me, and I wished Miss Fauth could be my mother, although Pops said Mommy was in heaven, watching down on me every day.

She had just disappeared one day when I was three; she had re-appeared briefly four years later, and then disappeared again. Pops had never explained her resurrection, but Pops had never been one for explaining. I just accepted that it was easier for Pops to believe that Lucinda Watkins was dead. When you came down to it, there wasn't much difference between being dead and simply having run away to Utah or Nevada or wherever she had ended up. When it came to unsolved mysteries that held no interest, I was used to it.

With Lucinda Watkins dead to me, I was free to create a mother out of any nice woman who happened along. That way, instead of being stuck with just one mother, who didn't appear to care much about me, I had found dozens of mothers who, in my fantasies, adored me.

"Whatever you've got, Miss Fauth," I said politely, eyes cast down as always. "I'm not that particular so long as it's a good story."

"You come back tomorrow," she said with a grin. "I'll do my best."

When I got there, Miss Fauth had set aside a pile of possibilities, most of which I'd had already read. I had consumed Russian and Italian and German stories over the previous year, and the one in the pile I hadn't read was a slim book called *Zen Stories*. I thanked the librarian, and disappeared to the comfiest seat in the children's room, where I read about this old farmer whose horse ran away. When they heard the news, his neighbors came by to offer their condolences.

"That's terrible," they said, sympathetically. "What awful news."

"Could be," the old man said philosophically. "Could very well be."

The next day, the old horse came back, bringing with it three wild horses. Again, his neighbors came by, this time to offer congratulations.

"So, virtue is rewarded," they said. "What excellent news."

"Could be," the old man said. "Could very well be."

The next day, the old man's son tried to break one of the wild horses, but was thrown off and broke his leg. Again, the neighbors came by to commiserate.

"Oh, what a terrible thing has happened to your son," they said. "This is horrible."

"Could be," the old man said. "Could very well be."

The next day, army recruiters came by to draft all military-age men to go to battle, but because the son's leg was broken, he was spared. Again, the neighbors came by to congratulate the old man.

"Your son will not have to risk his life," they said. "What wonderful news."

"Could be," the old man said. "Could very well be."

The story then abruptly stopped, but three dots and a number eight on its side followed it. At school the next day I asked Mrs. Zelonis what three dots meant.

"It's called an ellipsis," she said gently, kneeling down to put her face at my level. "It usually means that something has been taken out, but sometimes it can mean that the story is going on or is going to be continued."

"What about an eight on its side?" I asked.

"An eight?"

"Well it looks kind of like an eight. Let me draw it for you."

I made the symbol on a piece of paper on her desk.

"Oh. That is the symbol for infinity," she said. "Infinity is never ending."

"So, three dots and an eight on its side could mean that something is going on forever?" I asked

"Why, yes. I guess it could," said Mrs. Zelonis, a look of surprise crossing her face. "But now it's getting to be time for math." I have thought about that farmer and his son ever since, and have made up a series of continuing good news and bad news situations. Even in real life I had tried to convince myself that things that seemed at first like bad news could actually be good news, a notion for which I had a hard time finding examples. It took no effort to convince myself that good news could turn bad, because my entire life was evidence of that. Lying in bed at night, I would spin the story good to bad to good to bad.

It was about this time that I started having visitors in my room when I was going to sleep. I would close my eyes, and at first objects would appear and mutate, so that brown ooze would be transformed into a river and a pattern in the river's swirl would become a goat, but a friendly goat. This swirling chain of flashing images was like the trailer for the real movie.

If I was patient, managing to float lightly without drifting into sleep, then, one by one, the letters of the alphabet would wander in

and entertain me. Soon, I was making friends with the letters.

Unable to sleep, I would summon the alphabet to come and talk with me. I could talk telepathically with them, if I just concentrated without concentration.

Each letter had its own personality.

"A," for example, was daring and brave, willing to go to the ends of the world for a noble cause.

"X," on the other hand, was a hypochondriac, always complaining of vague symptoms and generally feeling under the weather.

"M" was a bore who would sit on my pillow and tell long, pointless stories, then trail off before even finishing them.

"T," though, was my favorite, because she spoke in an Irish lilt, and sang lullabies to me as I lay in bed. Oftentimes, she would wrap her soft, loving arms around me until I was fast asleep. Then she would kiss me on the forehead before disappearing until the next night.

It may be that at an early age we decide whether life has no miracles or life is all miracles. We decide whether to curse the rose for having thorns or bless the thorns because they have roses. I always feared that the first was the case, but tried to live as if the latter were true.

During the day, I might not have any friends, but once it was time for bed, I was the most popular kid in his room. The letters would dance around, sometimes putting on musical shows for me, sometimes arguing over which was my favorite and sometimes just pulling the covers over me when it was time to sleep.

Gramper and Cookie and I sat at the picnic table in their yard, waiting for Pops to rouse himself. I felt like a traitor, knowing Pops was in the flowerbed around the corner. The only sounds were a bird in a tree and Gramper buttering his toast.

Cookie broke the silence.

"Clayton, did your grandfather talk with you yesterday about our offer?"

"Yes, Ma'am."

When I was born, Cookie had told me, she started forgetting the bad things Pops had done to make space in her brain for all the amazing things that I would do. Now, though, her son's sins sat again at center court.

"And?" she asked.

"I just don't know. Four years is a long time. I don't know if I could live without Pops, and I really worry about whether he could live without me. It would break his heart if I stayed here. Plus, if he keeps on drinking he'll need some help from me. And if he's not drinking then maybe our lives could get better."

"Clayton Clevinger," Cookie said sharply, "When it comes to being a good father, my son is so far over his head he might as well be on the Titanic. Your father's drinking is his problem, not yours. You can't throw your high school years away to be a nursemaid to a drunk. Your grandfather and I are tired of his drinking. Not just because of him but because of its effect on you. We're going to give him an ultimatum. Today. 'Quit drinking completely or move out!' But we want you to stay."

"Yes, Ma'am."

Pops walked from the side of the house, his eyes at half-mast. Pops looked at the grass as he slowly weaved across the lawn. He almost fell as he dropped onto the picnic table and gestured for a cup of coffee. He took small sips of the coffee, repeatedly licking his lips. No one said a word and he stared at the table.

"Well," Pops said after a minute. "That's enough of that business. I've got to find that little man and give him what for."

Without looking up, Pops laughed. When no one asked him to explain, he continued.

"That little man who tells me to drink, and then when I do drink he comes around and takes a crap in my mouth when I'm sleeping,"

Pops said. "I'm gonna get that guy."

Pops had told me a bunch of times he was plagued by an invisible little man, dressed like an elf, who lived on his shoulder and whispered to him how good a drink would taste. The little man would remind Pops how he would feel if he drank. Pops said he tried to ignore the man for as long as he could, but that eventually he had to give in, the little man's arguments were so convincing.

I figured Pops' elf could just say, "Why don't you have a drink, David?" Pops made his shoulder companion sound like a leprechaun, but I pictured Pops with a beast inside, a creature whose only desire was alcohol, caring for nothing and nobody but his precious substance. In my picture, the beast was not cute, and I'd do anything to get Pops to kill it.

"Yes sir," said Pops, finally looking up, though not looking at anyone. "I'm done with drinking for good. Time for me to start working my program for real."

After a long awkward pause, Gramper spoke.

"David, you are my son, and I love you, but you cannot stay here any longer if you're going to drink. Period. This is your last chance."

"Aw, Dad, didn't I just say I was done? Didn't you hear me? I can change. Really I can. You just wait and see."

Pops looked at our faces, apparently hoping to see excitement at this new and improved David Clevinger.

Instead, he was met with stones.

"David," said Cookie, "We mean it. Absolutely no drinking or out you go. Period."

"Sure, Ma. I understand," said Pops. "I'm getting sick and tired of being sick and tired. I'll continue in AA, and I'll get a sponsor, and I'll read the Big Book and I'll get a job. Then Clayton and I will be able to move into a place of our own."

I was drawn into a conspiracy of silence with Cookie and Gramper, none of us mentioning their offer. I hoped this time Pops really would manage to not drink.

* * *

Pops was remarkably good for the next few weeks. He went to his meetings, read his AA books and didn't drink. He told me he thought this time he'd really licked this booze thing and would never

40

drink again. It was only about the forty-seventh time I'd heard this speech.

Gramper and Cookie planned a cookout for the Fourth of July, inviting neighbors and some fairly distant relations. Pops said he'd marinate some steak tips and man the barbecue. Despite myself, I looked forward to breathing holiday normality, a rare occurrence.

The Christmas before, for example, we'd been living in South Boston, an hour's drive from Mastricola, and Gramper and Cookie were picking us up at one for Christmas dinner. Although we'd never owned a car, Pops was proud he still had a driver's license when so many men in his various AA groups had lost theirs. Still, we needed rides to get anywhere beyond walking distance.

Pops nursed a bottle of brandy and some beer on Christmas Eve, singing along badly with Bing Crosby, Burl Ives and whoever else was on the radio. Sober, Pops would no sooner sing than he would put on mascara; drunk, Pops was a one-man karaoke bar. Whether he knew the words or even the tune, Pops would join any song, much to my annoyance and embarrassment.

Christmas morning, Pops didn't get up until nearly noon. He didn't have any presents for me, as usual, although he did slur a "Merry Christmas" before stumbling into the shower to try to sober up. When Gramper and Cookie arrived, I noticed the way they looked at the bottles in the trash and the lack of holiday decorations. The ride to Mastricola was highlighted by Pops leaning his head out the window and vomiting on the side of the car, leaving a frozen stain still visible the next day.

Pops said he thought he must have gotten food poisoning from some Chinese food a few days before. Alcohol was on his breath and seeped through his skin, stinking up the warm car. Cookie made a sly reference to an outbreak of the "cocktail flu," which was kind of funny, but also pretty sad.

When we got to Mastricola, Pops was too sick to eat and went to sleep on the couch. Christmas dinner was punctuated by Pops' snoring, not exactly a Norman Rockwell moment.

Holidays were difficult for Pops. More accurately, holidays were excuses for Pops to drink and difficult for me.

As I lay in bed on July third, I tossed up a prayer of thanks Pops had not had a drink in a two weeks, and a request the next day go smoothly. It was a warm night, and a fan hummed in the back-

ground as I closed my eyes. Soon, I had company. Four letters joined me for a short visit. Before rolling over to sleep, I wished my friends, H, O, P and E a good night.

When I got up Pops was already outside, loading the grill, even though the picnic wasn't scheduled until the afternoon. Cookie came into the kitchen for a cup of coffee.

"How'd you sleep, Sweetie?" she asked.

"Good. Real good, Cookie," I said.

Pops came in and grabbed some coffee.

"Mom, can I have your car keys? I think we're going to need some more charcoal for the cookout."

"I just bought a bag the other night," Cookie said. "That should be plenty."

"I know, but just in case," Pops whined. "Can I have the keys?"

Pops took them out of Cookie's purse and left. That was at eight o'clock. By noon, Cookie was going crazy.

"Where is that boy?" she demanded of Gramper. "He should have been back three hours ago."

"I know, I know," said Gramper. "And I think you *know* where he is, or at least what he's doing. I just hope to God he doesn't wrap our car around a tree, or hurt some innocent person."

"Do you want me to go look for him?" I asked. "Maybe I could stop him or at least I could distract him and bring him home. It's not like this is the first time."

"No, Clayton," said Cookie, gently but firmly. "You just leave your father to his own devices. You help Gramper with the grill and me with taking care of guests, and we'll just let your father be."

The picnic itself was pleasant, although at first Pops' absence hung in the air like a bad odor. I met some second cousins I didn't know I had, and nobody asked about Pops. For a time, the bad smell disappeared and I was even able to forget about Pops and enjoy myself.

At nine o'clock, as we were starting to walk to a nearby hill to watch the fireworks, we heard singing in the driveway.

"If you knew Lucy, like I know Lucy" Pops' out-of-tune voice warbled. "You, you, you'd be in love."

When we got there, Pops reeked of tequila and had dried vomit crusted on his sandals. As the fireworks started over the trees, Pops cried about the beauty of Independence Day, the glory of the

United States and the indescribable flavor of Cookie's potato salad, which had been left out on the picnic table for hours and which he was shoveling into his drooling mouth by the messy handful.

"This is good. Really, really, really good, Ma," Pops said, from a mayonnaise-dripping mouth. "Best stuff in the world! Really."

"David, where exactly is our car? And where were you today?"

"The car's down by the river. Couldn't find the keys. Musta lost 'em. If you got extra set I can get it morning. Not right now. Eating salad. Ran into friend. Didn't notice time. Sorry."

"David, you're drunk again," said Cookie, "and there's no point talking with you now. Go to bed and we'll talk in the morning."

"Aw, Ma, do I have to?" Pops whined like a child and tried unsuccessfully to stomp his foot. "Always talking' bout how much I drink. Never how thirsty I am. Not ten o'clock! Not a baby! You're not the boss of me!"

"David, just go to bed," pleaded Gramper. "You're embarrassing yourself and your son."

Once again, I felt like a traitor and tried to cover up.

"It's okay, Pops. You'll be better in the morning. I've seen you a lot worse before. The picnic was real nice and everybody missed you."

"At least somebody understands," Pops muttered. "I'm feeling tired now, and I *will* go to bed, but not because *you* told me to!"

When the fireworks ended, I brushed my teeth and went to bed. I felt bad for my grandparents that Pops had embarrassed them. I felt bad for Pops that he had broken his vow to stop drinking and would have a hangover in the morning. Finally, I tried to feel bad for myself, but found it impossible. I accepted life, and this was just another helping of the same dish life served up.

Before I went to sleep, the letters came again. Four other friends this time joined the previous night's visitors. The eight letters danced around the room, trying to cheer me up, although their joy felt like mockery. Still, I did wish a good night to the visitors from the night before and their playmates L, E, S and S.

After sleeping off the alcohol, Pops awoke late, and joined us at the picnic table. Before Pops had his second cup of coffee, Gramper said he and Cookie were too old for Pops' shenanigans, and he would have to leave by dinner, no ifs, ands or buts.

"Where are we supposed to go? I don't have a job. We don't have

an apartment yet. I know you're mad at me but don't take it out on Clayton." said Pops, looking through bleary eyes, barely able to focus. It was painful to open his eyes.

"We aren't mad at you, David," said Cookie. "We simply can't have you here."

"As for Clayton, we have already discussed this with him. Clayton is welcome to stay with us," said Gramper, reaching up with a napkin to wipe his mouth. "*He* does not show up drunk at family occasions. *He* does not pass out in the yard. *He* does not bring shame on this family. If he ever did begin to do so, the consequences would be the same for him as they are for you. I don't believe he will, because I see a strength in him you have always lacked David."

"So you'd be willing to break up my family, take my boy away from me, just because of a little drinking? That's not fair!"

"It's not a little drinking. It's a lot," said Cookie. "And what's not fair is the way you're treating Clayton, moving him from place to place. He needs some stability. He needs a home."

"We've never lived in the street or in a shelter," shouted Pops. "It's not like I'm a bum. We've always had a home."

"It takes more than cancelled rent checks to make a home," responded Cookie. "It takes responsibility and respect and love."

"How dare you say I don't love Clayton?" Pops said, genuinely hurt. "I love Clayton more than I love life itself. Clayton, don't I love you?"

"Of course you do, Pops."

"I'd like to have a few moments alone with my only son, my flesh and blood," said Pops, his voice a sixteen-year-old's asking for the car. "Please let me talk to him alone. Please."

"Fine," said Gramper, and he and Cookie gathered up the coffee cups and left. Once they left, Pops relaxed back in his seat, an expert on begging for what he needed.

"Let me just catch my breath, Son," said Pops. "That's a lot to take in."

He took a long sip from his coffee cup, and then sat slowly forward.

"So, what do you want, Clayton?" Pops asked. "Do you want to stay here with your grandparents, go to Mastricola High School and break my heart or do you want to throw your lot in with me, an old drunk? I can't promise you much, but I can promise to love you."

"Pops, you're forty-two. That's not old. And you don't have to be a drunk. Just stop drinking and you won't get drunk," I said, using a logic foreign to Pops.

"Clayton, it's not that easy. I've got a disease called alcoholism. Getting drunk, for me, is a form of temporary insanity. Alcoholism is a progressive disease, which means it only gets worse. I can't just quit on my own. I need help to stop. That's what Alcoholics Anonymous is for. I promise I'll get back to working my program. Promise. Now, do you want to live with me or your grandparents?"

"That's hard to say, Pops," I said. "Could we talk about it later?"

"No, we'll decide right now," said Pops. "If you have faith in me, then I can do anything. If my own son wants me to quit drinking, then I'll start going back to meetings. I'll go to ninety meetings in ninety days. I'll find a really good sponsor, the best there is, and do whatever he tells me to do. Your faith will pull me through and maybe change our luck. If you don't believe in me, though, just tell me flat out right now, and I'll leave without you."

"Pops, it's not that I don't believe in you. It's just that . . ."

"Course I can't say where I'll end up," said Pops. "You know what they say about alcoholics, they either end up in recovery, in jail, in an asylum or in a pine box. You decide, Clayton."

"Pops," I started, only to be interrupted again.

"Clayton, God never gives us more than we can handle. You know that. I honestly believe that my worst day sober is better than my best day drunk. I know that I've got another drunk in me, but I don't know if I've got another recovery in me. When it comes to AA, I'll just fake it 'til I make it. This time I really mean it."

I've heard Pops talk this AA-speak forever, and none of it added up to action. Pops drank and then he repented. Repeat. It was empty doubletalk, but it made Pops feel he was getting somewhere. As long as I could remember, Pops had been in Alcoholics Anonymous, although his membership seemed to have no great effect on his sobriety.

In fact, one of Pops' most valued possessions was a medallion symbolizing five years of sobriety. He always kept that thing in his pocket. Of course, Pops had never stayed sober for five years or anything like it. Three months was about his record. He'd found it while cleaning up after an AA meeting. He carried it around, though, hoping, at first, it might inspire him to actually stop drink-

ing. It hadn't, and over time Pops forgot that he'd never earned it. Now, Pops treated it with honor, proud of the accomplishment he'd never achieved.

Pops would mouth the slogans he'd memorized in the various church basements he'd visited, mourning his last drink. Still, when it came to the next drink, Pops found relief that alcoholism was a disease, and that he just hadn't found the cure yet. These slogans, though, satisfied Pops' hunger for sobriety.

From my perspective, any "program" to quit drinking should have not twelve steps but two:

1. Don't drink, and
2. If you feel like drinking, go back to number one.

All the other stuff just complicated what should be a simple process. After all, when I'd been teased about picking my nose on the school bus, I hadn't labored to "give it to God" or looked for a "spiritual solution." Nope, I just decided I wasn't going to be a nose-picker, no matter what. That simple. That effective.

I listened vaguely to Pops' lecture on quitting drinking. When he mentioned "a moment of clarity," I too had a vision: my life was what it was, my father was who he was, and I might as well accept things and move on.

"Let's go, Pops," I said during a brief break. "We're a team."

"We're a family, Clayton," said Pops, ruffling my hair like Andy Griffith might do to Opie. Still, I couldn't picture Aunt Bea kicking Andy out for covering his face with potato salad and passing out on the side lawn.

When I was eight, I collected scrap wood from a building site near our apartment. Using Pops' saw, I cut long pieces of two by four into eight four-foot lengths. I nailed four pieces together in a square, using one nail per corner, then nailed the other four pieces on as legs. I was finished when I placed a cracked piece of plywood on the top. My creation was shaky, unfirm and incapable of bearing any weight, but it met the dictionary definition of a table: "An article of furniture supported by one or more vertical legs and having a flat horizontal surface."

Using this same generosity of definition, Pops found us an apartment.

"It's a good deal, for the price. We were lucky to find it," Pops said, as we rode in the smallest U-haul truck available, its rental a going-away present from Gramper and Cookie, who had relented and let us stay for an extra week, while Pops got things in order.

With just a few bags of clothes, a box of plates and pans and a crate of various knick-knacks, including Lucinda's needlepoint work, we could just as easily have rented a two-seat convertible to move. Pops liked the appearance of a moving truck, even a nearly empty one.

"The landlord cut me a deal. In exchange for us doing some light maintenance—snow removal, painting, that kind of thing—he's only going to charge us five hundred a month. Plus, he's going to let us pay weekly. And, like I told you, it's already furnished."

Somewhere inside, I knew regular adults didn't have a problem setting money aside for the rent.

Somewhere inside, I knew any landlord who "cut deals" did so from a weak position in the marketplace, not as an act of goodwill.

Somewhere inside, I knew other families had furniture of their own, and didn't need to look for furnished apartments.

Somewhere inside, I knew the "here we go again" feeling in my stomach was right on the mark. I was used to it.

Looking out the window, I saw a sign reading "Oxford—A Good Place to Raise a Family" followed by an advertisement for the Episcopal Church.

"That's where my Tuesday and Thursday meetings are," said Pops. "I've got a temporary sponsor here and he's the one that got me the job at the plant."

"The plant" was a chicken-processing factory a ten-minute walk

from our new apartment. Pops' workday started at six in the morning, which might prevent his drinking for a while. Pops would spend his days up to his elbows in dead birds and blood. I figured we would be eating a lot of chicken from now on.

Pops turned off the highway and onto Main Street, stopping in front of a double storefront, Virginia's Pizza Emporium on the right and Val's Beautette, a hairdresser's, on the left.

"Val said we can use her phone number and she'll take messages for us if we need her to. We're right over here," said Pops, heading to the left. We turned the corner and I saw a large pile of weathered cardboard, through which Pops kicked a path.

Twenty-seven and a half Main Street, Second Floor, Oxford, New Hampshire was: "A room or suite of rooms used as a residence." But not much more.

We climbed an exterior flight of stairs to a bright green door, fluorescent almost, as if a blind person had chosen the paint. The color turned my stomach, and I noticed it had no window. In fact, it seemed a misplaced interior door, as if I were standing in an invisible room.

To the right of the door was a small wooden box with the name "Finnerty," written on an index card in black block letters, the card attached by two browning pieces of adhesive tape. I thought of all the mail we never got, and wondered whether it was worth the trouble to change the name.

A foot-long piece of grey metal jutted out of the mailbox, a flag holder, I guessed from its shape. Pops was not patriotic, so I thought the flag holder could be used the way hobos during the Depression made strange marks on brick walls, giving directions to houses that offered easy food. Instead of food, though, the flags could let me know Pops' current condition. White would mean he was currently and safely sober. Blue would signal he was cranky and headed for a bender. Red would mean he was drinking and black would let me know Pops was four sheets to the wind, sleeping in his own vomit, drunk.

I opened the door and walked into a tiny rectangular room, with just space enough for a couch to fill one wall and an easy chair to take up most of the furthest wall. Pops' old cassette player was on a small table in the corner, a dozen tapes sprayed around it. Pops liked music when he drank.

Although the room had the musty smell of a place shut up far too long, I knew Pops would use his own personal air freshener to change the odor. Even with every window open wide from March until December, Pops' three pack a day cigarette habit changed the air wherever he was. The tobacco smell became part of the walls' DNA, and I was used to gagging when I arrived home.

Two people couldn't comfortably walk past each other in this room. A lighting fixture, designed to hold four light bulbs but only containing two, hung down in the center. This room, though, benefited from less not more illumination.

"This is the living room," said Pops with pride. "I'm sure we can pick up a few things and fix it up real nice."

Other than nailing up each of Lucinda's needlepoints, I couldn't remember Pops doing so much as putingt up a curtain, but I didn't say anything. I followed Pops into a smelly room with a sink, a table, a refrigerator, two straight-back chairs, one with a cracked seat, and a counter with a two-burner hot plate sitting next to a stain-encrusted coffee percolator. Given Pops' complete lack of ability in the kitchen the almost complete lack of a kitchen was not really a liability.

"The bathroom's back there," Pops gestured to the far end, if there could be a far end of the cramped kitchen.

I popped my head in the closet-sized bathroom, which contained a rusted metal shower stall and a toilet, yellowed with age.

"And that's the bedroom," gesturing to a small windowless room, with a queen-size mattress, and a tall pine chest of drawers taking up most of the space.

"Welcome to your new home!" said Pops, proudly. "Now, let's get going on those boxes."

In the half hour it took to move our stuff in and put it away, I accepted this is where I would be living for now. Gramper and Cookie had whispered I could always come back, but I had made my decision and that was that. As for the apartment, I was already used to it.

We now lived fifty miles away from Gramper and Cookie, and would only see them when they made the drive. I hoped that would be often.

* * *

Oxford had ten thousand people and most had lived there their entire lives, as had their parents and their grandparents. The chicken processing plant and a large lumberyard were the major employers, reliable if not well-paying work. The only natural landmark deserved to have quotation marks around it; Blue Jay Mountain was a hill that dominated the landscape west of town, but it could be climbed up and down in an hour.

While Pops hated his job, Pops had hated almost all his jobs. His major complaints about the plant were that he could never get the smell of blood off, and everyone who worked there was a moron. Pops did not have a higher opinion of anyone than he did of himself; since he despised himself, that left the rest of humanity without much of a chance. When it came to listening to Pops complain about work, though, I was used to it.

Once we moved in, the rest of the summer passed like all summers before. While other fourteen year olds were working at the parks and recreation department, falling in or out of love or just hanging out with friends, I spent most of the summer reading library books in the bedroom. Although Pops suggested we could share the large mattress, I slept on the couch, and used the bedroom to store clothes and as a private reading room.

The summer dribbled away, and soon it was time for the first day of school. Pops believed back-to-school shopping was a scam dreamed up by the department stores to increase their sales. Of course, given our finances, shopping for any kind of clothes was out of the question. Either way, I was used to not having new stuff, ever.

As usual, my clothes were nondescript, not having been bought with any kind of foresight or planning, not having been bought hardly at all. Pops' idea of creating a wardrobe was grabbing someone else's wet t-shirts and jeans at the Laundromat, bringing them home dripping, and hanging them over the shower rod, kitchen chairs or any other available horizontal space. Pops hoped they would fit one of us.

Unfortunately for me, Pops had a flexible idea of what "fit" meant. I, who had a thirty-two-inch waist and a thirty-two inch inseam often had to wear a thirty-four inch waist and thirty inch inseam. Whatever absolutely didn't fit, Pops would trade in at the thrift shop down the street, pleased if he could bring home another outfit.

Luckily, the first day of school was a Thursday, which meant I would only have two days before the weekend and the big Essex Fair, where Pops was going to be working. He promised to take me on Saturday. While going to a fair broke was not as good as going to a fair with fifty dollars, it was still better than not going at all.

Lying in bed that morning, the alarm clock having gone off, and having hit the snooze button, I felt tired, not just because I had grown used to sleeping in over the summer, but a bone-tiredness.

"I want to lie here forever," I thought. "I want everything to go away. I want Pops to stay stopped drinking."

I knew I might as well want a brand-new pony. I remembered what Pops had told me when I had said I wanted to go to Disney-world someday.

"It's fine for you to want anything, Clayton, but remember people in hell want ice water and that doesn't mean they're going to get it."

With that in mind, I got up, did my exercises, showered and went into the kitchen to have breakfast and make something for lunch. Opening a jar of mandarin oranges and pouring it down my throat would do for breakfast, but the pickings for lunch were slim. Chicken parts Pops smuggled home in his pockets smelled up the old refrigerator. Because Pops didn't make a lot of money, the county gave us boxes of food each month. These crates were heavy on canned beans, dried mashed potatoes and jars of apple sauce, but hardly anything that I could put into a brown paper sack and carry to school.

Once I got the paperwork filled out, and Pops to sign it, I would get free lunch at school, my lunch ticket a different color from paying customers. For today, though, I was on my own.

I made two bread and sugar sandwiches for lunch, and then sat down at the kitchen table. I looked at my sneakers, holes in the toes and a floppy heel on my right foot. I knew every other freshman was right now wearing new shoes, new pants, new shirts, and, for all I knew, fresh new underpants.

Then I looked at my backpack, grabbed from the lost-and-found at Mastricola last spring. Each day I had carried my books and stuff, I prayed its rightful owner wouldn't recognize it and demand it back. Now I was in Oxford, and could find new things to worry about, a task for which life had prepared me well.

Although it was just the first day, I was already tired of school.

Even before setting foot in Oxford High School, I knew ninth grade was unlikely to be any different from eighth grade, which was no different from fifth, which, when you came right down to it, was no different from kindergarten.

As I thought about school, I recognized the taste in my mouth, the same aspirin flavor school always gave me, the sense I carried this great emptiness inside that sucked the life out of life itself. My greatest dream or fantasy was that I could someday transform myself from being a loser, despised by everyone, to being merely an underdog, who everybody cheers for.

Once again, I would be the immigrant to a clan where some of the members had been in diapers together. Once again, I wouldn't understand much of what went on the first day of school. It didn't much matter whether I was in a city like Boston or a Podunk town like Oxford. Wherever I was, I didn't quite fit in.

I walked the mile to Oxford High School. Like most schools and prisons, it was set out of town in a solitary place and had all the architectural vision of a giant box of Kleenex.

I went to the guidance office. Pops had forgotten to have my records shipped, and my guidance counselor, a sour-faced woman who looked like she had a lot of cats, took my lack of records personally. After tutting and fussing, Miss Bradshaw finally told me I would be in Ms. Prince's homeroom, room two-seventeen, with other As, Bs and Cs, and gave me a copy of my schedule.

I found room two-seventeen, and saw that the teacher had put a name on every desk. Since I wasn't on her list, there was no desk assigned to me. I took a seat toward the back of the room, planning on explaining my situation when the teacher arrived. Before the school day officially began, I had my last peaceful moment. Looking around the room at the twenty or so other students, I tried to dream the dream that maybe this year could be different. Maybe, just maybe, I might be able to make a friend.

As each new student came in, I imagined he would be my friend, my buddy, somebody to talk to without being mocked. Even though I hadn't ever had a real friend, I had read a lot of books about friendship and thought I could be a pretty good friend if someone would give me the chance.

I looked at one blond boy, who seemed to have a nice smile, although his head was shaped like a pumpkin, and thought maybe he was a possible buddy. He wore a Red Sox jersey, and I imagined striking up a conversation about baseball, which might lead to sitting together at lunch, which might lead to friendship. Like Jews declaring at each Passover Seder, "Next year in Jerusalem!" I tried to believe that friendship truly existed and this year it would be mine. Maybe this kid and I would have secrets and I could introduce him to Cookie and Gramper.

The thought of Cookie brought me back to earth. Two months ago, when Gramper and Cookie had kicked Pops out, I'd been sure that Pops would go into a tailspin. Instead, he had a remarkable run. He had not been drinking all summer, he had held down his job, and he was going to AA meetings three times a week. While I had faith that the good times wouldn't last forever, that couldn't stop me from enjoying the peace now.

My thoughts were broken however, when a large, angry-looking boy, whose notebook read "Josh Brazelton," but whom everyone had called "Blaster" when he entered the room, sat down next to me. Blaster was heavy-set and his teeth were crooked and gapped, making him look like a well-nourished pickerel. He was nicely dressed, name brands sprouting from his pants and shirt, and I guessed that that his family had money.

Blaster looked around the room, catching the eye of another boy sitting at the front. Clearing his throat, he announced in a deep voice, "Guess the lilacs haven't bloomed yet, but I have to take a big steaming dump if that'll help."

The rest of the class laughed loudly, while I was left confused and alone, knowing I didn't have the secret decoder ring. This must be some inside joke from last May or June, when these kids had all been looking forward to high school in the fall, back when I had just been starting to fit in at Mastricola Middle School.

"Blaster Brazelton," said an extraordinarily short girl in the front row, raising herself up in her seat as high as her four feet ten inches would allow, and turning disdainfully toward the back of the room, "you need to be the master, instead of the disaster."

Once again, laughter built a jail cell around me, cutting me off from the rest of the group. Blaster then delivered the coup de grace.

"I don't know about that, cause I haven't ast *her!*" said Blaster, pointing his thumb at me. "What do you say, Dickweed?"

"What are you talking about?" I asked, a tightness in my guts I'd

felt hourly in classrooms ever since kindergarten, not knowing what to do or say, but knowing that whatever I did would be wrong.

"Not 'What are you talking about.' You're supposed to say 'faster.' Haven't you ever played the game, you idjeeeeeot?" said Blaster, holding the eeee sound out to the laughter of the class.

"I'm confused. What is it?" I said.

"If you don't know what 'it' is, then you've never done it," declared Blaster. "And by the way you're dressed I bet you won't be doing it any time soon. Even Jasmine wouldn't kiss you, and she's kissed everyone."

"Shove off, Blaster," said the tiny girl in the front.

"Shove off?" said Blaster. "Why I was just giving you some free publicity for your after-school activities. Wouldn't you like to kiss this kid? He looks like he could use some charity, not to mention deodorant."

"Ha. Ha," said Jasmine. "Sure, pick on the new dweeb. You talk a good game, but I'll bet you spent your entire summer Blasterbating."

Blaster lifted one enormous butt check off the wooden seat and proceeded to pass gas, a sound and smell demonstration, I guess, of why he had been given his nickname. The sound was foghorn-like, but the smell was what gave the fart its power. It was a pig farm in August, or maybe a crypt, and I wished I could change seats. Since Blaster had already targeted me, though, anything I did would lead to more attention.

"Four burritos and a bag of Fritos," announced Blaster, as if we'd asked for an analysis of the odor spreading through the room.

At this, Ms. Prince came in, signaling an end to the conversation, if not the smell. Her nose twitched almost imperceptibly, and she walked over to the window and opened it wide indeed.

"Good morning, Ladies and Gentlemen," said Ms. Prince, a thirtyish woman wearing a double-knit plum-colored pants suit which showed off her abdominal bulge, a kangaroo pouch which might hold a few joeys. Ms. Prince wore oversized round glasses, which magnified her hazel eyes to the size of half dollars. "Welcome to Oxford Regional High School, and the beginning of the best four years of your life."

I laughed to myself. I'd never really thought of life as having "best" times. I just measured time by how badly it didn't meet my desires.

I studied Ms. Prince, her eyes twitching around the room, not really stopping on anything, like a drunk who can't quite decide where to sit down.

I noticed something weird about her cleavage. The tops of her breasts were not large or small, but they were covered with light-colored downy hair. Ms. Prince had a hairy chest, like some peroxide gorilla. I'd never seen a woman with hairy breasts. I felt sick to my stomach looking at furry boobs. It was like sulfur perfume or garlic ice cream.

"I will be teaching many of you Earth science," Ms. Prince went on. "Earth science is an important subject because the Earth is the planet on which most of you will spend the rest of your lives."

Like many teachers, Ms. Prince had terrible comic timing; the things they thought funny were generally lame and predictable. She paused, thinking she had gotten off a one-liner. When no laughter came, the silence was awkward, and the poor teacher's eyes still darted around the classroom.

Blaster leaned over to me and stage whispered in a feminine voice, "And morning is an important time because that is when I forgot to shave my boobs."

"Do you have something you'd like to share with the rest of the class?" asked Ms. Prince, looking in our general direction.

"No, Ma'am," said Blaster, quickly looking down at his desk.

"Not you. The boy next to you who was just speaking so rudely."

"Me?" I asked. "I didn't say anything about shaving."

"That will be enough of that kind of talk. And why are you sitting there, young man? That is not an assigned seat. It is an unassigned seat. What is your name?" asked Ms. Prince, still not quite focusing on any individual student.

"Clayton. Clayton Clevinger, Ma'am," I said, the notion growing that Ms. Prince was perhaps legally blind, and that she relied on some faulty teacher radar to maintain discipline.

"Clayton Clevinger," repeated Ms. Prince, looking down at a clipboard she held in her hands, just barely close enough for her faulty eyes to see. "I don't have you on my home room list. You are not even assigned to this classroom. Why are you here?"

"My guidance counselor told me to come here," I stammered. "We just moved in a couple of months ago. My Pops isn't so good

at taking care of paperwork. He must have forgotten to sign me up. Or maybe the papers got lost. I don't really know."

"Well, whether your 'Pops' is good or not, I expect you to behave better in this or any other classroom. Is that clear, Clayton Clevinger?"

"But Ma'am, I didn't do anything," I said, not wanting to finger Blaster, but not wanting to be punished either.

"Either way, you just watch yourself," said Ms. Prince, still without having made eye contact.

Having fired a warning shot fired across my bow or any other student who might mock her, she returned to the tasks ahead of her. First day meant insurance forms, field trip permission slips, information on dropping or adding classes and all the other bureaucratic trivia that kept principals and guidance counselors employed.

As Ms. Prince was handing out a list of extracurricular activities, none of which I cared about, Blaster leaned threateningly over.

"Listen, Doofus, don't ever try that again," Blaster hissed.

"Try what?"

"Getting me in trouble."

"But I didn't . . ."

"You were *going* to say something, weren't you?"

"I was just going to explain to her that it wasn't me that was talking about her having hairy boobs," I protested lamely. "The whole thing freaks me out too much to talk about it."

"That's what I mean," said Blaster. "You were going to get me in trouble."

"Clayton Clevinger," came Ms. Prince's voice from the front of the room. "Is that you talking again?"

"No, Ma'am," I said, sliding down into my seat. "Well, sort of."

"Young man, I've never sent a student out of the room on the first day of school, but I think you might need to have a little talk with Mr. Platine, the principal. What do you think?"

"I don't think I really need to see anybody, Ma'am," I said.

"So you think you know better than I do how to maintain discipline in my own classroom?"

"No, Ma'am. I just think I can be quiet on my own without having to meet a principal."

"I don't like that tone, young man. You leave this room right now!"

I left, having made an enemy in Blaster and having been pegged as a troublemaker by Ms. Prince. I went to the office, overflowing with students and parents filled with first-day questions.

Luckily, before I had a chance to meet with the principal the bell marking the end of homeroom rang, and I managed to drift out, hidden among the other students.

The rest of the day was uneventful. Because of stupid block scheduling, I only met my Spanish, algebra and world history teachers, all of whom were nice enough. At the end of the school day, I went to the same lame school assembly I had been in at every other school I had ever attended.

Mr. Platine, who would be looking for me the next morning, stood behind a podium in the gym. He didn't look evil, but he also didn't look like someone who was going to be interested in hearing my side of any story, either. With an anxious look on his slightly frog-like face, Platine seemed like a man who tried to live his life by a to-do list he was forever misplacing.

He was a squat man who wore brightly-colored ties with plain blue shirts and stared down troublemakers in assemblies. He held tight to the podium, as if he feared a strong wind might soon enter the gymnasium. He blathered on about rights and responsibilities and the importance of respecting yourself and others and don't forget to cover your books and the soccer team plays on Tuesdays and Thursdays and I'm sure this is going to be the best year ever. Blah, blah, blah.

I was glad when the end-of-the-day bell interrupted one of the blahs and I was free to leave.

Walking home, I decided to walk into the woods and explore a while. Cookie and Gramper had woods behind their house and I had spent a lot of afternoons making forts out of sticks and abandoned houses out of piles of pine needles. I was too old for that stuff now, but I still liked having a private spot, a place to go and think.

After I pushed through the undergrowth beside the road, I found a large granite rock, the size of a living room. I climbed it.

At the top, I put my backpack down and had a seat. For being so high there was no great view. I looked at tree trunks ten feet up, but they weren't much different from the same trunks at ground level. Climbing the rock was its own reward. With the trees over me, I felt I was in a cathedral. I fought off a temptation to become some modern-day St. Francis and deliver a sermon to the trees and whatever animals might be within earshot. All in all, I was pleased with this thinking spot.

Pulling the second sugar sandwich out of my backpack, I sat back and wished that I had something to miss, some part of my life that had been so good that its absence bothered me. A life of gray punctuated by black spots was all I could really conjure up.

I prayed for color.

When this prayer was not immediately answered, I stood up and looked down from my perch. Even if there was no color in my life, there was plenty in the woods. September in New Hampshire is not October, but it's still something. It was a very pretty spot.

Sometimes, and now was one of those times, that's enough.

Walking home, I thought, like always, about Pops and his drinking. In some ways, it would be easier if Pops drank all the time, instead of now and then in binges. Then I wouldn't be waiting for the other shoe to drop, the inevitable quitting of a job or being fired from it and the two-day or two-week binge that would follow. Of course, better still would be for Pops to actually stop for good. Come Christmas time, I would have to ask Santa for that.

I studied mythology in eighth grade, and I thought of Charybdis, the monster who lived in the straits of Messina, forever doomed to swallow the sea down twice a day for having stolen Heracles' sheep, which had struck me as a pretty harsh punishment. Across the strait lived Scylla, who was human to the waist down, but consisted of snapping, biting dogs below that. If sailors tried to avoid the danger of Charybdis, they were bound to be hurt by Scylla and vice versa.

With Blaster as Scylla, ready to bite me hard at the first opportunity, I now had to return to the apartment where dwelt the dangerous Charybdis in Pops, who could right then be drinking a sea's worth of booze, no matter what his intentions.

Leaving the woods and turning on to Main Street, I saw the Oxford library was having a sale, getting rid of books that nobody had signed out in five years. They were set out on a flimsy card table at fifty cents apiece. The library hadn't bothered to man the table, instead leaving a tin can for people to drop money into.

I glanced at the titles, but with no money and no prospect of getting any, I would need to stick to the books that were still free. Someday, though, I might have money to spend on books and then I would be the richest person in the universe.

I thought on this, dreaming the dreams of the literate rich and walking down the sidewalk on Main Street. When I was only footsteps away from the apartment, I heard a brief laugh followed by a whizzing sound. I turned around and was hit in the face by a small, green book.

"That's for being a rat, you A-hole," shouted Blaster, as he rode away on his mountain bike. "Don't worry. There'll be more. Next time I'll rip your arm off and beat you with the wet end!"

I felt blood dripping from my nose, but didn't reach up to wipe it away until Blaster rounded the corner. I didn't want to give him the satisfaction of seeing the damage he'd done. After cleaning my

face onto my sleeve, I bent over to pick up the book that Blaster had stolen.

The slim volume had blood dripped on it, so I figured the library wouldn't want it back, and even if they did, I didn't feel like explaining how the book had been damaged. I read the side of the book and saw "The Ballad of Reading Gaol," misreading the last word as "goal" and assumed it was about a soccer player. Still, I could always use something to read, so I shoved it into my backpack.

I walked up the steps to the apartment. Although the steps had a roof above them, which would keep rain from slicking them and snow from piling up in the winter, they had no exterior wall, so that anyone on Main Street could see my progress up the stairs, floating up step by step as if toward heaven, although no one would ever confuse our apartment for paradise.

Arriving at the door stoop, I wished the flagpole could let me know what Pops was like. I paused and muttered the same incantation I had prayed almost every day since before I could remember. Every time I arrived home, I sent up a prayer, "Please let him be sober," and then unfolded my mental checklist to scan before entering the apartment.

I first listened for music, for Pops loved music when he was drinking, although didn't care about it sober. I had no use for music ever. It just reminded me of drunken foolishness.

Loud rock music? No. Good. Any time Pops had Lynyrd Skynyrd or Led Zeppelin or Deep Purple blaring, it meant I would be in for a long series of less than true stories about Pops' life. If Pops started talking about carnival life he could be entertaining, but other than that seven or eight year stretch, Pops' life had consisted of getting fired from or quitting a series of laborer jobs or sitting in filthy apartments with me watching him get drunk. This life didn't generate much to hold anyone's interest, so Pops had to improvise and exaggerate a life for himself. I had heard these tired riffs over and over.

Loud folk or county music? No. Good. If Pops was listening to Gordon Lightfoot or George Jones or James Taylor, he would be in his weepy phase, and I would spend the rest of the afternoon assuring Pops that his life had meaning, that he was a good father, and that it would all work out if he went to his AA meetings and "Let go and let God." Then Pops would tearfully declare me a saint and quietly pass out on the couch.

Loud Salsa music? No. Especially good. That meant he was alone. Dance music of any kind signified women and Pops' taste in women tended toward those who lacked subtlety throughout their lives. If they had large breasts, they didn't believe in bras. If they had large butts, they thought their short skirts should fit like ace bandages. Regardless of their other attributes, they always wore too much makeup like a seven-year-old girl who's gotten into Mommy's make-up.

They laughed too loud and fawned over me, as if I were a toy poodle, until they were ready to disappear into another room with Pops. Then I became invisible.

How many times I wished I could make Pops' women disappear, when I walked in on them shaking their bodies frantically, as if they had itching powder in their panties.

The women never stayed long, thank God, because, like Pops, they were drunks happy to have someone to booze with. I imagined each woman with a female beast inside her who would only be satisfied with more alcohol, the answer to all of life's problems. I pictured the beast inside wanting to drink with Pops' beast. Once the booze was gone, so were they.

With no loud music blaring, I narrowed my checklist down to the three meanings of silence.

First, Pops could be sitting on the filthy couch, a cup of cold coffee in front of him, a cigarette in the overflowing ashtray, studying the newspaper for a better job. He would greet me, and I could disappear into the bedroom and have a quiet afternoon reading before doing my chores.

Second, Pops could be gone, which kept all judgment up in the air until his return. Still, I could read peacefully until then.

Third, Pops could be passed out anywhere in the apartment, floor, bed, couch, bathtub, leading to my version of hide and seek, followed by a long night. It's myth that alcoholics can drink more than normal men. Pops was a lightweight drinker. The time between the first drink and Pops' passing out was no more than two hours.

I remembered a day when I was in the fourth grade in Boston, when I had come home from school and tried to open the apartment door, but it stopped after six inches. As I pushed with my shoulder to force the door a little more, I peeked around the corner and saw that I was pushing Pops' head at a precarious angle against his shoulder.

"Gallant recognizes that alcoholism is a disease, and that his father's drunkenness is no different from the diabetic's response to sugar. Gallant sympathetically slides through the barely open doorway, hoists his father's body off the floor and lays him out on the couch. Once his father is safe, Gallant prays the Serenity Prayer: 'Grant me the serenity to accept the things I cannot change, the courage to change the things I can and the wisdom to know the difference.' Accepting his father's alcoholism, Gallant is free to move on with the afternoon, letting God do His magic on Gallant's dad. Gallant leaves the apartment to look for baby birds to return to the nest."

"Goofus curses his father for his weakness, and uses his shoulder and weight to force the door open, even though he is using his father's head as a fulcrum for movement. Once inside the apartment, Goofus slams the door in shame and anger, and then kicks his father's right side three times for good measure. As a final act of contempt, Goofus spits on his father, then goes into the kitchen to make a sandwich, only to find that his father has finished off the bread, leaving Goofus nothing but sugar to snack on. Instead of giving up his fear and confusion to God, Goofus returns to his father's inert body and kicks him three more times, this time on the left side, and leaves the apartment to search for some kind of snack."

With a shake of my head, I closed the door slightly, to relieve the pressure on Pops' body. Sliding a foot through the slight opening, I pushed Pops' head out of the way, and then slid sideways into the living room. Carefully placing my hands into Pops' armpits, I slid him away from the door and put a pillow under his head. I had kissed the sleeping man, and gotten out my multiplication homework.

Now that I was in ninth grade, nearly grown up, I had given up many of my illusions. I knew Pops was going to be Pops. Still, coming home with uncertainty every day was like buying a lottery ticket where the winner gets to play Russian roulette.

Like a contestant on some demented version of "Let's Make a Deal," I chose the green door and put my hand on the doorknob. Turning it slowly, I walked in.

"Hey, Clayton," Pops said, looking up from the paper, an ashtray full of cigarette butts in front of him. "How's the boy? Good first day of school?"

"Sure, Pops. You know, the first day's always the same. "'You're not a child any more,'" I mocked in my deepest voice. 'You are in ninth grade, now, not in middle school any longer.'" I can remember the same speech from when I was a little kid. 'First grade was fun and games, but second grade is time for hard work and learning.'

"I think things will be okay here, though. I'm already starting to make friends and all my teachers seem okay."

I was used to lying to Pops about school and life in general. As far as Pops knew, I had a passel of friends in every school I'd ever attended. I would tell Pops stories and anecdotes I'd overheard, submitting my own name for one of the true actors. Many afternoons spent at one library or another were retold to Pops as play dates with kids in my class. It just made things easier.

"Well, Clayton, you've always managed to find your way. I don't have to worry about you. Sometimes I feel like luck has skipped a generation, and all my bad luck has been turned good for you," Pops said.

I wondered about the universe in which Pops resided, a place where I was the poster boy for good luck.

"Don't forget," Pops continued, "I've got a meeting tonight. One of my AA buddies is going to pick me up around six. While I'm gone, there's a pile of clothes that need washing."

Since I was seven, I'd been responsible for doing our laundry. It wasn't bad as chores went, and I'd grown used to sitting in Laundromats, listening to the washers and dryers hum. A Laundromat was warm in the winter, and a good place to read.

"Sure, Pops. No problem. Can I have a ten?" I asked, never sure what the response to this question would be.

"I suspect we can manage that," said Pops, as though he were offering me a kingdom. "I ran into a guy today that I used to work with years ago, guy named Jonas. Jonas Zoller. Used to run the carny circuit back in the day."

"Oh."

"I knew him back when your mother and I were together," Pops said, a dreamy sound coming into his voice. "I haven't seen him for years. Nice enough guy. Turns out he's got a landscaping business in Manchester, offered me a job for next spring. And guess what else he had to tell me?"

"What?"

"He's been in touch with your mother. Saw her last winter. Said she's doing well, looking good. Had been down south traveling with a carnival but now she's settled down and living in Albany. She might even come to visit him at Thanksgiving."

Great, I thought. Just what I needed.

I remembered Lucinda Watkins' appearance at our apartment one afternoon when I was seven. It was the middle of January and Pops was out buying some groceries when someone knocked at the door. I answered it, opening the door half way and found a tall woman, her hair a bright red, but a red not found in nature, teased to an unnatural height.

It appeared this woman's fashion philosophy was anything worth doing is worth overdoing in spades. Although she was chunky, bordering on fat, the woman wore a Band-Aid sized leather skirt and a crop-top shirt, so that her not inconsiderable belly oozed out for all to see. She was tottering on six-inch cork heels that made her belly undulate in front of my face in a way that made me queasy.

Her make-up did not accentuate her features but concealed them. Bright blue triangles expanded over her eyes while her lips were painted a fire-engine red and then outlined in brown pencil. Although her jowls drooped a while, she had applied a lot of base makeup; unfortunately, the makeup was a cocoa shade and she had neglected her ears, which shone brightly like moons.

Hanging from one ear was a glass earring the size and color of a robin's egg; from the other dangled a bright green wooden ball. This gave her head a strangely unbalanced look, a look matched in her eyes.

Each finger had a ring, as if she were attracting raccoons with shiny objects. Although the rings covered them up some, home-made tattoos peaked out from each of her fingers. Her left hand had my old friends H A T and E, while her right hand had the letters L I F E. A grainy green, the ink appeared to be fading, although not quickly enough for my taste.

"Hi, Sweetie," the woman said. "You must be little Clayton. I'm your Mommy."

I screamed and slammed the door, but the woman reopened it. Here was my mother back from the grave and she looked much the worse for her resurrection. I eyed her suspiciously.

"My mom's dead," I whispered.

"No, I'm not, Sweetie. I've come for a little visit. We can get to know each other."

Lucinda, having grown up in Ohio, had that accent that passes for no accent at all. When she spoke, if I closed my eyes, I could almost picture a newscaster reading the weather or farm futures,

except for her grammar. And the swearing.

In fact, Lucinda's visit was spent mainly with Pops and mainly drunk.

My clearest memory of her stay was a night when she and Pops were drinking brandy. Lucinda was doing a needlepoint that showed an American flag and fireworks.

I was playing with brightly colored plastic refrigerator letters in the corner of the kitchen, listening to Pops and the woman. I was thinking about what to do with my Christmas money, a crisp twenty-dollar bill, given to me by Cookie and Gramper a few weeks before. I had placed it in my piggy bank, along with four dollars that was already there.

At seven, I felt rich with twenty-four dollars, and thought about the toys or the books or the candy I could buy. Maybe I would buy Pops a colorful tie, although I had never seen him in anything more formal than a button-down shirt.

Pops and the woman had been drinking and talking about the olden days, back when they first hooked up at the carnival and how they had traveled the country until I was born. They started comparing notes on different carnys they had known.

"Do you remember Doctor Strange?" asked Lucinda.

"Which one was he?"

"Used to run the show 'Monsters and Misbegottens,' freak-show kind of thing with two-headed babies, frog babies, headless babies. Had the tape about the dangers of drug abuse. You remember him."

I sat on the floor playing and tried not to picture the deformed babies, but found it impossible. Those babies would wander my nightmares for years, even after I understood that the so-called "babies" were either fetuses in formaldehyde or, more likely, plastic sculptures in pickle juice.

"Always wore a black cape and high hat?" asked Pops, appearing to remember the man. "Had that deep booming voice? Kind of a crazy old guy?"

"That's him."

"What about him?"

"He got fired and then a couple days later he got killed," Lucinda said with a giggle. "I was running a Star Dart game, plushies for prizes, right down the midway from him, so I'd watch him every day."

"We were at the West Virginia Fairgrounds, the one with all the free parking, and one night he showed up kind of, let's say, feeling no pain, and when he was making his opening, building his tip, let's just say that he got kind of weird and that's when the trouble started."

"Weird how?" asked Pops.

"Weird like," and here Lucinda made her voice as deep as possible, "LADIES AND GENTLEMEN! What we have here on the stage behind the curtain is an extra attraction, an attraction not fit for boys and girls, but designed for the scientific edification of adults. It is an attraction so strange, so frightening, so educational that we keep it in its own tent. What we have behind this curtain is 'MONSTERS AND MISBEGOTTENS,' stark evidence of how cruel Mother Nature can truly be. If you have a heart condition, please leave now. If you are easily offended, please leave now. If you do not have a seeking mind, please leave now. If you want to be educated, please step right up and pay your two dollars, two dollars for an experience you will never forget."

"That sounds like a pretty standard pitch, Lucy," said Pops.

"Let me finish," said Lucinda, and then returned to her deep voice. "You there, Miss, yes you with the pizza face and the boyfriend who looks like his uncle and his father might be wearing the same pair of pants. Come the both of you, and see what your children will look like. And you sir, yes the one with the teeth so yellow I can't believe it's not butter, come and see some creatures whose mothers had the good sense to kill them rather than let them grow into you. And you miss, yes you with the nasty rash covering an even nastier face, come on in."

"By this time," continued Lucinda in her own voice, "people were rushing the stage, screaming and calling for his head. Took security five minutes to prevent a riot and drag old Doctor Strange off."

"And they killed him," asked Pops, horrified. "Didn't they understand he was just drunk? It wasn't his fault."

"No. Security didn't kill him, you idiot. They protected him, but once they were done protecting, they threw him out on his butt."

"I don't know if you remember," she continued, "but Fairlea, West Virginia has about a thousand residents, and if you're a carny without a carnival it's not the greatest place in the world to be stranded. Doctor Strange was out in the parking lot without a penny or a pot to put it in, so he did what carnys before him have done in

that same situation."

"No!" said Pops. "He didn't!"

"He did," Lucinda responded. "The Question Mark. He set one up."

I was confused. I had learned in school what a question mark was, kind of a hook with a period under it. I couldn't see anything evil about a piece of punctuation, or how you could "set one up."

"What's so bad about a question mark?" I asked Pops softly.

Lucinda appeared to have forgotten my presence, and sounded annoyed when she responded.

"None of your business."

I looked down at the floor, and even Pops seemed to feel bad for me.

"It's not a normal question mark, Clayton," he said reassuringly. "It's a way to make some money outside a carnival. You take anything, a hat, a pan, a big rock and set it up behind a white sheet. Then you draw a huge question mark on the sheet, along with a price, usually just a dollar or two. Then you stand there with a hat in your hand and people pay you to look behind the sheet.

"If they get mad," continued Pops, "usually you give them their money back. Most people, though, just feel stupid for having paid you and walk away. You can make ten or fifteen dollars before it's time to close up shop and move away to set it up again.

"Doctor Strange pressed his luck with the wrong mark, though, and ended up dead."

"What happened?" I asked.

Lucinda didn't look at me, acting as though Pops had asked the question.

"Well, Doctor Strange had used his dentures as the hook. Five liquored-up good old boys from outside Rupert came along. The first one paid his money and he was plenty angry to be seeing a set of choppers instead of some freak-show kind of thing or a naked girl or, best of all, a naked freak-show kind of girl."

"Right then and there, Doctor Strange should have laughed it off and paid that hillbilly double his money back, but instead he went and got cute. And you know what they say, 'Too smart'"

"is stupid," completed Pops.

"Amen to that," said Lucinda, glad to damn intelligence. "He didn't give double the money back, instead he offered to go double or nothing on the sneaker grift."

"What's a sneaker grift?" I asked, picturing a frightening monster throwing sneakers with their laces tied together, like the ones I'd seen thrown over electric lines.

Again, Lucinda ignored the question, but Pops came to my rescue.

"A grift is a way of getting money off a mark through tricking them," Pops explained. "With the sneaker grift, you walk up to someone and say something like, 'I bet you five dollars I can tell you where you got your sneakers.' Who wouldn't take that bet? Almost nobody. Then you say, 'You got those sneakers in the parking lot of the West Virginia State Fair in Fairlea, West Virginia,' which is absolutely true, although the mark thought you were going to tell him where he'd bought the shoes. Then the mark either laughs and pays you or laughs and walks away."

"Or he and his four friends drag you to a darkened corner of the parking lot and beat you to a bloody pulp and leave you to die," said Lucinda with a laugh.

"Yup," said Pops, laughing out loud at Lucinda's wit. "Or that."

I couldn't see the humor in the violent death of someone they had both known, but I was only seven and just assumed there was some part of the story I was missing.

Pops and Lucinda kept on drinking into the evening. Once they were pretty tight, they had gotten into an argument about me.

They weren't arguing about the way Pops was raising me.

They weren't arguing about the fact that Lucinda had left her son.

No, their argument was about whether I would have made a pretty girl. Lucinda was convinced that I could have won beauty pageants if I'd been a girl.

"No way, Jose," said Pops. "He's all boy all the time. Just like his old man."

Pops smoked cigarettes, but he only smoked cigars when he was drinking. He had a cheap smelly stogie going, its cherry-red end reflected in the beads of spittle on his lower lip. Lucinda was a cigarette smoker, too, and a chipped glass ashtray in front of her was filled with smelly white caterpillars crawling out of a filthy nest.

The conversation had flowed over me without having much impact; I had learned a little about various carnys, but it didn't really concern me. Now, though, they were talking about me, and I felt

caught in a riptide, as if I were being sucked under.

Cookie and Gramper and Pops all told me my mother had left because she needed to and because she had things she had to do. They all tried to convince me it had nothing to do with me. It was nothing I had done that made her go and there was nothing I could have done to prevent her from leaving. Still I felt, somewhere deep down inside, my mother must have found something distasteful in me and that it was this discovery that caused her to walk out of my life.

After all, even at seven years old, I knew that it was men who were supposed to be shiftless and irresponsible and untrustworthy, not women. Mommies didn't leave their children behind; daddies did.

"You give me ten minutes alone with Clayton, and I'll make him into the prettiest little thing you ever saw. Right now, David, you take that smelly old cigar of yours and go for a walk. Pick me up a pack of smokes. I'm almost out. When you come back, you won't believe your eyes."

"I'll bet you another bottle of brandy that you're dead wrong," said Pops, slapping Lucinda on the behind before he walked out the door, an action that caused me to look away in disgust.

"Well, now, my little Clayton," said Lucinda. "Let's see what we can do to fix you up nice and pretty. Come sit across from Mommy."

I dutifully got up from the floor and walked across the cracked and dirty linoleum, then sat down on a straight-backed wooden chair that faced this woman, who sat in an identical chair.

The woman cradled my chin in her hand and lifted my head gently, brushing my hair off my forehead and licking the ball of her thumb to remove a smudge. Her boozy breath made me blink.

I had no memories of being alone with this woman, Lucinda Watkins, whom I was now supposed to call "Mom." She had never taken a splinter out or put a thermometer in, yet when she appeared two weeks before, Pops acted like she'd just come back from the grocery store, instead of having ditched us.

I looked Lucinda Watkins in the eye; although she was only in her early thirties, Lucinda's face showed all the drinking she'd done and the life she'd led. Spider-web lines surrounded her eyes and the corners of her mouth. Even the thick base make-up she wore could not hide the splotchiness of her skin. The crimson lipstick smeared on her lips did not hide an oozing cold sore on the left side of her mouth. As I gazed into this woman's face, I wanted to see a mother, a mom, a mommy; instead, I saw a withered hag who wanted to smear make-up on me.

"We'll make you into a pretty girl," she said. "You just wait and see."

"No!" I said, crossing my arms over my chest.

"No what?" snapped Lucinda. "Don't you tell me 'no.' I'm your mother."

"No."

"Don't say that, you little piece of garbage," she shouted. "You can't tell me that. I brought you into this world and I can take you out of it. I'm your mother."

"No makeup," said I emphatically. "And you're not my mother. You're just a smelly old drunk lady and I hate you! Why did you even come back? Nobody wants you here. We don't need you."

Lucinda Watkins stared hard at me, her son. She picked up her jelly glass of brandy, took a small sip, then a larger sip and then placed it back on the kitchen table. For a moment, I thought she would cry, and I felt the beginnings of some small seed of regret for what I had said.

Before I had a chance to say or do anything, though, Lucinda's face changed and without warning her right hand came up, cupped slightly and slapped the side of my head, hard, making my left ear ring.

Lucinda again cupped my chin, this time harshly and pulled my head up sharply and stared into my eyes. I had read enough fairy tales to know I was looking at the Wicked Stepmother, even if she was my mother. Lucinda showed no regret, no mercy, no compassion; if anything, she wanted to exact more suffering, not soothe any she had already caused.

"Now you listen up, Bucko," she hissed. "If I had been a knitter instead of a needlepoint artist, I would have had a knitting needle and you wouldn't be here right now. I'm your mother and I'll tell you what you can and can't do. First, don't you ever tell your father, your grandparents, your teacher or anyone else about this. If you do, I'll find out and I'll kill you. Do you understand?"

I didn't say a word. Lucinda shook my head up and down so hard that it made my neck scream.

"Do you UNDERSTAND?"

"Yes."

"Yes what?"

"Yes," I said softly, although through a clenched jaw. "I understand."

"Yes, I understand, Mommy," Lucinda corrected me. "I'm your mother and you have to love me. 'Yes, I understand, Mommy.' Now say it."

I looked the woman dead in the face.

"I said 'Say it!'" she barked at me.

Without any change of expression, I spoke clearly and forcefully. "It!"

Whack! Another cuff on my head brought tears to my eyes and more ringing in my ears. Against my will, tears started flowed down my face.

"You said to say 'it,'" I protested, but the woman stood up and walked away.

Across the room, Lucinda Watkins stared at the stove, then turned on a burner. Taking a cigarette off the pack on the counter, she bent over and lit the smoke. After a moment to compose herself, she turned and faced me and in a quiet but steady voice said,

"Clayton, do not say a word. Period. Not one single word. I am your mother and I have punished you for your smart mouth. That is my right. Now just keep quiet about everything that has happened here."

Moments later, the front door opened.

"Hi, Guys," said Pops, fresh cigar in his mouth, holding another bottle of brandy by the neck in one hand and a pack of cigarettes for Lucinda in the other. "I brought back a little treat."

Looking at me, he could see undried tears. Lucinda's blows had left no mark, except for a slight redness on my ear.

"What's the matter, Buddy?" asked Pops. "What about the make-over? Did your mother have to admit defeat and give up?"

"He just got scared of being made into a girl," Lucinda quickly responded, not taking her eyes off me. "He was afraid he wouldn't be able to play with trucks any more. You know how kids are. They get spooked easily. Isn't that right, Clayton?"

I wanted to tell Pops what had happened, wanted to run to him and throw my arms around him, but I couldn't.

"I'm tired," I said. "I'm going to go to bed."

"Sounds good, Kiddo," said Pops, "Don't let the bedbugs bite."

With the fresh bottle of brandy and Lucinda to share it with, Pops forgot about my tears.

I often felt my birth had been like being kidnapped. With Lucinda's return I felt like I had been sold into slavery.

Lying there, my ear still aching, I closed my eyes, watched the pictures and conjured up my friends, the alphabet. One by one they appeared, some of them tiny, like the print on a medicine bottle, others as huge as a symbol on a billboard. They filled my vision, recognizing that I was sad.

T leaned down over the bed and softly sang Toora Loora, my favorite lullaby, then took me into her arms, the only place in the world I felt safe weeping. The tears and sobs flowed, and after a while I felt spent but spent in a good way. I hugged T a thank-you hug. I wiped my face without opening my eyes, not wanting to break the spell.

"If there's anything you guys can think of to make her go away, I'd really like that. I'm just a little kid, and I don't know what to do.

"S" was the most frightening of the letters. Sliding snakelike, S slithered to the forefront of my mind, curling himself around and around.

"Don't worry," he hissed into my ear. "We'll take care of everything."

"Who's with me, gang?" I heard S shout, as I relaxed myself into the pillow. I heard some of the volunteers, then I listened as S, C, A, R, and E vowed they would protect me. As I drifted off to sleep I heard the five of them banding together.

When woke up the next morning, I jumped out of bed and ran into the living room. The couch was empty. I ran into Pops' room and saw that Pops was alone.

Lucinda was gone.

Then I rushed over to wake Pops, and tell him the big news.

"She's gone!" I shouted into his ear. "She's really gone."

He rolled over slowly and looked groggily into my eyes. For me it was like looking into the eyes of an animal. Then he shut his eyes, rolled over and went back to sleep.

I gave Pops up for hung over. Looking for something to eat, I found a piece of paper on the kitchen counter. I picked it up and saw it was a note written on the back of a school-lunch menu I'd brought home from school.

"David," it read in a shaky hand, "Sorry to rush out like this, but

I need to get away from Clayton. He is nothing but a monster. I should have killed him when I found out I was pregnant.

"Last night, while you were out, he tried to tell me a lot of lies about you. He said you beat him and scream at him and call him names. When I tried to make him stop, he told me he hated you and wished you were dead. Then he begged me to take him with me, so that he could get away from you.

"I don't believe a word he says, David. I know he is an ungrateful liar and that you are a very good father.

"I just think you deserve to know what he says about you behind your back.

"Also, and this is hard to say, I wouldn't blame you if you gave him up. Although I swore up and down he was your child, the truth is I never bothered to learn the last names, or sometimes even the real first names of a lot of the carnys I was with. I knew yours, and that's why I said you were the father. No hard feelings, I hope.

"If you need my signature on anything to give Clayton to the State, feel free to forge it. Ha, Ha

"Yours, Lucinda

"P.s. I found some money lying around. I'll pay you back the next time I see you."

The note did not really surprise me, and some of it I didn't really understand until I was quite a bit older. I couldn't really picture Pops giving me away, but the note would hurt his feelings.

I took the paper into the bathroom and tore it into forty tiny pieces and dropped them into the toilet. Looking one last time at Lucinda's message, I flushed the note away.

Later that morning, Pops finally got out of bed and stumbled into the kitchen.

"Where's your mother?" he asked through his first cup of coffee.
"She's gone."
"Gone? What do you mean gone? I'm sure she'll be back."

If I tried to prove she was gone gone, I would have to admit I'd read and destroyed the note. Instead, I stayed quiet

When Lucinda didn't return that night or the next, Pops never mentioned her. Life went back to our version of normal, and I put my mother back into her grave. This time, I hoped she would stay there.

A few days after Lucinda left, I looked in my piggy bank and discovered my Christmas money was gone. I didn't think money in a piggy bank was exactly "lying around," but I couldn't say anything to Pops, who was just starting to get over the sadness of having been dumped again by the same woman.

I wasn't surprised, but I was sad. Now Pops wouldn't get a tie.

* * *

The news Lucinda Watkins might be reappearing in a few months was hardly comforting. I hoped that maybe Pops and I could stay with Cookie and Gramper over the long Thanksgiving weekend, to keep as much distance as possible between us and her.

As I walked into the bedroom to lie down and read, I thought of a book I once saw in a Boston library. It was a biography of Dorothy Parker. I hadn't had any interest in the book, except for its title, which I now found myself repeating over and over.

"What fresh Hell is this? What fresh Hell is this? What fresh Hell is this?"

Dinner was nothing much. Pops was a man for whom food was nothing more than fuel, and there was no need to get fancy about it. It was Thursday night, so we had macaroni and cheese from a box with a couple of pieces of heavily salted chicken. Tomorrow night would be Friday, so we would have macaroni and cheese from a box and a couple of pieces of heavily salted chicken.

Pops had only once in memory served a vegetable of any kind, and that was pre-chopped lettuce for tacos. After that meal, Pops decided that tacos were too much work, so we never had them again. Likewise with fresh fruit, Pops saw it as a luxury that rich people could afford. He was not going to spend money on food that could go bad before you could eat it. Pops valued two things in a food: shelf life and, in the case of the chicken, the right price.

"So, what did you think of my news?" Pops asked, finishing up his second piece of chicken.

"What news?" I evaded.

"About your mother maybe visiting. I thought you'd be excited. You haven't seen her in a while."

Pops spoke with the casualness of mentioning that it hadn't rained in two weeks, not that of a man who has been walked out on twice by the mother of a boy he was raising on his own. I could never decide whether I respected Pops for maintaining this tone of affection toward Lucinda Watkins or despised him for the dishonesty it betrayed.

"Yeah, Pops. I am," I said. "Really excited. Can't wait to see her again. After all, it's been seven years."

"Clayton, even with her having left us, that doesn't stop her from being your mother. She'll always be that, no matter what," Pops said in Lucinda's defense. "She's as low on luck as I am. Aladdin rubbed a lamp and got a genie. If Lucinda or I rubbed it, we'd probably get an ax murderer. She's had her share of problems, you know."

"I know, Pops," I said in the tone of a catechism. "She's got alcoholism. In a lot of ways, she can't help herself."

"That's right. It's a progressive disease. It gets worse and never gets better. The best you can hope for is to halt the progression. Always remember that."

I did have to give Pops credit for consistency. He blamed his life on alcoholism and bad luck, and he was willing to share the blanket

of irresponsibility with Lucinda and anyone else who drank under an unlucky star.

"I will, Pops," I said. "It's hard to beat alcoholism."

"But that's what I'm doing," said Pops, with a pride that made me nervous. "One day at a time is the secret. That and working the steps and getting a sponsor."

After dinner, Pops got picked up for his meeting. When he had left, I realized he hadn't given me the ten-dollar bill he'd promised. This would make things harder, but I had spent a childhood developing an ability to discover found money.

I grabbed the army-surplus duffel bag we used as a hamper, then walked around the apartment looking for any stray items that might have turned up missing. In the sofa, I found two socks and a pair of Pops' briefs. In the kitchen, three t-shirts had been used as potholders. In they went. Finally, in the bathroom Pops' sweatpants and a Red Sox sweatshirt, worn as pajamas, were balled up in the corner

I looked under the kitchen sink for laundry detergent and bleach, neither of which were there. This was no surprise; Pops had promised to pick up laundry supplies, and Pops' memory was not what it used to be; in fact, it never had been. I cursed myself for not having done the shopping myself and factored in the expense of laundry supplies in my need for money.

Next, the search for that money. Starting in my wallet, I found two one-dollar bills, a promising start. Next, I went to Pops' change jar, on top of the chest of drawers in the bedroom. Six quarters, five dimes, eight nickels and a lot of pennies. I prayed I wouldn't be reduced to having to stop at a convenience store to cash in pennies.

I next poured the clothes in the bag onto the floor so I could look through the dirty pants. Pops' work pants had a few dimes and a nickel, and my second pair of jeans held three quarters and four dimes. I was getting closer.

Finally, I went to the nails we hung our coats on. Payday! Pops had somehow left a ten-dollar bill in his suede fall jacket. I could now get a soda and even a candy bar while I did the week's laundry.

I had some algebra homework to do, and a chapter of world history to read, so I placed books and a notebook in the laundry basket and picked up two pencils, just in case one broke. On a whim, I threw the soccer book into the bag and headed out the door.

I had spent time in a lot of Laundromats. The Oxford Sudsomat was no better or worse than others. It was just a place to do clothes.

I walked in through the front door off Main Street. The place was empty of people and filled with what I thought of as "dryer scent," a sweet, thick smell, not unpleasing at all. Before me was a bank of washers to the left, a bank of dryers to the right and in between orange plastic ice-cream scoop chairs found only in Laundromats. At the far wall was a bank of machines—candy, soda, detergent and a bill changer. At the back right-hand side was the back exit, leading into what appeared to be an alleyway.

I went to my left and chose a metal basket on wheels that would be mine for the next hour. I opened the duffel bag and removed the books I'd tossed in, setting them on top of the washer, then poured the week's worth of clothes into the basket. Opening two adjacent washers, I separated the clothing, darks into the left one, lights into the washer on the right.

Finished with sorting, I walked to the back of the Laundromat and bought two boxes of Tide and, feeling rich, a box of dryer sheets that guaranteed Pops and I would smell like summer rain.

Once I started the washers, I picked up the books and sat down in my very own half-orange.

To me, school was like riding a bicycle; if you hadn't figured it out, it looked impossible. Once you had, it was neither exciting nor stimulating. Although math had never really interested me, I had a knack for it. Somewhere along the line, I started thinking about math problems as puzzles, which made them both easier and slightly more fun. Since I'd studied algebra at the end of last school year, the ten problems went quickly.

The world history chapter was boring, as all history textbooks are. Written in boilerplate, it showed no voice or point of view. The book's purpose was be to provide facts to be spat back on a test. That world history had something to do with human beings was not made clear.

This first chapter was a ten-page overview of early civilizations near the Tigris and Euphrates Rivers, the same civilizations I had read about in fourth and sixth grades. Still, I knew how to play the school game well enough, so I wrote down the pertinent facts, or at least those pertinent to Mr. Halloway, the teacher.

Done with my homework, I picked up the little green book. The book's cover was faded, and its pages were roughly cut. This was

an old book. Very thin, it had a black ribbon attached to the spine, used as a bookmark. I was used to reading paperbacks, or, at best, new mass-produced books from the library, so simply holding an old hardcover felt special.

I opened it up to the title page. "The Ballad of Reading Gaol," which I thought must be a typo of some kind, but it would be weird to miss a typo in a title. Some guy named Oscar Wilde wrote it in eighteen-ninety-nine. I turned to the first page, and saw it was a long poem. I almost closed it because I had never read a poem that interested me.

I read the first stanza, though, and recognized this poem was not like any I had read in school. It wasn't a Hallmark card. It didn't pound me over the head with a message. Instead, it read as real as a newspaper story. The poet, a prisoner, was writing about another prisoner scheduled to be hanged, and he was both moving and funny. I laughed out loud at some points, but I felt sentimental at others.

> "It is sweet to dance to violins
> When Love and Life are fair
> To dance to flutes, to dance to lutes
> Is delicate and rare
> But it is not sweet with nimble feet
> To dance upon the air! "

I could smell the brick dust in the prison, see the bit of blue sky prisoners were granted through their bars, and taste the gruel and bread. Then I looked up from the poem and found myself back in Oxford in the Sudsomat, the sweet smell of drier air hanging in the room.

Poem or no poem, I was hooked. While the story of the last days of the hanged man was gripping, I was really grabbed by the images and the words, which worked together to create an effect. Never had a poem so moved me, or forced me to read it. Never had I felt a poem had been written for me personally, a little gift-wrapped present waiting patiently for its true recipient more than a hundred years later.

> "The vilest deeds like poison weeds,
> Bloom well in prison-air;
> It is only what is good in Man "

That wastes and withers there.

I didn't even notice the washer moving into its rinse cycle or the click it made when it finished with our clothes, because I was too busy back in prison. When I looked up, I felt sucked out of a dream.

Noticing the laundry, I slowly put down the book and walked over to empty the washers. Feeling more alive than I had in a long time, yet slightly disoriented, I unloaded both washer loads into the box on wheels, and then walked it to the driers. Choosing two dryers, I threw in the clothes, opened the drier sheets, inserted quarters and pressed buttons. The two dryers started their humming.

Needing to clear my head, I walked to the vending machines and bought a Coke, holding it to my forehead before opening it. The first drink tasted delicious. When I was young, I used to fantasize about being rich enough to eat just the first, best bite of any food, and throw away the rest.

I looked at all the candy, before choosing peanut butter crackers, their fluorescent orange color attracting me. I had trouble getting the plastic open and finally used my teeth. This, as always, resulted in one line of crackers being cracked.

I went to the back door and walked outside. There was not much to see, really, just a small brick courtyard made by the backs of apartment buildings, each with a rusted fire escape crawling up it. Three separate alleys led out, a short dead-end one to the left, a long one directly ahead that led through a block of buildings and a long one to the right that eventually led to Main Street.

A large pile of trash filled half of the alley directly across from me. I went to see if there was anything interesting.

Bending over the pile, I saw a bunch of old newspapers, some cans with bits of food starting to rot and the remains of what looked like a chicken parmesan sandwich, its tomato sauce coagulating like blood. I picked up a broken stick and poked a while.

At first, I heard scurrying, and thought it might be rats in the alley, but the sound continued. Interested, I poked the pile of newspapers off the trash heap and looked into an aquarium. A black plastic lid with metal mesh covered the box. The scrabbling sound continued and when I looked a little longer, I saw that I was being looked at.

A little brown mouse leaned up against the glass and stared at me, its nose twitching madly.

I guessed that the mouse had jumped in, looking for something to

eat and had found himself trapped, unable to get any traction on the plate glass walls. But when I looked at the lid, there was no hole for the mouse to have entered through. Unless the creature had found some way to pull the lid over the aquarium, this was its home and someone had placed the cage out in the trash, mouse and all.

"Poor little thing," I said aloud. "How you doing in there, Mister Mouse? Where's your owner and what's wrong with him? I mean, what kind of person throws away a perfectly good mouse?"

I broke off a piece of cheese cracker and gently pried the lid off the box to toss it into the aquarium. The mouse pounced on it.

"There you go, Mister Mouse. I hope that helps."

Some people are "animal people," folks who are just naturally drawn to animals and have a way with them. These people have a need to have pets the way others need indoor plumbing.

I am not an animal person. Oh, I don't hate animals, or want to see them tortured or anything, but a world without any animals wouldn't affect me much at all.

Still, I did feel bad for the mouse. I looked down at him trapped, trapped in his glass prison. I lifted my foot and pushed the aquarium gently over on its side. The mesh lid fell to the ground and I expected the mouse to hightail it for freedom.

While it had to hop from the black plastic bottom of the cage to the glass wall that had now become the base of the aquarium, the mouse did not scamper, neither did it bolt, dash, dart or flee. Rather, it sat, still looking intently at me.

"Hey, Mister Mouse," I said gently, kneeling to get a better look. "Don't you think you might want to be moving along, looking for a mouse hole or something? I mean, there might be a cat coming for you."

The mouse continued to stare back at me. While I am not an animal person, Pops is a cheap person, who would not accept spending money on even a dog or cat, much less a mouse. Pops might go along with having a cow, so long as it gave more milk than it ate in feed, but to have a pet for pet's sake made no sense to Pops, so I couldn't bring the little guy home.

Still, I felt some crazy kind of responsibility for the mouse.

"Hold on a second, Mister Mouse. I'll put things back to normal for you."

I gently tipped the aquarium aright and removed the almost empty plastic water bottle, and snuggly fit the plastic lid back on the box.

"Be right back, Mister Mouse."

I went into the Laundromat and filled the water bottle at the communal sink in the center of the room, making sure to tightly close the lid and create a vacuum. I bought two more packets of cheese crackers and went back to the alley and pried open the top, using my teeth to open the crackers and crumbled them up for the mouse. I placed the water bottle snugly back in its holder and reattached the mesh lid.

"There you go, Mister Mouse. Now, I keep on calling you Mister, because I don't know your name. I'm guessing that most mice are pretty sick of the name Mickey, so we'll forget about that. How about I just call you Mister, okay? Now, let's get you out of the trash before someone comes to pick you up."

I hoisted the aquarium and stood up, looking for a safe place to hide the box. I chose the left alley and wandered halfway down before coming to a boarded-up door, with a set of steps leading up to it. The door itself was set deeply in a doorway, deep enough so no one would accidentally find the mouse. This would also protect him from rain. I didn't want to think about him swimming in a flooded aquarium, using up his strength before drowning and floating.

"There you go, Mister," I said, placing the box as far in as I could. "That's about the best I can do for you right now. I'll try to think of something, and I'll try to see you tomorrow night. Good luck, Mister."

Inspired, I ran back into the Laundromat and got pencil and paper. With my fanciest and neatest handwriting I made a sign. Using a rock to hold it in place, I stepped back to admire my work.

"MISTER MOUSE'S HOUSE—THE MOUSEQUARIUM," read the sign.

I took a deep breath of the cool night air and went inside. Although I couldn't say what, I felt as if he had really accomplished something.

Settling into my seat, I drifted back into my cell in Reading Gaol.

> " And all the while the burning lime
> Eats flesh and bone away,
> It eats the brittle bone by night,
> And the soft flesh by day. "

I had no idea how much time had passed while I'd been reading. For all I knew, I could now be a middle-aged man, a beard dripping down my chest. I looked down at hands. No sign of aging, so I felt safe to look up and around the Laundromat. Nothing had changed but me.

And the fact that the clothes were now dry.

I roused myself from my seat, stood and walked over to the dryer, folding each piece, and building one pile for Pops and one for me. All the time, though, I had one foot in my cell.

Once I had folded and packed the clothes into the duffel bag, I picked up the book and swore to myself that I would memorize the whole thing, even if it took me a year. Repeating the first lines like a mantra, I shouldered the laundry and walked home.

> **"** He did not wear his scarlet coat,
> For blood and wine are red,
> And blood and wine were on his hands
> When they found him with the dead,
> The poor dead woman whom he loved,
> And murdered in her bed. **"**

For the rest of the evening, I found myself returning to the poem, wanting to memorize as much as possible so that I could recite pieces of it whenever I wanted.

When I woke up Friday morning, I still had Oscar Wilde's verse in my head.

> " I never saw sad men who looked
>   With such a wistful eye
> Upon that little tent of blue
> We prisoners called the sky. "

I had started a list of the words I didn't know in the poem, and planned to look them up in a dictionary in the school library during his study hall. These words were so exotic that I couldn't even begin to guess them, even using the context. Words like "seneschal" and "anodyne" and "rigadoon" that felt good in my mouth but carried no meaning.

Now, though, I needed to get out of bed and get ready for school. The night before, Pops had gone out for coffee after his meeting, so I had had a little time for myself before going to bed. I had laid out a clean shirt and underwear for today and made myself another pair of sugar sandwiches for lunch.

As soon as I finished my exercises, I went into the bathroom, brushed my teeth and turned on the shower. As I got into the warm water, I relaxed and let time stand still. Working shampoo into my hair, I gently massaged my head, then lathered up my body. I felt my face, which was just starting to sport a downy mustache and little tufts of hair on my chin. Pops was never going to teach me to shave. In fact, I had never seen Pops clean-shaven. I figured I would buy a razor on my own and figure things out as I went along.

My thoughts turned ahead to school, which killed my pleasant trance. I remembered Blaster's threats. I also remembered Ms. Prince sending me to see the principal. Although she might not see very well, she didn't seem like a person who would just let things drop. Before I knew it, any relaxing the shower had done was disappeared by all my nervousness over school. Angrily, I turned off the water.

Getting dressed quickly, I didn't even bother looking in the mirror to admire myself. I ran a brush through my hair, not that it helped a lot, and went to the kitchen, where I ate a left-over chicken breast, cold, out of the refrigerator, then loaded books into my backpack and headed out.

I left about twenty minutes earlier than I had the day before and decided to take a different route to school, keeping an eye out for Blaster, wanting to avoid any more book bombs. I still had to walk down Main Street, but I took a different cross street, even though it meant I would not be able to stop at my cathedral.

As I walked up Beards Street, I recognized it was a poorer street than its parallel cousin. Lawns weren't well maintained, and trash seemed piled in unlikely places. I had no judgment of this; I had lived with Pops in cramped apartments and these houses were at least stand-alones.

I remembered Blaster and looked around. I noticed a scrawny boy standing in front of a shining trailer with broken lawn ornaments and no evidence of upkeep. To the left of the trailer was a ramshackle shed tilted to the right, its roof needing a lot of shingles.

As I got closer, I saw the boy had a mouthful of braces, which sparkled in the sun when he smiled. He looked to be no more than ten or eleven and he was hunched forward, shoulders raised, as if he were trying to keep a cloak from falling off. In addition to being short, the boy was scrawny. I had seen pictures, in Gramper's war books, of concentration camp survivors, emaciated and sexless. This boy would have fit right in, except for one thing. He wore a black t-shirt with large yellow letters that read "Girls Don't Poop."

I laughed out loud at the shirt, and approached the boy.

"That's some shirt," I said admiringly.

"Thanks," said the boy in a high-pitched voice, smiling what looked like a mouthful of staples, paper clips and tin foil. "Mommy says it all the time, so I had this shirt made up special. My Aunt Margaret hates it, but she's not the boss of me."

I tried to take this information in, but couldn't figure out how any woman would work that phrase into conversation once, much less all the time. I thought it was unusual for even a little kid to call his mother "Mommy." I'd never had cause to use the word, but I knew most kids switched over to "mom" or "my mother" by first grade. I couldn't sort things out and assumed I had missed some crucial piece of information.

"I'm Clayton," I said.

"Mommy named me Sebastian, but everyone I know calls me Shiny," he said.

"Why Shiny?" I asked.

"On account of because it's my nickname," he said, as if that answered any questions I might have.

I didn't know how to respond, so I just looked at the ground.

"Do you go to the public high school?" asked Shiny, breaking the silence.

"Yeah. Just started yesterday. I'm new this year. We moved in over the summer. I'm in ninth grade. What grade are <u>you</u> in?"

I expected to hear that Shiny was in fifth or sixth grade.

"I'm in ninth grade, too, but I don't go to the public school. I go to private."

Two things shocked me. First, the boy was tiny for his age and, second, my picture of private school students had them living in mansions with freshly rolled lawns, not silver trailers with broken lawn gnomes.

"You're in ninth grade?" I asked, trying not to sound surprised.

"Yep. Mommy always said I was proof that good things come in small packages."

"And you go to private school?"

"Yep."

"And you call your mother 'Mommy?'"

"Why wouldn't I? It's her name."

"Her name is 'Mommy?' That's what it says on her driver's license?" I asked.

"Nope, 'cause she doesn't have a driver's license any more. It lapsed on account of because she couldn't get to the DMV. But it is her real name. Mommy's mommy felt so good about being a mother she named Mommy Mommy to make sure she'd know the pleasure of motherhood. I mean, imagine if a woman named Mommy didn't have kids. Think how confusing that would be."

Once again, I wasn't sure I understood what Shiny meant and didn't know what to say, so I gestured toward Shiny's trailer.

"Is that your house?"

"It's not a house. It's a trailer," he replied. "It's not mine, of course. I'm only fifteen. What would I need with a trailer? It belongs to my Aunt Margaret."

I looked at the tiny silver trailer, grass growing up its side. The screens over the back windows were shredded.

"So you and your mother live with your aunt in the trailer?"

"No, of course not. I live there alone with Aunt Margaret. Well,

her and her cats. She loves cats and dresses them up for holidays."

"How many cats does she have?" I asked.

"At last count a dozen," said Shiny. "Of course, three of them are pregnant so that number will go up."

"You have twelve cats in that little trailer?" I was incredulous.

"Yup," said Shiny. "They make it real cozy for us."

I could not picture a dozen cats in a two-bedroom trailer as "cozy."

"So it's you and your aunt and her cats?"

"Yup, and I'll tell you, it feels good to be needed. I mean, she could hardly look after herself in her condition, now could she?"

"Her condition? What's wrong with her?"

"She's mad."

"Mad? What's she mad about?" I asked.

"Mad about?" he parroted. "Nothing. That's the problem. She's entirely too happy for a woman in her condition."

"But you said she was mad," I said.

"Yes, I did. You're quite right about that. She is mad, but not *about* anything. She is mad in the old sense of the word. She suffers from a rare form of mental illness that causes her to be happy all the time. Imagine the pain of being always happy, no matter what. You can watch the news and see a hurricane batter some little town, and all you think is, 'I'll bet they can rebuild that even nicer than before' or 'Well, at least now the Red Cross will have a chance to do their best.' If you lose your leg, you think, 'Well, at least I've got one good leg. Some people don't have that.' It's horrible being so happy, as I'm sure you can imagine."

"I guess," I said.

"When I think of the fun I've had being angry at people or being disappointed by situations or just cursing life in general, and know Aunt Margaret never knows the pleasures of anger, it makes me so sad inside. And then when I'm enjoying being sad and sorry for my-self, I get angry my poor aunt never ever gets to curl up in a blanket of sorrow and throw herself a good old fashioned pity party. It's just awful, really.

"Like halitosis or intestinal distress," he continued, "her illness is in many ways harder on those around her than on my aunt. Seeing that poor thing be so happy, day after day, just breaks my heart. She's been to psychiatrists and psychologists and phrenologists and even a paleontologist, but there's nothing that can be done.

"While the rest of us can enjoy a broad pallet of emotions--anger, fear, sorrow--poor Aunt Margaret is stuck with cheerful, heedless, lighthearted and content. Imagine if the only emotional forecast you had was chipper today, chirpy tomorrow with a one hundred percent chance of can't complain for the weekend.

"My grandparents are dead," Shiny continued, "so poor Aunt Margaret has what's called an 'orphan disease.' The big drug companies are willing to spend millions of dollars on antidepressants, but not one penny on depressants, which is what the poor woman desperately needs.

"The doctors have tried everything from daily screenings of war atrocities to listening to sad music to oral readings about good love gone bad, but there's nothing to be done.

"And, of course, there's also the pronoia, which would drive anyone crazy."

"Pronoia?" said I. "I don't think I know what that is."

"Not many people do," replied Shiny. "And they should be thankful about that. I wish I'd never had to hear of it.

"You've probably heard of its opposite, 'paranoia,' which is perfectly healthy. In a world like ours, it just makes sense to watch your back and assume that people are out to get you. Instead of fearing that everyone wants to hurt her, though, Aunt Margaret lives with a sneaking suspicion people are working together in a secret conspiracy to make her happy. Aunt Margaret, if I let her, would hug everyone she meets and thank them for their hard work. The authorities would have to lock her up.

"Think of it, Clayton—that was your name, wasn't it? —Clayton? You probably know from math class that when you multiply two negative numbers together you get a positive number. What they don't tell you is that when the positives start multiplying, as they have for Aunt Margaret, it's a very negative situation for everyone. That's why it's good for her what happened to Mommy, even though it's bad for me."

"What happened to your mother?" I asked. "And what about your father?"

"Well, to begin with," said Shiny, "I never really knew my dad, or anything about him, not even his name. All I know is that he hated his father, whose first name was Sebastian, and that's why Mommy

named me that. He wasn't ever really even Mommy's boyfriend, just a come and go kind of guy, if you know what I mean. Mommy always says that life is a sexually transmitted disease, and that I'm one of its most gorgeous symptoms.

"Mommy is about the most beautiful woman I ever saw. She has a gap between her front top teeth that she could stick two Popsicle sticks in. I don't know if you know it, but all the prettiest women have gaps between their teeth. You could look it up."

I wondered what reference book I'd use to track down this information.

"Mommy's nose is nice and big, with a part up at the top that looks like it's been broken, but it never was. I don't know about you, but I like a woman's nose to be clear that it's a nose instead of a button. A nose should be proud, not trying to hide itself.

"And her hair? Talk about pretty. Not all thick and covering her head like most women. Instead her hair is thinning, so you can see parts of her skull. I'll tell you, men would always go crazy for her.

"Mommy never really bought into the whole world of responsibility, you know, all that make sure there's dinner and that the electric bill gets paid and that the clothes are clean," he said, vaguely. "We moved a lot when I was little. Sometimes we'd move twice in a month. Mainly in Florida, but not the Florida they always show on TV, with everybody in bathing suits and running on the beach. I lived in Florida until I was twelve, and I never saw the ocean, just a lot of two-room apartments without pools. Mommy was kind of a free spirit, and didn't like to feel pinned down.

"One tradition she had, though, was she would always subscribe to the newspaper wherever we lived. We'd get the *Crestview News Leader* when we were there, then the *Branford News* for a while, then the *Palatka Daily News* or the *Citrus County Chronicle*, all depending on where we lived. She never really read them, she just liked having them in the house. I think it showed her that we were real people, getting the newspaper.

"As soon as we'd get to a new town in her big old white truck, she'd call the newspaper and set us up with a subscription. It was also a tradition for Mommy to use a fake name for her subscriptions, usually some minor TV or movie actress, whose name you'd think sounded kind of familiar, but not really. It could be Regina King or Rita Wilson or Amy Acker. That's what our life was like, moving and getting the newspaper. Mommy may not read any of them, but when I was little I used to like taking a ballpoint and drawing horns and beards on people. By the time I was eight, I was reading most of the paper each morning, just because it was something to do.

"We had a tradition of piling up newspapers in the corner of whatever kitchen we were in. Sometimes the pile would get taller than me, but usually we moved before that happened. Like I said, Mommy likes to move a lot. Moving is a tradition for her."

"So did your mother have a hard time keeping a job or something?" I asked, thinking of Pops' long-running difficulties.

"Oh, no, Mommy could have kept any job she had. She'd just get bored. Sometimes she'd get a job cashiering at the Piggly Wiggly or taking tickets at a movie theater. Lots of different jobs. What she likes best, though, is just sitting around the house, waiting for something to happen. Then Jack happened."

"Jack?" I asked.

"He was the love of her life. She met him at a Bingo game and she won twenty dollars that night, so that's why she fell in love with him. He made her feel lucky and special, kind of like getting the newspaper. Maybe they'd even have gotten married if it weren't for Stella."

"Stella was his wife?" I asked.

"No, Mommy could have handled that. She's had lots of married boyfriends. Stella was Jack's dog. Jack loved that little Chihuahua like she was his daughter. She'd sit on his lap at meal times, and he'd feed her right off his plate. Even though Mommy knew that Jack loved her, too, it was the *too* part she couldn't stand. Mommy wanted Jack to love her *more than*, not just too. When he'd be drinking, he'd joke about how he didn't know which he'd choose between the two of them. That hurt Mommy's feelings. Still, if it hadn't been for me and Chinese food, Mommy probably would have married Jack and he'd be my stepfather today."

"Shiny, forgive me," I said, "but I'm really confused here. Stella is a dog. Jack and your mom were friends. You and Chinese food? What does that have to do with it?"

"When I was younger, you see, I was crazy about Chinese food, especially egg rolls. I'd always beg Mommy to take me out for Chinese. One Saturday afternoon, when Jack was at work, she got lucky at bingo again and won fifty bucks, and as soon as she came in the

door, I was all over her, asking for Chinese food. Whenever Mommy was happy and feeling lucky she liked to spread the love, so she said okay. We got into her truck and we drove across town and parked a couple of blocks from the restaurant."

"Why?" I asked.

"Why what?"

"Why did you park a couple of blocks away from the restaurant instead of *at* the restaurant?"

"It was a tradition. Mommy loves traditions. We ordered a pu-pu platter and Mommy had three or four of those colored drinks with the umbrellas. It was real nice. Until the fortune cookies."

"Fortune cookies, Shiny?"

"Yup. We had this other tradition where I would choose her fortune cookie and she would choose mine. My fortune was nothing to remember, but when Mommy opened hers, she got a faraway look in her eyes and a smile on her face."

"What did it say?" I asked.

"It said, 'Stop ignoring your destiny. Remove the obstacle.' So, of course, right then and there, Mommy knew what she had to do."

"Of course," I replied, having no idea where this story was going.

"We left that restaurant without paying. That was another tradition we had. Mommy always said only rich people pay for restaurant food. We ran the two blocks to the truck and Mommy reached up under her skirt and started taking off her panty hose."

"Why?" I asked, feeling more confused with each new piece of information.

"Because she was going to need them for Stella."

"Why would she need them? I thought Stella is a dog."

"*Was.* She's dead now."

"I see," I said blindly.

"Then we drove to Jack's place and Mommy and I went in and poor little Stella was sitting on an easy chair. This little Chihuahua was looking like she was just getting ready to turn on the television.

"Mommy went into the kitchen and got some doggy treats and put them down at the toe of one leg of the panty hose. In case Stella got hungry. Then Mommy told me to hold the thigh as wide open as I could and she snatched up Stella and shoved her, nose first, into the panty hose.

"Once she got Stella all the way in, Mommy told me to tie off the crotch with a double knot. Of course, there was no way that little dog could have turned herself around in the panty hose, but Mommy wanted to make sure we did the job right. She was a stickler for that kind of thing."

"She shoved a dog into tights? Why?" I asked.

"On account of because that was how she wanted to do it. Once Mommy had Stella in the panty hose, she lifted that sack of dog over her shoulder and left Jack's apartment, like Santa Claus in reverse.

"Course, a Chihuahua is a yapper, so once we got her in the truck, Mommy took some duct tape and started trying to wrap Stella's snout through the panty hose. The problem was, Stella didn't really want her snout wrapped, and the tape wasn't on her nose, it was on the hose, so Stella kept on backing and backing up toward the thigh and Mommy kept on wrapping and wrapping until finally Stella couldn't back up any more.

"By the time Mommy was done, she'd used up so much duct tape that she'd made herself a stick out of the panty hose. When she held the staff of duct tape with the little ball of dog at the end, if that dog had been painted red, Mommy would have been holding an old-time thermometer."

"So, you're in her truck in her boyfriend's driveway," I said, "with a duct-taped set of panty hose containing a ball of dog at the end of it. What exactly, was her plan next?"

"Like I told you, Mommy was never much for plans. She just kind of liked to let the fur fly and see what happened. So I can't really tell you about her plan or even if she had one. But I can tell you what she did, and that's she drove us home and carried Stella inside, with the stick on her shoulder and Stella hanging down on her back. She looked like a hobo in one of those old movies.

"She went straight into the bathroom—she always did like the bathroom—and she left the door open. I followed her and watched as Mommy started the water in the tub, but she didn't bother checking the temperature with the back of her hand. Just turned both faucets on full. Didn't put in any bath salts, either, and Mommy was always very particular about her baths. Used to take a bath two, maybe three times a week.

"Stella was really quiet, just a whimper or two, on account of because her nose was finally taped up, and she wasn't really moving that much anyway, 'cause there wasn't much space. I thought may-

be she was going to take a nap, but Mommy's lawyer said at trial she was probably already dead."

"Her *lawyer* said she killed the dog?" I asked. "Why did she have a lawyer and why wasn't he trying to prove she *didn't* kill the dog?"

"Everybody knew she killed the dog," replied Shiny. "People don't go to prison just for killing a dog, Clayton."

"Prison?" I asked.

"Yup. The thing was, the story gets kind of weird now."

"Really?" I murmured, wondering what adjective Shiny would have used to describe the story so far.

"You see, once the water was about half way up the tub, Mommy held on to the duct tape handle and used poor Stella like a plunger. Just held her under water and kept pushing. After a couple of minutes, Mommy pulled the panty hose and duct tape stick out of the water, and using both hands pointed the dog at me.

"'Sebastian,' she said, 'this is what love leads to.'"

A dead dog on a stick, I thought.

"With the way Mommy was holding her, Stella looked kind of like a marshmallow that's ready to fall off the end of your stick into the fire. Except, of course, she was brown, not white.

"Mommy carried the Stella-cicle into the kitchen. I followed and we both sat down at the kitchen table. Mommy leaned forward and put all her weight on the stick, so that Stella, or what used to be Stella, dripped water all over the floor."

"'It's time to think,' Mommy said.

"I didn't know what to do, so I tried to think with her, but it was kind of hard, 'cause I couldn't stop watching Stella puddle up our floor like a dog mop."

"After about five minutes, Mommy looked at me and said, 'Sebastian, don't ever fall in love with a person who likes dogs. Things get way too complicated.' Then she got up and turned the oven on to about three hundred fifty degrees and started unwrapping Stella."

"Shiny, I'm starting to get confused again," I said. "Why the oven? Why the unwrapping? Why not just leave the dog wrapped up and throw it in a dumpster?"

"On account of because that would be cruel to Jack, and Mommy loved Jack," Shiny said with a hurt tone. "Mommy didn't want Jack to spend the rest of his days thinking Stella might have run away from him. She said she wanted him to get closure, so that his love for Mommy could grow and grow

"Mommy said we were going to take Stella back to Jack's street and leave her there for Jack to find. We were going to run over Stella's body three or four times, so Jack would think a car had hit Stella. Problem was, no matter how happy he might be to find Stella and no matter how sad he might be that she was dead, he'd still have to notice she was dripping wet. Mommy said that grief might cover up a lot, but not the smell of a dead wet dog. Jack would get suspicious.

"So Mommy had to dry Stella off. She'd never really had to dry a dead dog before. She'd only done one thing with dead animals. That's why she turned on the oven. There was a problem, though."

"Hard to believe there could be any more problems, Shiny," I said.

"Well, there was. See, Mommy thought that after thirty minutes at three-hundred-fifty degrees, Stella would be all dried out. That's where Mommy figured wrong, because after half an hour in a closed oven, Stella was starting to cook, and smell like she needed to be basted, but she was still as wet as when she'd been lying on the kitchen floor.

"Mommy didn't know what to do, because the smell of roasting dog meat was starting to spread through the kitchen. She was kind of spooked, so she turned the broiler on and sat back, thinking that broiling with the door open might work. Next thing you know, smoke and flames are pouring out of the oven and filling the kitchen. Seems Stella had caught on fire instead of drying off.

"Mommy grabbed a couple of oven mitts with pictures of peacocks on them. Then she picked Stella up by the tail and yanked her out of the oven. Now she was standing in the middle of the room, holding a burning Chihuahua by the tail, kind of spinning herself like one of those hammer throwers in the Olympics."

"I wanted to help, so I opened the kitchen window, to let some of the smoke out. Mommy told me to shut it, because she didn't want the neighbors to know. Then she spun one last time, and Stella's tail came off in Mommy's hand. Stella's burning body flew into the corner of the kitchen, right beside our pile of newspapers, Mommy still holding on to her tail."

"Well, if you didn't know, newspapers are pretty good for starting fires and a burning dog beside a pile of newspapers turns into a big fire pretty quickly. Mommy started crying that she didn't know what

to do. She went to the fridge and opened a beer. With the beer and Stella's tail in one hand, she grabbed me with the other hand and pulled me out of the apartment.

"She didn't try to put out the fire?" I asked.

"Nope. On account of because it was just an apartment and I think Mommy figured that if Stella's body burned up that maybe she'd get away with what she'd done. Unfortunately for her, some nosy neighbors smelled smoke and the fire department was there in about five minutes.

"They went right into the kitchen and sprayed down the fire and Stella was all burned, but she was still recognizable as a dog, a very dead dog. Mommy was going to try to talk her way out of things, but the fireman who was talking with her noticed Stella's little tail, still grasped firmly in Mommy's hand.

"When Mommy got arrested, I went into foster care with a real nice family. I lived on a farm and everything. I even got to be a ward of the state on account of because they didn't know where my father was and they had to sort things out. That's how I got these," here Shiny smiled broadly and pointed to his braces which had red, white and blue bands.

"They're a gift from the people of Florida, kind of a going away present. Of course, now that they're on and I'm in New Hampshire I won't be able to get them off for at least three years."

"Why's that?" I asked.

"On account of because Mommy went to trial last June. Her lawyer convinced her to plead guilty to animal cruelty and arson and she's doing three to five at Jefferson Correctional Facility. It's a very nice place from the brochures and Mommy writes me every week.

"Mommy told me on the day she went away that soon I'd be going to stay with my Aunt Margaret here in New Hampshire, but first I'd be with a foster family. She told me that while she was in prison I was to do everything Aunt Margaret told me to do. I was to treat her like she was Mommy herself. I was even to call her 'Mom,' but not 'Mommy,' 'cause I only have one Mommy.

"She also said that once she was out, we'd never have anything to do with dogs again.

"So that's how I ended up here in Oxford," concluded Shiny.

"And you moved here in June?" I asked.

"Yup."

A woman came to the door of the trailer. She was wearing a flowered housedress, her hair tied back with a ribbon. Shiny's Aunt Margaret looked normal enough to me, but she did have a broad smile on her face.

"Sebastian, who's your friend?" she called out with her grin growing.

"His name's Clayton Clevinger, and he's just walking to school, Mom. He's got get going and doesn't have any more time to chat."

Then Shiny turned his attention back to me.

"See what I mean about Aunt Margaret?" asked Shiny. "Any normal person would have been suspicious and thought you were harassing me and come out to break things up. Instead, she assumes we're friends."

Shiny shook his head.

"It's really sad, isn't it? But you should be going along now, or else Aunt Margaret will be inviting you in for breakfast and who knows what that might lead to."

10

I arrived at homeroom only a minute or so late, but as soon as I walked in the door, Blaster glared at me and called out, "He's here, Ms. Prince

Without looking in my direction, the teacher said, in a matter of fact voice, "Mr. Clevinger, you failed to carry out my request yesterday. Please now report to the principal's office. Immediately."

"Um, I did go yesterday, but the principal was too busy to see me," I muttered, knowing that this excuse was not going to work.

"When I told you to report to Mr. Platine yesterday, I did not say to leave before seeing him, did I, Mr. Clevinger? Did I ask you to use your own judgment?"

"No, Ma'am."

"Of course I didn't. You demonstrated your lack of judgment yesterday with your behavior in this classroom."

"Loser," stage-whispered Blaster. "Don't think you're going to get away with what you pulled yesterday."

"That will do, Mr. Brazelton," said Ms. Prince to Blaster. "I believe Mr. Clevinger has enough other things on his mind without having you threaten him. Now, Mr. Clevinger, gather up your belongings and go to the office."

"Yes, Ma'am."

My "belongings" consisted of a backpack I had not had time to take off. Inside the backpack were two sugar sandwiches and the copy of "The Ballad of Reading Gaol." As I left the classroom, I could vaguely hear Blaster making some new threat, but I ignored it and walked down the hallway to the main office.

"I'm here to see Mr. Platine," I said to the first secretary whose eye I could catch.

"What's your name?" she asked.

"Clayton Clevinger," he replied.

"Send him right in," came a voice from a large office to the right.

"Mr. Platine will see you now," said the secretary.

I had always been a pretty good student and a quiet kid, so I had no real idea of the flavor or texture of trouble, although I supposed that's what I was in now. I got to the open door and knocked on the frame. Mr. Platine motioned for me to come in, and then to have a seat across the man's desk from him.

"So you're the Clayton Clevinger who has upset Ms. Prince so," said Mr. Platine, in a not-unfriendly way. His tie today was a cra-

zy-quilt combination of yellow, red and green, as if a cartoon character had thrown up on his chest. The man was firmly planted, almost toad-like, in his chair.

"Yes, sir," I said.

"And, overall, how are things going for you so far here at Oxford?" asked Mr. Platine.

"Okay, I guess," I said.

"Okay? How unusual. I've been a principal here for more than six years now, and I don't believe I've been referred a single student for whom things were 'okay.' Usually, students who are referred to me are having serious problems of some kind, usually disciplinary problems. Would you like to start over again?"

"Well, I kind of got off on the wrong foot yesterday with Ms. Prince," I conceded. "She thought I was talking during homeroom, that I was saying some things about her, so she sent me to you. I came down here to the office, but the bell rang and I had to get to class, so I left before seeing you."

At this, Platine said nothing, simply sat back and looked into my face. After a moment, he smiled a smile that was sandpaper on poison ivy to me, as if he had figured out the answer to some extraordinarily hard riddle that had been puzzling him for years.

"What?" I said, unnerved by his silence. I was used to adults interrupting me, ready to begin their own lectures before I had finished explaining myself.

Platine continued smiling at me for a good thirty seconds before responding.

"What what?" asked the principal.

"What were you smiling at, Sir?" I asked. "You just smiled at me and stared."

"Really?" said Platine. "I was thinking about how masterfully you avoided taking ownership over any of your behavior. Ms. Prince *thought* you were talking about her, which implies that you weren't. Then, when you were told to meet with me, you appeared briefly at the office, then snuck out like a little boy, without seeing me. It's as though, in your worldview, you are just a victim of life's circumstances, not an agent of your own destiny. That's one lesson we try to teach here at Oxford High School. You are in control of your life, for good or for ill. That's why I think Group will be good for you."

"But I wasn't talking," I protested. "And what do you mean, 'group?'"

There was more silence from the principal, this time without a smile of any kind, just a sort of impatiently patient look. He was not going to answer questions.

"Well, I <u>was</u> talking, but I wasn't the only one. And it wasn't me that said the rude stuff about her. It was this kid sitting next to me."

"Regardless of what anyone else in the universe was doing, you were, in fact, talking, when Ms. Prince had asked you to be silent, weren't you?" asked the principal, in his best television prosecutor tone. "Weren't you?"

"Yes, but . . ."

"Let's just stop at 'yes' and declare a little moral victory for ourselves, shall we?" said Platine in a harsher tone. Then, like butter melting in a warm pan, the principal switched back to being conversational. "What do you like to do outside of school, Clayton?"

This kind of question drove me crazy, because I figured there was some correct answer to it, an answer I could never quite put my finger on. Whatever it was that normal kids did, from riding bikes to shooting hoops, I had no clue about. Still, I couldn't tell him I'd never had the money for any hobbies other than hoping that Pops wasn't drunk, or taking care of him if he was.

I had never been a scout, never been on a team, and never stayed after school for any club. Not only couldn't we afford that kind of stuff, nobody had ever asked me to do them. The only hobby I had was reading, because I could be near Pops to protect him from himself, and yet a million miles away.

"Reading," I said. "I like to read."

"Really?" asked the principal. "And what kind of things do you like to read?"

"Anything that seems interesting," I said. "Outside of school I'll read anything from science fiction to regular novels to magazines. Sometimes I even read poetry."

"Poetry?" asked Platine. "How unusual. I used to be an English teacher myself. Not many boys are interested in poetry. Any poetry in particular?"

"It's funny you should ask. Just last night, I read this poem by a guy called Oscar Wilde. It's called 'The Ballad of Reading Gaol,'" I said, pronouncing that last word 'gay-ohl.'

"I believe that's pronounced 'jail,'" said Wunderlich. "And what did you think of it?"

"It is, without a doubt, the best poem I've ever read," I said, excited at my new discovery. "I've even started to memorize pieces of it."

Although a part of me was embarrassed by my enthusiasm, I couldn't stop from reciting.

> "For oak and elm have pleasant leaves
>   That in the springtime shoot:
> But grim to see is the gallows-tree,
>   With its adder-bitten root,
> And, green or dry, a man must die
> Before it bears its fruit!' and 'Some kill their love
>   when they are young,
>   And some when they are old;
> Some strangle with the hands of Lust,
>   Some with the hands of Gold:
> The kindest use a knife, because
>   The dead so soon grow cold."

"I've got the book right here in my bag!" I said, opening my backpack. "If this isn't great poetry," gesturing at the book, "Then I don't know what is. It's so dark and yet so beautiful."

"So dark and yet so beautiful," repeated the principal. "Unusual words for a male high school freshman to use in describing a poem. Usually, I hear words like 'boring' or 'confusing' or 'stupid.' You must be quite a sensitive young man."

I didn't know what to make of his use of this adjective. "Sensitive" meant someone who cries a lot and can't take being teased. I had been teased almost non-stop, yet almost never let tears appear. I didn't think the word applied, and wasn't sure why he had used it here. Like rinsing my mouth with water and finding a piece of food I didn't remember eating, this word made me nervous.

"I'm not really sensitive," I said. "I never cry, and I keep my feelings to myself."

"I don't mean that kind of sensitive," said the principal. "I just meant you must be in touch with the deeper chords of nature and humanity to appreciate poetry the way you do. Especially that kind of poetry."

What did "That kind of poetry" mean, I wondered. Poetry about murderers? Poetry about death? Poetry about prison?

"Well, I don't really know what kind of poetry it is," I said, "but I know I like it."

"And that particular poet?" asked Wunderlich. "Oscar Wilde? Isn't he a bit, oh I don't know, 'outrageous' might be the word I'm searching for."

"I don't know anything about him," I said. "I just like the poem."

"Oho," said the principal. "You don't know anything about the poet. Still, you must have suspected some things from the flowery tone of the poem. Didn't you, Clayton?"

Once again, I was baffled by what he was saying. Every phrase seemed to have an obvious meaning, but underneath he implied some hidden information. This conversation felt more like a chess match than a discipline session.

"What do you mean?" I said.

"The poet's orientation, perhaps?" asked the principal.

"Orientation?"

"Oscar Wilde was flamboyantly gay. Isn't it interesting that you would be drawn to his work? Well, isn't it?"

I was sick to my stomach. This man was suggesting I might be gay because I liked a poem. I thought back over the authors I liked and tried to mount a counter-offensive against his suggestion. As I thought of my next move, I felt like a novice player eying the board, recognizing that the mistakes were all there to be made.

"But, Mr. Platine," I began, "Just because I like an author's work, that doesn't mean anything. I mean, Dr. Seuss was not a real doctor, I don't think, but you wouldn't ask a second grader who liked *Green Eggs and Ham* if she was thinking about writing phony prescriptions for medicine.

"And Shel Silverstein published a lot of cartoons in Playboy, but you wouldn't ask a kid reading *The Giving Tree* whether he wanted to see naked pictures of women.

"And Beverly Cleary could be a middle-aged man in pajamas eating Spaghetti-Os out of a can for all I know. I still liked Beezus and Ramona.

"All of those guys sent their work into the world on its own. I don't know anything about Oscar Wilde or his life. I just know I like that poem."

"I see I've hit a nerve," said Platine. "'Methinks thou dost protest too much.' Maybe that's something you can discuss in Group."

"Group?" I asked. "Like group therapy?"

"Let's just call it Group for now," he said. "Our school psychologist, Mr. Wunderlich, facilitates it every day at lunchtime here in the office conference room."

"That's okay Mr. Platine," I said. "I'm not really much of a joiner."

"Clayton, you don't seem to understand," he said. "I am meeting with you right now because you have violated the rules of Oxford High School. Group serves as diversion from the disciplinary system. That is, it is a way to avoid a Saturday detention or even suspension from school. It is *voluntary*, of course, but do you really want to start off the school year with a black mark on your record? This is a way for you to avoid all that."

"Mr. Wunderlich is currently working on a doctorate in psychology," continued Platine, "and he uses an experimental methodology he's developed, combining the study of philosophy with an experiential piece in group dynamics. He claims it's very effective."

It was times like these I hated Pops the most. Oh, I could accept his drinking, although I hated it. I could live poor for I'd always been poor. No, what I hated most was not having a real, respectable father who could appear at times like this and make the world treat me fairly. If Pops ever showed up at school, they'd probably call the cops on him. I had to accept, as always, life was what it was. I was used to it.

"So, then, I would say one group session would be sufficient for a first offense," said the principal. "Let me write you a pass. What class do you have now?"

I looked down at my schedule.

"English," I said. "With Miss Buonardi."

"I think you and Miss Buonardi are going to get along very well," said the principal. "Very well indeed."

I took the piece of paper from him and left the office. Walking down the quiet hallways to class, I happened to glance into a room and see Blaster, who didn't look up. Well, at least he wouldn't ruin this class.

I prayed that English, my favorite subject, would be good this year. I got to the assigned door and lightly knocked on it.

11

"Excuse me, Ma'am," I said, walking into the classroom. "I was in the office. I had to meet with Mr. Platine. I have a note."

I walked toward the teacher with the admit slip clutched in my hand.

"Well, you have a note. May I ask if you also have a name?"

"Clayton. Clayton Clevinger, Ma'am."

"Well, Mr. Clayton Clevinger, I am Eleanor Buonardi, Miss Buonardi in the classroom. Why don't you stand right next to me for a moment, since you're already on your feet. I was just explaining to your classmates that they haven't discovered their love of poetry, which got a fair amount of laughter. Do you happen to have a favorite poet, Clayton?"

I answered before I realized it was a rhetorical question.

"Well, not a favorite poet, but I do have a favorite poem," I said.

"Yes," she said gently," and what would that favorite poem be?"

"'The Ballad of Reading Gaol,'" I said, pronouncing the English word correctly. "It's about a prisoner who's going to be executed, and the poet keeps on studying him until he is finally put to death."

"That's quite a long poem, isn't it?"

"There's a hundred and eight paragraphs," I said, "but it doesn't seem like that much because it's pretty interesting."

"And so are you, Clayton," Miss Buonardi said softly. "Just for the record, paragraphs are usually used in prose. 'Stanza' is the word usually used in poetry. Why don't you take that seat over there and we'll prepare to spin the Wheel of Fortune. Now, do any of you happen to know the source of the Wheel of Fortune?"

"I think it's syndicated by Sony Pictures Television," answered a thin boy in the second row, cursed with pasty skin and a squeaky voice. "At least that's what they say in the voiceover."

"I was looking for an answer a little earlier than that, Jim," Miss Buonardi said, having glanced quickly down at her seating chart.

"In ancient Greece," she explained, "Aristotle put forward the classical definition of a tragedy, basically that bad things happen for a reason, there is some fatal flaw in a person's character that leads to mishap. This is also the notion we have today, so that in just about every Hollywood movie or contemporary novel, the so-called good guy wins because of his moral superiority and the bad guy loses because of his character flaw.

"Of course, it's not just the losing that makes a tragedy, it's that the protagonist almost wins. In some ancient Greek dramas, when things had reached a crisis point for which there seemed no possible resolution, the playwright would have a god intervene, sometimes actually wheeling him on stage in the form of a complex machine. This "god from a machine" was called deus ex machina. We don't have machine gods brought in to end our stories, but any time a cavalry rides over the hill or the hero stumbles upon the villain's weakness or the heroine's long lost love returns in the final reel, it's an example of *deus ex machina* and it demonstrates our need for happy endings and justice in art. Chekhov told us that if there is a revolver on the wall in the first act of a play, it will be fired in the last act. This need for resolution, with good rewarded and evil punished, is so universally accepted that it can't be seen because it's everywhere. It's so common an understanding in our culture that we don't even realize there is any other way to view art or life

"A thousand years ago in most of Europe, though, this idea would have made no sense. Indeed, placing the individual at the center of the universe would have been seen as blasphemous. It would be as unthinkable to an Englishman of that day as the notion that we can tell the future through the entrails of dead animals would be to you today.

"Instead, all acts of the universe were conjoined on the *Rota Fortuna*, or the Wheel of Fortune, which lifts the beggar up to power and drives the king off his throne. In the words of Thomas a Kempis, the Fourteenth Century mystic, 'Man proposeth, but God disposeth.' People can wish and work and plan, but it is fate that determines itself.

"To the Medieval mind, the idea of human responsibility was ridiculous, like blaming a cork for bobbing in the ocean. The Wheel of Fortune was at the center of the universe, determining all events, charting all courses. To think otherwise would have been heretical.

"Interestingly, this notion was displaced during the Renaissance by the classical notion of tragedy at the same time the Copernican Revolution was removing man from the center of the astronomical universe. In one realm, man was more important than the universe; in another, he was moved from the center to the outskirts. Things were reversed, just as the Rota Fortuna would have done. But I digress."

Miss Buonardi was a teacher who was so full of real knowledge and even occasional wisdom that she couldn't keep it to herself. As with many of the best teachers, her asides and perambulations through history and literature were every bit as educational as her prepared lectures.

"The study of literature *can* be the study of ideas, but it should be much more than that," she said excitedly. "We will have chance to live other people's lives through literature, like children playing dress-up to better understand the adult world."

Miss Buonardi gestured behind her.

"I will now introduce you to another Wheel of Fortune, one that corresponds to one-hundred-twenty different poems. Each day we will spin the Wheel of Fortune and read the poem selected. If the Wheel determines that we read Emily Dickinson's "Because I could not stop for death" every single day for the entire school year, then that is what we will do.

"Each day, I will come up with a brief assignment related to that day's poem; each night you will do that assignment, in addition to other reading and writing you may be required to do."

"Although each of you will have a chance to spin the Wheel, I believe today should be Clayton's day. Clayton, would you do the honors?"

"Yes, Ma'am," I mumbled, walking slowly up to the wheel, grasping it and giving it a fling. As the Wheel spun, I looked into it, hypnotized by the motion. Finally, the wheel stopped on number thirty-four.

"Feel free to sit, now, Clayton. Let's see, thirty-four is from A. E. Housman's *A Shropshire Lad*. The first time I read it aloud, just listen to it. I'll then read it again, so you can write it down. Listen:

> Oh, when I was in love with you
> Then I was clean and brave,
> And miles around the wonder grew
> How well did I behave.
> And now the fancy passes by
> And nothing will remain,
> And miles around they'll say that I
> Am quite myself again.

The class stared at Miss Buonardi, waiting for her to tell us what to think about the poem. All the class, that is, except me. I thought for a second and then I laughed. The other students gave me sideways looks; after all, I was a new boy, and some of them had seen me sent out of homeroom the day before.

"Why the laughter, Clayton?" asked Miss Buonardi gently.

"I guess I thought it was funny, ma'am," I said. "I mean, it's like the character talks about love as if it were a spell that made him act differently than he usually would. Then he just throws away the line about the fancy leaving him, and he's back to being himself again. I just thought it was kind of funny, not meaning any disrespect."

"Clayton, it's perfectly okay to see humor in poetry. I agree that the character seems to treat love as if it were forty-eight-hour flu. I also agree it's amusing. The best thing is that you listened and had a response to what the poet was saying.

Miss Buonardi turned her attention to the rest of the class and read the poem aloud again for us to write it down in our notebooks.

"While this poem uses very simple language that you all know, chances are over the next months you will be introduced to a number of words with which you're not familiar. Please ask what a word means if you don't know it. I promise I won't send you to a dictionary to memorize a definition. If anyone goes to a dictionary, it will be me.

"Your assignment for tonight is to copy the poem and take it somewhere into the town of Oxford and hide it, not so that it will never be found, but so that it won't be discovered right away. Then I want you to go home and write an imaginary scene about the person who finds your poem and what effect it will have on her life."

The same squeaky-voiced boy who knew about Sony raised his hand again.

"Yes, Jim?"

"Does it have to be a woman who finds it? Because you said 'her.'"

"No, Jim, of course not. There are millions of men who use the word 'he' for the indefinite pronoun. I think one English teacher in Oxford, New Hampshire, can try to strike some kind of balance."

A freckle-faced girl in the second row raised her hand. Miss Buonardi glanced again at her seating chart.

"Yes, Margaret?"

"So we're supposed to hide a poem somewhere in town for someone to find?"

"Yes."

"And then imagine a person finding it?"

"Yes, Margaret."

"Isn't this kind of a weird assignment?"

"Yes, Margaret, I suppose it is. On the other hand, it could be that you will enable another human being to really read a poem for the very first time in his life. Perhaps poetry is something your character has long since forced himself to forget, an assignment he hated in high school. Now suppose you've hidden your poem by folding it up and putting it into the change box of a pay telephone and your character is calling home to say that he's running late and that he still needs to buy eggs. After this call, he reaches down for his change, finds your poem and really reads it, wondering why the universe has floated this poem to him. It could change his life, or it could just be an annoyance. You decide, Margaret. You decide."

"I guess," said the girl, uncertainly.

"A man named Walker Percy," she said, "put forward the notion that reading poetry in an English class is like dissecting a dogfish in biology class. Students are simply going through the motions, doing whatever students do when their teachers tell them to do something. Percy suggested that perhaps the only way to truly see a dogfish is to hand it out in English class and allow the students to use whatever bobby pins or keys or pencils they had to dissect the fish.

"Likewise, the only way to read a poem truly might be to nail it to a dissection table in biology, so that students would have to approach it from the back door, instead of from straight on. I'm not saying I completely agree with Doctor Percy, but I do believe there's an element of truth in what he says."

A frantic hand waved in the front row.

"Yes, Kathleen?"

"What are we going to be graded on?" asked Kathleen, pen in hand to write down where the money lay.

"Oh, I don't grade you on your homework. I'll write a response most times, but it's just important that you're doing it. Aim for quality in your writing and don't worry about the grade."

"But how will we know how we're doing if you don't grade us?" Kathleen asked, truly confused.

"I imagine by reading my comments you will see how I think you're doing. You could also ask classmates or family or friends to read your pieces and respond. Or, when you think you're done, you could go for a long walk, then come back and read your piece aloud to see if it sounds like you on a good day or you on a bad day."

The rest of the class period was fairly typical for a first day. As incoming ninth graders, we weren't used to ninety-minute classes and Miss Buonardi was varied the style of activities before the class had a chance to lose interest. Miss Buonardi lectured on the history of literature, trying to keep it as light as possible. This was followed by an interactive activity which involved Miss Buonardi's having taken the lines from Robert Frost's "Acquainted with the Night" and placed each line onto a strip of brightly-colored construction paper; as a class, we had to determine how best to order the lines, then listen to how Frost had done so. She followed this with a request that we write a letter to someone who had had some kind of impact, positive or negative, on us..

At the end of class, as the other students were leaving, I approached Miss Buonardi's desk.

"Miss Buonardi," I said. "You remember how you said if there were any words in poems that we didn't know that you'd help us learn them?"

"Of course, Clayton."

"Well I have these."

I pulled out the list of words from Reading Gaol, and handed it to Miss Buonardi.

"Could you help me out with these, Ma'am?"

"I would be delighted, Mr. Clevinger. Let us begin."

12

At lunchtime, I got my sugar sandwiches from my locker and reported to the office conference room. Filled with students, the room had the hemmed-in feeling of a halfway house for prisoners who are near the end of their sentences and need to practice social niceties before their release.

The room already reeked of nervous sweat, and I couldn't wait for the twenty-eight-minute lunch hour to end, a feeling that seemed to be shared by the rest of the group, judging by the way they sat sullenly.

Eight students, all boys, sat in chairs around the table, their body language screaming that this was the last place in the universe they wished to be.

An effeminate, tidy man, wearing a lavender sweater, sat at the head of the table. Mr. Wunderlich, I guessed. He appeared to be leading a discussion, if you can call it a discussion when an audience stares at the leader blankly

"Hi," the man said. "You must be Clayton. I'm Peter Wunderlich. Good to have you on board. You're joining us at an excellent time, a time of great progress and great process. Ha, ha. I think you're really going to like Group. I know the other boys have gotten a lot out of it. Why some boys like it so much they can't seem to help from coming back. Ha, ha."

Here Wunderlich had to ignore a semi-loud Bronx cheer from a heavy-set boy to his left, who rolled his eyes before shutting them, looking ready for a nap.

"The progress we're making, both individually and in terms of group dynamics, is remarkable, if I do say so myself. I think what we're doing here is creating a model of personal growth and transformation."

I looked around the circle, and saw cocktails of anger mixed with boredom. Despite Wunderlich's proclamation, this room did not look as though it were a crucible of miracles. It felt like a place where kids came to let time pass, and that it couldn't pass quickly enough.

"Well, it's the second day of school, and we've already got a new member," Wunderlich said to the other students. "And he's new to our school to boot. I'm very excited to have Clayton here in Group. The rest of you have all been in Group before, so why don't you all introduce yourselves."

The other boys met Wunderlich's request with silence

"Clayton," Wunderlich continued as if nothing had happened, "to your right is Edward, then Ricky, then Daniel . . ."

Wunderlich continued to name names, but I stopped really listening, knowing I would never remember them all. I just noticed that none of the kids in the room appeared to pay much attention to Wunderlich. Instead, they squirmed, poked each other and generally showed contempt.

"Does anybody have anything to say to Clayton before we begin Group proper?"

"Welcome to the monkey house," whispered one student, although I couldn't see who.

After a brief pause, Wunderlich continued.

"If nobody has anything more to say, let's begin.

"And so, Clayton," said Wunderlich, drawing me out of my study of the group, "we need to go over some of the ground rules of Group. These are important for the nurturance of trust, and the plant of trust brings forth the fruit of personal growth.

"The first rule of Group is that whatever is said here stays here. We need to have confidence in our confidentiality. Ha, ha."

I didn't expect that a lot was said at Group, except by Wunderlich, so I didn't see any problem with obeying that rule.

"The second rule of Group is that nobody has to share if they don't want to. We encourage sharing, but we don't mandate it."

Ditto.

"The final rule of Group is that when somebody *does* share, we have to be supportive. No matter what, we keep on supporting each other. You may find that when you choose to share, the empathy of the rest of the group helps you discover parts of you that you didn't know existed.

"As a wise man once said, 'We must hang together, or we will surely each hang alone.' Ha, ha."

I had never known a man who actually said "ha, ha" when he thought he was funny. Normal people either laughed or they didn't. I pictured a cartoon of Wunderlich next to Little Orphan Annie's dog, white balloons coming out of their mouths reading "arf-arf" and "ha-ha."

"One of the reasons we have rules in group is so you will know how to behave," said Wunderlich. "A common theme among the philosophers we will be discussing is the importance of following the rules."

"Now, Clayton," Wunderlich said, "you will have a chance to witness the exciting marriage of philosophy and psychology that we are embracing in Group. It's really the heart of the Group process, and the most exciting thing I've come up with in all my years of facilitation. To give some quality focus to our conversations, I like to deliver a little talk on a individual philosopher before we start with the sharing portion of Group.

"Yesterday, I gave an overview of existentialism, beginning with a quote from Jean-Paul Sartre: 'Man is nothing else but what he makes of himself.' Would anyone like to review for I what that quotation really means?

Silence.

"Christopher? Would you like to bring Clayton up to snuff?"

Christopher was the fat boy who had given the Bronx cheer. He sat sullenly with a bag of Doritos in his lap and an unopened quart of chocolate milk on the floor beside him. He reminded me of a sea tortoise, as he opened his eyes and slowly looked around the room, as if he wasn't sure where the voice had come from.

Christopher's response was to lean forward and pick up his jug of milk, slowly removing the half-dollar sized blue plastic cap, and inverting it. I noticed that Christopher's forearms were huge, probably the size of my thighs, as he slowly poured five or six drops of the gooey liquid into the mini-cup.

Finally, focusing his eyes on the piece of blue plastic, he brought it to his lips and tossed it back like a movie cowboy would a shot of rye. He closed his eyes, a smile spreading across his face. Eyes still closed, he nodded twice, as if he were the host of a restaurant dinner party and approved of the bottle of wine brought by the steward.

"Christopher?" said Wunderlich. "Jean-Paul Sartre? Existentialism? Remember?"

Christopher slowly opened his eyes and looked at Wunderlich.

"What? Did you say something?"

"I asked if you could tell our new friend I about existentialism."

"Nope."

He returned to his chocolate-milk tasting, as if the teacher's interference had been a bug flying around the room and his negative response had been pesticide.

"What about you, Jerry? Would you like to take a shot at it?"

I looked at a thin boy wearing a black winter coat, even though it was still late summer. His coat was zipped all the way up to his chin, and his head was covered with an oversized Duke University baseball cap, pulled down so that his ears were half covered by the body of the hat.

"Why me?" the boy whined in a voice surprisingly deep for someone his size. "Why do you always have to call on me?"

"Why not?" asked Wunderlich playfully, appearing to think he was a well-loved leader. "Just tell us about Jean-Paul Sartre."

"I don't remember," said Jerry, reaching up to his throat to make sure his coat hadn't become unzipped even an inch.

"Sure you do," coaxed Wunderlich. "Just one thing about Sartre."

"I said I don't remember!"

"Just one little fact about Jean-Paul Sartre. C'mon, Jerry. You can remember one fact, can't you?"

"Fine. His first name was John! Is that enough?"

"Why don't we take a break in our seats and regroup," said Wunderlich.

Wunderlich motioned for me to lean over to him.

"I think you can see what I was talking about," he said. "There's a give-and-take here that you just don't get in a typical classroom. The dynamics of the group are fascinating, aren't they? You're going to like it here. I promise."

With all the authority of a man who has declared it is time for the tide to go out, Wunderlich cleared his throat to show that break was over.

"Thanks for all the help, guys," said Wunderlich, as if anyone had been listening to him. "Let's listen to the quote one more time: 'Man is nothing else but what he makes of himself.' Along with that, Sartre believed that how one acts in private is what matters and Kafka asked how we could exist without other people and love.

"I think we can safely say that what Sartre meant and what existentialism is about in general is that it's important to follow rules, whether in school or out of it. Even if nobody is watching you, don't run in the halls or write graffiti on the bathroom wall or steal from the school store. If you follow the rules, you won't get in trouble. Remember that, guys, and you'll do okay.

"Why don't we move on to the heart and soul of Group? It's sharing time."

A groan went up from the boys, which Wunderlich completely ignored.

"How can something have two hearts?" asked Christopher, opening his eyes. "You said your stupid little talks were the heart of your stupid little Group. Now you say that 'sharing' is the heart and soul. Which is it?"

"It's an expression, Christopher."

"So's this," said Christopher and burped a long, chocolaty burp. The boys all laughed, while Wunderlich got a pained expression on his face.

"Christopher, I don't think that behavior is very appropriate, do you?"

Christopher smiled and looked around the group. He swallowed deeply, then burped out a huge

"YURRRP."

"Christopher, that will do! Remember Group rule number three. I'm a member of Group, and I'm not feeling very supported right now."

"Awwwww," said Christopher softly, and then closed his eyes again. "Too bad."

"Christopher, please open your eyes. Group is not a place to sleep. In fact, some people feel more awake here than at any other time in their day. Again, Christopher, please open your eyes."

"Anyone who feels more awake here than outside of here might want to check his pulse to see if he's still alive," said Christopher, not opening his eyes. "Anyway, when you went over your stupid rules, I didn't hear anything about not sleeping.

"No, but common decency says that you don't close your eyes in a group," said Wunderlich, losing the rhetorical battle.

"What about blinking? Aren't our eyes going to dry out if we don't blink?"

"That's different," said the psychologist. "You need to blink. And blinks don't last very long."

"I also need to sleep, you idiot. It's a biological need, just like blinking or going to the bathroom. Tell you what, Wunderlich—"

"Peter."

"Tell you what, Wonder Peter, I won't blink at all tomorrow

during Group. I'll just stare a hole in your face, if you want. All those blinks I don't use tomorrow, I'm going to cash in right now and go to sleep."

"But you don't need to sleep right now."

"Sorry I can't hear you," said the fat boy. "I'm fast asleep."

Apparently recognizing it's impossible to wake someone who's pretending to sleep, Wunderlich turned his attention away from Christopher and tried to stimulate "sharing."

"So, Daniel, yesterday you were telling us about what you did over the summer and how it made you feel," said Wunderlich in a silky voice.

A longhaired boy with a heavy metal t-shirt glared at Wunderlich.

"No I wasn't," he spat at the psychologist. "You were grilling me about my life, trying to get me to 'share," just like you did any time I was in here last year. Why can't you just leave me alone?"

"I'm sensing some hostility there, Daniel," said Wunderlich placidly, leaning back into his seat. "Anybody else picking up that vibe? So, Daniel, what is so threatening about last summer? Why have the defenses gone up? Did something happen?"

"No! Nothing happened. I sat around my house just like I do every summer. I went swimming in the pool at my apartment, just like I do every summer. I watched a lot of TV, just like I do every summer. Now, can you drop it?"

"Sat around the house all alone, huh, Daniel? That's all you did over the summer? Sounds to me like you're in some kind of denial, which, contrary to popular opinion, is not just a river in Egypt. Ha, ha."

"How can I be in denial about nothing? That's the stupidest thing I've ever heard," Daniel shouted. "You talk nonsense all the time, and you get paid to do it. It's stupid and you're stupid."

"That's right, Daniel, let it all out. Catharsis is a good thing. Go with that anger. Don't swallow it. You don't want to bottle up your feelings or they'll escape through other means."

"Why don't you pick on the new kid, Wunderlich? Maybe he's got 'issues' that would interest you," said Daniel. "Or at least get you to leave me alone."

"I like the fact you're expressing interest in your peers, Daniel. That's a really good thing and a sign of growth. Keep it up, Pal!"

"So, Clayton, sounds to me like Daniel wants to know how your summer was."

"Fine," I said. "It was fine."

"Well, where I come from the word 'fine' an acronym for 'messed-up, insecure, neurotic and emotional.' Is that what you meant?"

"Wouldn't that spell 'mine' instead of 'fine,' you stupid dork?" asked Christopher, before shoveling another handful of Doritos into his mouth, still keeping his eyes firmly closed.

"Even though it's just us guys, I still feel the need to be appropriate," responded Wunderlich, girlishly. "I know you might think of me as a friend, a buddy, one of the guys, but I'm still a professional and I need to set a good example for you."

"Nobody here thinks of you as a friend, Wunderlich. We all think you're a weird, pathetic little man. If you think you're an example to anybody, you're crazier than a bedbug," said Christopher. "Nobody would be here if you hadn't worked out some deal with Platine so that you get subjects for your stupid doctor's thesis thing and he doesn't have to do as much discipline. We hate you."

"And you don't know what you're talking about when it comes to philosophy either. Some French guy says we are what we make of ourselves, and you tell us it means 'Follow the rules.' Last spring, you went on for a week about some stupid Greek guy and his chair—The Platonic chair, the perfect example of a chair, is what you're referring to, Christopher," said Wunderlich, apparently thinking his help would be appreciated.

"Whatever," said Christopher, brushing off the explanation. "You told us that the chair was a symbol of how we should stay in our seats during class and do our work well. No matter what stupid philosophy you're talking about, it all comes down to you telling us to behave. It's like listening to some dorky Nazi lunatic with limp wrists. To hear you talk, every single damned philosopher was a control freak who wanted nothing more than for us to remember to wash our hands after we go to the bathroom.

"I don't think using the D-word is appropriate, Christopher," said Wunderlich, "but I really do like the way you're taking ownership of your feelings. I'd like to give a shout out to all my peeps about it."

Wunderlich looked around the room, but none of his "peeps" would catch his eye.

"Would you shut up? Please just shut your stupid mouth," said Christopher. "You're an idiot, but you're so full of crap you don't

even know it.

"Very good," said Wunderlich, who turned to look at me. "Now we're going to move on to what I like to call the synergistic portion of our session, where we tie everything together. Briefly, we learned today that Jean-Paul Sartre was one of the leading proponents of existentialism and that he thought it was important that people play by the rules and do what they are supposed to."

Wunderlich might as well have been reading in Finnish from a phone book.

"With that in mind, anybody want to synergize with what you heard today from Christopher about his anger or Jerry about his denial?"

"C'mon, fellas. It's important that each of you practices some empathy and put yourself in Christopher and Jerry's shoes. That's what Group is all about."

With that, the lunch bell rang, freeing them.

"*That's* what group is all about," said Christopher, opening his eyes and heading toward the door.

"See you guys next Monday," said Wunderlich. "Good talk. Real good talk."

13

After school, I walked to my cathedral. Tomorrow, I would be at the fair while Pops, who was already there tonight and wouldn't be home until one in the morning, worked one of the rides or took tickets. Pops was closing in on a new personal record for not drinking. Right now, I focused on Pops' last drink getting further away instead of on his next drink drawing closer.

I climbed to the top of the rock. From my chancel, I looked down onto the nave, empty of course. I thought about what Miss Buonardi had said about the wheel of fortune, and it made a lot of sense to me. I mean, I hadn't done much to create myself or to put myself in whatever situations I'd been dropped. Old Rota Fortuna had just kind of grabbed me by the collar and done her magic. Having spent so much time down, maybe it was time for me to be lifted up.

I pulled out my second sandwich and thought about Shiny. It must be tough having a mother who's in jail, I thought, and having to live with a crazy aunt in a ramshackle trailer. Pops was far from perfect, but at least he was always around. I thought I should be getting home, and decided to cut back and take the alternate route, past Shiny's house. Maybe he'd be outside.

When I got to Shiny's aunt's trailer, I saw movement inside. I stood there and watched for a moment, then Shiny himself came out, having changed into a new black and yellow t-shirt, this one reading: "Helen Keller says: Talk to the Hand."

"Hey," he called from the wooden porch attached precariously to the trailer. "Whacha doing?"

"Hey. Nothing much," I said.

"We're all out of milk," said Shiny. "Want to walk to Cumberland Farms with me?"

With Pops gone, there was no real reason to go home, not that Pops was any great drawing card himself.

"Sure," I said and waited for Shiny to walk up the short driveway. Shiny whistled while he walked, a pleasant, not overpowering, whistle, very good actually, coming from his metallic mouth. "So, this morning I told you all about myself, and you didn't tell me anything about you," said Shiny. "Tell me the story of Clayton Clevinger

"There's really not much to tell," I said. "I live downtown in an apartment with my Pops. I go to school. I read books sometimes. I even read poetry. That about sums it up."

"You live with your father? What happened to your mother?"

asked Shiny. "She dead?"

"You could say that," I said. "I mean she's gone for good. But tell me more about your aunt. She sounds pretty interesting."

"I guess other people's diseases are always fascinating," said Shiny. "Still, living with Aunt Margaret isn't all bad. I mean, with her condition and all, she does the best she can. I try to put the best face on her putting the best face on everything.

"It's just that she's just got some quirks that can get on my nerves. Mommy had quirks, too, but they were pleasant and comforting. Like, for instance, one thing was that she likes the sound of running water, so as soon as we moved into a place, she would turn on the water in the sink and leave it run. Mommy says she's always wanted to live near a mountain stream, and that was as close as she supposed she would ever get.

"Also, Mommy loves to listen to Spanish talk radio at night."

"So do you speak Spanish, too?" I asked.

"Too?" Shiny said. "No, and neither does Mommy. That's what makes it a quirk. If she could understand what the people were saying it wouldn't be a quirk, it would be a hobby. She likes to pretend that she knows Spanish, but she can't tell whether she's listening to people talk about baseball or cooking or Costa Rican politics.

"Aunt Margaret's quirks, though, are just kind of weird and unexplainable. For instance, she really likes to watch television, but she also needs for the house to be quiet, dead quiet, so she turns the sound off. I mean, I've known people who watch football games or even nature shows with the volume turned down, but Aunt Margaret will even watch soap operas or game shows or situation comedies in silence, just staring at the blue box and sometimes laughing or cheering, but I never know why.

"That's the kind of quirk that can really get on your nerves," said Shiny. "It's not funny or sweet. It's just weird.

We walked silently for thirty seconds or so, before Shiny appeared to need noise.

"You still haven't talked about yourself. I want to hear you talk for a while."

I'd never liked talking about myself. I've known enough to hide Pops' drinking ever since I was old enough to tell a lie. Once you get used to hiding one part of your life, it gets pretty hard to uncover the other parts.

"Pops doesn't let us have a television," I said. "He thinks television is filled with stupid people talking about nothing, and he says we can talk just as good nothing as anybody else."

"No TV?" said Shiny, "How do you get along without TV? I wouldn't know what to watch without it. That's where I've learned just about everything I know."

"We had television when we lived with my grandparents," I said. "So it's not like I've never seen the thing. I know what television is. It's just that we don't have it now, and with cable TV costing so much money, and us not having a television set anyway, I don't see any way we'll get it soon."

"It's funny," said Shiny, "You always think your family's nuts. Then you talk with other people and you realize everybody's crazy, just in different ways. It kind of makes me feel better."

"I guess," I said. "Pops is the same way with a telephone. No matter where we've lived or how much money we've had, he never wants a telephone. 'If I want to make a call, I'll put a quarter in a pay phone,' he says. 'And there's nobody out there that I really want to hear from bad enough to let them interrupt my peace and quiet.' So, no phone.

"I mean, the lady that runs the beauty parlor downstairs takes messages for us, or would if there were anybody to call. But besides my grandparents, there's nobody really who needs or wants to talk with us."

I was enjoying walking and having someone to talk to. I tried to think of a new topic, any new topic, so that the conversation wouldn't end, but before I could say any more, an apple hit me in the side of the head.

"There's plenty more coming, you loser!" shouted Blaster, as he rode by on his mountain bike. "You might be able to hide during the day, but I'll find you."

"Go kiss your sister!" shouted Shiny defiantly. "She needs the practice."

Blaster slammed on his brakes, turned and rode at us.

"What did you say, Weirdo?"

"I told you to go teach your little sister how to kiss. She always drools when she does it. Of course, it must be hard for her to find guys to make out with, what with her having a butt that's larger than a pool table and breath that smells like tuna fish."

"If you weren't a little shrimp who goes to a retard school, I'd kill you for talking about Melanie," Blaster said menacingly. "She's only in seventh grade, you disgusting pig!"

"But I bet it's her third time!" yelled Shiny into Blaster's face.

"Listen, Sebastian, I'm not going to touch you because I feel sorry for you, but just shut your pie hole," said Blaster. "And as for you, Clevinger, just wait. Your turn is coming soon."

With that, Blaster rode away.

"What a jerk," I said. "I hate guys like that."

"He's probably having a bad day," said Shiny philosophically. "Maybe his extra chromosome got loose or something."

"Shiny, I'm a little confused. I thought you told me you just moved in last June. How does Blaster know you? And why would he say you go to a retard school?"

"I've never seen that boy before in my life. I suspect Mister Blaster has been spying on me and is jealous that I go to private school. It happens all the time," Shiny said with certainty.

"But he knew your name. And you knew he had a little sister in the seventh grade," I said, confusion settling in on me.

"I've always been good at guessing things like that," said Shiny, while I wondered what "things like that" were. "He just looked like somebody who would have a sister. And Sebastian is a fairly common name for people who look like me. I think I'm a case in point. I'm sure he's mistaking me for somebody else, or else he has the gift of guess, too."

I looked down at Sebastian with his crazy blond hair and mouthful of braces, and, try as I might, could not imagine that there were two Shinys in the world.

Shiny had stuck up for me with Blaster, and diverted attention from me, so maybe the strange explanation was some form of the truth. Anyway, when it came to living in a world of confusion with a side order of deceit, I was used to it.

14

"You were saying this morning you go to private school?" I asked Shiny. "What's that like?"

"Oh, I've always gone to private school, from kindergarten on. I've never had to go to public, although I've heard that some of them are quite nice. Still, Mommy always made sure I was in private."

"Schools are schools, pretty much," I said, "is the way I see it."

"Maybe that's true for public schools up here, but down in Florida I went to a school that was pretty different."

"Different how?" I asked.

"Well, it was an experimental school in Palatka. Its name was The Experimental School and the headmaster had some unusual ideas about making sure students did their best, let's just say that. He had a theory that students learn best when they aren't so sure of themselves. He liked to keep everybody guessing about how well they were doing, not just in class, but with the other kids in the school. He even had a big sign over his desk that read 'COMPLA-CENCY BREEDS INDIFFERENCE!'"

"But don't those words mean kind of the same thing?" I asked.

"That's why they can breed," replied Shiny, "sort of like a horse and a donkey can get together and make a mule, but if a man and a horse get together it just makes a jail sentence. Anyway, he had a special system he had created to make sure nobody got too full of themselves. The first day of school, every kid was told he had to bring in a shoe box on Friday or he'd be expelled."

"Expelled for forgetting a shoe box? That's crazy," I said.

"It was a private school and he could do whatever he wanted to," said Shiny, "and that's what he wanted to do. Luckily all the kids from first through fifth grade did bring in their shoebox. Of course, there were only eighteen kids in the whole school, so it wasn't as hard to do as it would be for you public school kids."

"How could you have a school with just eighteen students?" I asked. "There would only be like four kids in each class."

"They actually had room for twenty, but there were only eighteen when I was there. It was just like the old days, except different."

"Even twenty students," I countered. "How could you afford to have a school that small and still pay for teachers and books and janitors and stuff?"

"Like I said, it was an *experimental* school, so all those things were

probably already paid for out of a grant or something. There were only two teachers and three or four helper ladies. I was only in third grade, so I never asked those kinds of questions.

"Anyway, we all brought our boxes in on Friday and first thing, before we even pledged allegiance to anything, we had to decorate those boxes as pretty as we could and put our names on them. Then we had to deliver them to the headmaster. His name was Chauncey Mittlereschule. That's German for middle school, which is funny because it was an elementary school.

"Once Mr. Mittlereschule had all the boxes, he nailed them to the wall in his office in alphabetical order, by first names not last. That's when The Experiment started. That day, before we could go to lunch, we were each given seventeen index cards. I don't know how he had managed to do it, but the headmaster had found eighteen different shades of index cards. It might be that he knew somebody in the experimental index card business, but I don't know. I do remember that my card color was Canary Yellow.

"On each card we had to write down something we disliked about each student there, each and every one, no matter how well we knew them. Once we had written something mean about each person, we walked down to Mr. Mittlerschule's office and put the card in the other student's box.

"At the end of the day, Mr. Mittlereschule came into our class and announced that we were going to have a special presentation, so we rearranged the desks and lined up the chairs for the assembly. Once we were seated, he explained why we had written on the index cards.

"'Boys and girls,' he said, 'Is there anyone here who is proud of the work he or she has done today?'

"Of course, everyone raised their hands, me included. He looked at the class and chose me, so I said I was proud of a picture I'd drawn. He asked me to come up to the front of the room and he put his hand on my shoulder.

"'I think you've all heard the expression 'pride goeth before a fall.' Well, this year we are going to put those words into action. Sebastian here is proud of his painting, which could mean that he is satisfied with it. But since we seek perfection in our studies, satisfaction is the last thing we will be satisfied with. Sebastian, because of your pride, I'm going to tell you a few things your classmates wrote about you.'

"Then he told me that I was a big-mouthed shrimp who moved

his lips when he reads. 'I hope,' he continued, 'this is of assistance in curing your false pride and keeps you working hard.'

"I told him I thought it would help a lot and then he let me sit back down and told us he'd be watching us closely throughout the year for any evidence of pride. If he saw any, he would know how to fix it, so we could get back to work and improve ourselves."

"Now that was a pretty lousy thing to do," I said, encouragingly.

"Lousy?" said Shiny. "No, that wasn't the lousy part at all. After all I *was* a loud-mouthed shrimp who moved his lips when he read. The lousy part came the following Monday, when he announced that *every* day before we could eat lunch, we would have to find something new that we disliked about each of the other students. I mean, filling that first card was nothing, because there's something to dislike in just about everybody. Mother Theresa always bothered me because she looked like a squaw from an Indian tribe, for instance, and even Jesus was kind of cranky a lot of the time. But to go on complaining in new ways about people takes a lot of work.

"I remember about two weeks into the school year, Mr. Mittlereschule called me into his office and said that I had called three people fat, and that I had to be more creative about my complaints. 'Sebastian,' he said, 'from now until Christmas you may not make any reference to people's physical appearance when complaining about them. It's what's inside that counts.'

"I said it's easy to come up with one thing that annoys you about a person, but there are a hundred eighty days in a school year. That's more annoyance than anyone has. I mean, Mommy and I moved by the middle of January, but even if I had been writing daily complaints about Hitler, at some point, I would have wanted to say 'He seems well groomed' or 'He does kiss babies, not just kill them,' but we had to go on relentlessly picking apart our classmates.

"By the time we moved, it took most of my waking hours to focus on annoyances and imperfections in other people. Of course, the positive side was that my schoolwork suffered, so I didn't show pride in it and didn't have to hear what other people thought of me."

"So after you moved, did you ever hear what happened to the school?" I asked. "Is it still around?"

"About six months later, I was reading in one of Mommy's newspapers and I saw a story about Mr. Mittlereschule, only because he got his Ph.D. he had become Doctor Mittlereschule. In the paper,

he said that the school had been closed. He said the experimental school had been a success as an experiment even though it had been a failure as a school because the experiment had proven that the hypothesis was false and that's all an experiment can be expected to do.

"I didn't really understand what he meant, but I was glad that the kids wouldn't have to come up with even more complaints about each other the following year."

"That really happened?" I asked. I've been to a bunch of schools, but none like the school that Shiny had described. "I've never heard of anything like that.

"That's because you go to public," Shiny answered. "This was private."

"Oh," was all I could muster. "Is that what most private schools are like?"

"No, no, no. Most are a lot more traditional, like the one I went to for a while in Wakulla Springs. It's still around and it's called Outsourcing Academy and some of the foremen are really cool."

"Foremen?" I asked. "What kind of school has foremen instead of teachers?"

"The kind of school that Outsourcing Academy is. We were teamed up with a school of orphans in Pochampally, India. It seems that Indian kids are really good at doing schoolwork, and they like to do it and, most especially, they do it really cheap. Our headmaster figured it didn't make sense for us to be doing all this work against our will when these Indian orphans all wanted to be learning.

"What we did is email them our schoolwork and they did it for us. Out of our tuition we paid them thirty-eight cents an hour, which makes their orphanage the third wealthiest orphanage in all of India. When Mommy and I left that town, I had straight A's in all my classes and I was doing well in an independent study in calculus, all through the efforts of Lalit Samudra, a cute little nine-year-old girl with rickets in India."

"So what's the part about a foreman?" I asked.

"Well, before Outsourcing Academy came along, the Suryawanshi Orphanage had the kids chained to hand looms, making saris in the traditional way. They earned nothing but room and board, and two free handkerchiefs made in the Pochampally style, which is distinctive because the designs are created in the warp and the weft, not just the weft the way they are at Dubbaka. They're really beautiful, but two handkerchiefs is not really much for pay.

"Anyway, with the lucky orphans making pennies hand over fist, they didn't want to weave any more. They just wanted to study and prepare for the future."

"Luckily, the headmaster of Outsourcing Academy had some connections with a freight airline company. He had the orphanage ship us the orphans' handlooms. Since we were all doing well in our telestudies, we had plenty of free time to learn to weave in the ancient Indian style. After a while, we got pretty good at weaving.

"We marketed our saris and sashes under the brand name 'Blind Leper Boys Mission of Mumbai.' It seems people were fascinated by the idea of blind people weaving such beautiful cloth. We sold our stuff in boutiques in Miami and Fort Lauderdale. Our logo was a fly-covered leper boy with a Pochampally shroud. It was really pretty.

"Over time, we were making a lot of money. Some of it we used for upgrading our equipment, mechanizing the handlooms, and the rest we spent on advertising. Of course, once we mechanized, there wasn't much work for us to do, so the headmaster started looking around for other opportunities. When Mommy and I moved, the headmaster was negotiating with a software company in New Delhi that was interested in outsourcing its customer support to the school."

"Shiny, did you ever go to a normal school?" I asked.

"A 'normal school' is the old fashioned name for a public school, and I told you I've only been to private. You need to listen more closely. Anyway, as soon as we'd moved into town and subscribed to the newspaper, Mommy would get out the Yellow Pages and start calling around to find just the right school for me. Most of the better private schools have their own buses that come and pick you up and then bring you home in the afternoon.

"That can be a really nice service," continued Shiny, "but it can also lead to confusion. Like this one time, when I was supposed to be starting at a school that taught kids how to read by giving them chocolates when they got a word right and making them chew on tin foil if they got a word wrong—"

"They made you chew on tin foil?" I asked, horrified.

"Not me," said Shiny. "Like I told you, I was *supposed* to go there, but I went to a different school on account of because a bus came to

pick me up by mistake and took me to a school for the blind. The driver herself wasn't blind, but she couldn't see so well and must have misread the slip."

"You went to a school for the blind?"

"Yup. It took them two weeks to figure out I didn't belong there, and by then Mommy and I were moving again."

"Couldn't they see right away that you weren't blind?" I asked

"They couldn't see anything. They were blind, silly. On account of because it was a school for the blind."

"No, but I mean like the teachers," I said.

"The teachers were blind, too. It was the law in Florida that to teach blind kids you had to be blind yourself. It was the Blind Leading the Blind Law, I think. There were some sighted teachers who had been teaching blind kids for years, but once they passed that law, those teachers had to tear their eyes out or be out on the street without a job.

"Anyway, everyone at the school was blind, even the secretaries and the janitors. The simplest letter home could take a week to write, because it's hard to proofread when you can't see anything. And I've got to say that place was pretty filthy. Blind janitors aren't so good at sweeping or washing.

"I was only in second grade, so I didn't know that much about what schools were supposed to be like. I mean, I'd only been to twelve or thirteen schools at that point. I wasn't even surprised when they had Show and Smell."

"Don't you mean Show and *Tell*?" I asked.

"Nope. Show and *Smell*. Each kid had to bring something in that had a real distinctive odor, then the other kids would have to guess what it was. I remember one little blind girl who always had oatmeal on her dress, on account of she was a sloppy eater, even for someone who can't see her own mouth. That little girl, Marissa was her name, brought in a Tupperware box with a dead rotten goldfish in it, and held it out for everyone to smell.

"I was the only one who guessed the smell, so I got a prize. Of course, since I could see the dead fish, and other people had to just guess the smell, I guess it wasn't exactly fair."

"How did you finally figure out you were in the wrong school?" I asked.

"I never did figure it out," said Shiny. "They did. The blind kids figured it out on account of the clothes I was wearing."

"How would blind kids know what you were wearing?" I asked, confusion settling like a blanket. "They couldn't even see them."

"No, they couldn't see them, but they could *hear* them. Blind folks don't care what clothes *look* like—they'll wear any crazy color combination—but they do care what clothes *sound* like. Just like you wouldn't wear a striped shirt with checkered pants, a blind person wouldn't wear a silk shirt and a new pair of blue jeans. The 'swoosh' of the silk would clash with the crinkly sound of the jeans.

"One day, without thinking a thing about it, I wore some corduroy pants with a wool sweater. As soon as I walked across the room, every one of those blind kids held their hands over their ears and shrieked like if I had my underwear on the outside of my pants in a regular school. It caused quite a commotion, I'll tell you.

"Within ten minutes, they had Mommy on the phone, complaining that I was trying to pull a fast one. Luckily, Mommy was already packing up for our next move, so the school promised they wouldn't prosecute."

"Prosecute? Prosecute for what?" I asked.

"Impersonating a blind person," replied Shiny. "It's a big problem, but people don't know about it. For instance, every musician in Florida wants to be blind, because it's good for business. People just assume that a blind trombone player is better than a sighted one.

"The biggest problem, of course, is with the National Rifle Association. Every rifleman wants to pretend to be blind, because that makes their shooting all the more impressive. Being a good shot with a rifle is okay, but imagine how much better it would be to not even be able to see the target.

"Also, in Florida, blind hunters get to hunt at night, on account of because it doesn't make any difference to them. Night after night, you could hear blind men wandering through the woods, stumbling over stumps and now and then squeezing off a shot. 'Course the smart ones would have bird dogs for seeing eye dogs, cause otherwise they would have a hard time finding what they'd shot.

"You know how sometimes when you're walking through the woods and you see a dead deer lying on the ground?" asked Shiny.

I searched my memory, but couldn't think of a time when this had happened. Still, to be pleasant, I nodded.

"Nine times out of ten, that's a deer that's been bagged by a blind

hunter who couldn't find it afterward. It's sad, really."

"How do they see the deer in the first place?" I asked.

"They don't," said Shiny firmly, "on account of because they're blind. Did you miss that part?"

I tried to formulate a question, but I felt too confused to begin. Anyway we had arrived at the convenience store. Shiny stopped and turned toward me.

"Well?" he asked.

"Well what?" I said.

"Do you have any money for milk?"

"No. I'm broke. You don't have any money? Why would you walk to the store to buy milk without any money?" I asked.

"I didn't say I was going to buy milk," responded Shiny. "I just said we were out of milk and asked if you wanted to walk to Cumberland Farms."

"Oh," I said.

"But enough about me," said Shiny abruptly, as if he hadn't been speaking for the last fifteen minutes. "I don't know anything about you. Tell me about yourself."

"Like what do you want to know?" asked I.

"Nothing in particular, just tell me a story the way I've been telling you stories."

I had developed a filter preventing me from going into much detail about my life, not that there had been any great number of people overflowing with questions. I felt when you're going through hell, you shouldn't slow down to talk about it.

"Well, my life hasn't really been all that exciting or interesting," I said. "I mean, I've moved a pretty lot, but nothing like you. I've been to different schools, but they've all been public schools, so they've pretty much been the same. Sorry I haven't lived the kind of life you have."

"'Sorry's' not enough," said Shiny with finality. "I want you to tell me a story about you and your father."

I had never before been ordered to tell a story.

"Well, I live alone with my Pops here. At different times, though, we've lived off and on with my grandmother Cookie and my grandfather when I was younger. I remember back when I was about nine, we were staying with them. Pops was working at some machine shop place and making pretty good money. I remember it was summer. One day, I was reading in my grandparents' back yard and I heard Pops.

"'Clayton,' he yelled. 'Come here. Quickly.' His voice was so emotional, I was afraid he might be hurt."

"His voice had come from the tool shed. I was afraid he'd hurt himself."

"When I got there, and saw he wasn't injured, I was relieved, of course, but he held this weird contraption in his hand. It was a bent piece of steel, heavy steel and at one end it had what looked like two straps of surgical tubing connected to a small leather strap. I didn't have a clue what it was, but Pops was so excited you would have thought he'd found a case of diamonds.

"How do you like it,?' he asked."

"What is it?" I asked"

"Clayton, this is a genuine wrist rocket, the most powerful sling shot ever made."

"Now that I knew what it was, I could see the beauty of the design. Pops picked up a cardboard tube, slipped off the end and poured some ball bearings into his hand. He picked one up and showed me how to load the wrist rocket. Then we went into the backyard, and Pops held the wrist rocket up as if it were a revolver, sighting down his arm at a spot on an elm tree across the yard. Slowly, he drew back the piece of leather with the strips of tubing. When he got it as far back as he could, he took a deep breath, let the breath out, then let go of the strap.

"The thing moved faster than I could possibly see. Pops looked at me with a quiet grin and told me to follow him. We walked over to the tree, and we could see a small hole in the tree bark, but the ammo itself was buried deep in the wood.

"Starting that afternoon, Pops trained me in how to use it. Every day, when he got home from work we'd go out in the backyard and shoot at targets. Pops would make them with a Magic Marker on construction paper that we attached to a refrigerator box.

"Even though I got pretty good, I was never competition for Pops. He could shoot ten out of ten bullseyes. That was a good time for us, a real good time. Still, much as I love him, I knew that Pops had a way of distilling the poison out of even the sweetest nectar, so it wasn't going to last."

"What happened?" asked Shiny. "Did your father lose his job?"

"No, the job thing still lasted, but things had already headed south for me.

"Anyway, what with me and Pops shooting so much, we also started using the backyard more for other things too. We'd sit out there after we were done shooting and probably talked more during that time than we have before or since.

"One day, I looked at a bush in the back yard and I saw the reddest red I'd ever seen. It made every other red look gray. It was only the size of a quarter and it darted around a bush. It looked like the biggest bug I'd ever seen.

"'Can you see that red, Pops?' I asked him.

"'Sure. That's a ruby-throated hummingbird. Tiniest bird in the world. Darts around looking for nectar.'

"We sat and watched it for about five minutes, until it flew away. Then I said to Pops, 'I wish I could have had that hummingbird forever. It was about the most beautiful thing I ever saw.'"

"Pops looked at me and said, 'I'll see what I can do.' I figured he was just talking, and didn't think about it again. The summer went on, and each afternoon we'd go shoot targets. Sometimes we'd see that hummingbird. Sometimes we wouldn't.

"Anyway, my birthday is at the end of August, and I'd asked Cookie and my grandfather for a new bike. I didn't ask Pops for anything, because he doesn't really believe in giving gifts. On my birthday morning, though, I woke up and there was a sloppily-wrapped box about the size of a baseball. I figured that Pops had gone to the dollar store and gotten me a ball. There was a card attached to the box. It read, 'Clayton, enjoy forever, love Pops.' I tore off the paper and opened the box. It wasn't a baseball after all. There was crumpled up tissue paper, so I started to pull it out. There at the bottom of the box was that ruby-throated hummingbird, dead, with a hole in its chest and a similar one in its back. The bird had a little note wrapped around its leg. It said 'Think of me when you look at this beauty—love, Pops.'

Now "Pops was pretty pleased with himself, not thinking that he'd given me a body by destroying the bird I loved. I try to be careful what I wish for, because once in a great while you get it."

"Now, see, you told that story pretty well," said Shiny. "And here you said nothing interesting ever happened to you, as if you'd have to make up a story that would be interesting."

"Thanks, Shiny," I said. "I mean, I wouldn't just make up a story and pretend it was real. That'd be lying."

"People do it all the time," said Shiny. "It's easy to do. They just start talking and things start coming out, and then they keep building on what they've said. I've known people who can make up a story that you would swear was real, and I've known other people that make up stories that don't fool anyone. Some people think it's an art, but I think it's a craft that anyone can develop.

"For example, Mommy had a friend, Erasmo Essenwein his name was, who cried all the time out of sympathy for kings and queens. Erasmo Essenwein just felt so bad for all royalty, on account of because they've always got hired help. They never get to touch doorknobs. Erasmo Essenwein's two greatest joys in life were opening doors and making up stories that no one could possibly believe.

"Why he made up a whole life for himself. Every single thing he said was just made up off the top of his head. He'd just tell one crazy story after another.

"If you asked him if he wanted milk, he'd tell you about a friend of his who had died from poison milk, on account of because the cow had eaten some poisoned hamburger."

"Why would a cow eat a hamburger?" I asked.

"She wouldn't normally," said Shiny, patiently "but this cow was not a normal cow. She'd been traumatized as a calf by seeing a snake in the grass and so she wouldn't eat any vegetables. Now, just like a starving man will eat grass, a starving cow will eat hamburger, just to keep up her strength. Unfortunately, cows don't know anything about food safety or cooking meat properly and this particular cow—"

"Wait a second, I thought this was a story that your mother's friend made up. There *isn't* any particular cow, is there?" I asked.

"You're absolutely right," said Shiny excitedly. "This cow was made up by Erasmo Essenwein himself, so it's a good story, you can bet. Like I was saying this particular cow— "

I shook my head, trying to clear it, then gave up and just listened to Shiny's shaggy cow story.

15

W hen I got home, the apartment was pleasantly empty, and with Pops at the fair, I'd have the place to myself. Even if I didn't do anything but read alone in the living room, I looked forward to the solitude. I was lonely at school, where everyday events worked together to leave me out, but I was never less lonely than when I was alone.

I opened a jar of applesauce and drank it, then followed that with a handful of crackers, both items gifts from the county. The applesauce was generic, white label with black letters, but the crackers were genuine Ritz, a little bit of luxury from the people at the welfare department. The crackers weren't stale but, for name-brand product, they were not very crisp either. Still, they filled me up.

Because I would have to get up early in the morning to ride to the fair with Pops, and who knew when we'd get home Saturday night, I decided to get my homework out of the way, beginning with my Spanish assignment, conjugating verbs in spider-like charts.

Once I'd completed the mindless drudgery of Spanish, I moved on to algebra, another twenty problems of distilling X out of equations. Finally, I was able to continue to my English assignments, where I really wanted to be.

First, I finished the letter to someone who had had an impact on my life. While in class, I toyed with the idea of a letter to Lucinda Watkins, telling her I'd destroyed her note to Pops, so he didn't know anything about his possible non-paternity. Then I would go on to say Lucinda had offered a positive impact on my life through the graciousness of her having walked. Then I would close by telling her that, while I wished her no individual harm, I would not be altogether troubled if her body were ripped in half in some kind of construction accident.

That kind of letter might offer me perverse satisfaction, but I couldn't imagine poor Miss Buonardi's response to it.

Instead, I had written a joint letter to Cookie and Gramper, flavored boy next door, not boy eating government crackers. When Miss Buonardi read it, she would picture me with a shiny red bike in my driveway on Christmas morning instead of sitting in a cracked chair at a kitchen table.

The second assignment, planting that Housman poem somewhere in town and then writing about the person who finds it, was more of a challenge. This would take some creativity. Luckily, I had

all evening if I chose to use it.

I grabbed two more of the plastic sleeves of crackers and slid them into my jacket pocket, then walked down the stairs to find just the right place. I had five dollars left from doing laundry the night before, but I wanted to save most of it for the fair.

I had sat in a lot of different classrooms with a lot of different teachers, but I had never been given an assignment like Miss Buonardi's; her classroom seemed to have life itself, while all the other rooms at the school just had snapshots of life. I figured the best way to have a good idea is to have a lot of ideas, so I tried to loosen my brain, and let the ideas flow.

Reaching the sidewalk, I examined the storefront under our apartment. Looking first into the beauty parlor, I thought about going inside and slipping the poem into a months'-old fashion magazine or collection of hairstyles. I pictured some old lady getting her hair dyed. She'd open it and believe it was a message from God that her husband didn't love her any more.

That could be fun, I thought, but knew I would feel weird walking into Val's Beautette, being the only male and the only person under fifty. Val herself, who had offered to take all the telephone messages Pops and I never got, was already spying me suspiciously through the plate glass. She'd probably take the poem and tear it up in front of me. That was a story I didn't want to tell.

I looked in the next window, Virginia's Pizza Emporium. I'd never eaten there, but Virginia seemed nice enough back in August when I bought a soft drink. The pizza shop was tiny, though, and I couldn't picture any place to hide the poem, unless I asked Virginia to tape it like a flyer to a pizza boxes.

I pictured the pizza delivery to a nineteen-year-old boy with bad acne. He'd tear open the box to get a slice of pepperoni and pineapple pizza, then close the box to keep the rest of the pie hot. Spotting the poem on top of the box, he'd know that it wasn't a coupon or advertisement. Tearing another bite off with his teeth, the boy, I would name him Jeffrey, would rip the poem off the box to look at it more closely.

When Jeffrey found a poem along with his pizza, he'd call Virginia to complain that he had studied enough poetry in school to last a lifetime, and he damn sure didn't want any more now. He'd ordered pepperoni and pineapple, not poetry pizza. Virginia would apologize, and the next time I even walked by her shop, she'd call me inside to yell at me.

Even though it was just a story in my head, I knew I needed to fly under the radar of respectability. Making such a bizarre request of a neighbor would blow my cover. The pizza place was out.

I walked, hoping for inspiration. I thought about placing the poem inside a newspaper at the variety store, but since all New Hampshire newspapers are morning papers, whatever paper I hid the poem in would probably be picked up, unsold, and recycled the next morning. Even a great imagination would have a hard time telling how ground up newspapers had an impact on someone's life

The best I could do was create a woman who used the ground newspaper to keep her flowerbeds warm over the winter. The poem would be just what the plants needed and the following spring's daffodils would be the most beautiful ever. The woman, Belle, I would call her, would enter a flower show and the blue ribbon she won would be the high point of her life. That seemed a stretch, and I was already bored even before I finished creating the story.

As I walked, the words of Oscar Wilde started strolling through my brain, taking the place of the pretty daffodils.

> " They hanged him as a beast is hanged:
> They did not even toll
> A requiem that might have brought
> Rest to his startled soul,
> But hurriedly they took him out,
> And hid him in a hole. "

I thought about putting the poem into a sealed plastic bag, and searching for an open gravesite. I'd drop it into the hole, knowing the casket would cover it at the funeral the following morning. For centuries, the poem would lie beneath the ground, softly ticking away until, say, in the year twenty-three-thirty-seven, when real estate in Oxford had almost completely run out and the town fathers decided to dig up all the cemeteries and get rid of the bodies so another wave of hundred-story condominiums could be built.

One of the workers, a sensitive young man named Ibrahim (the United States having become a Moslem country in the previous century) is hired for the project and finds the Housman poem. When

he reads it, it is the first time anyone in the town has read anything other than the Koran or TV Guide in fifty years.

Ibrahim finds himself moved by the beauty of the words and is ashamed of his actions in disturbing the dead. He leads a protest against the building expansion and becomes the first non-religious poet in memory, writing poems about love and death. Unfortunately, it's hard to find open gravesites when you want them; there was no deus ex machina at work in my life. I was lucky to even have Rota Fortuna.

I came to the Laundromat. As I walked into the laundry with no clothes to wash, a young mother eyed me suspiciously, black stubs among her yellow teeth, with two small, dirty daughters, probably four and two, neither of them in shoes. The woman didn't have much energy to devote to studying me, though, because the younger of the two had turned on the faucet in the sink at the center of the room and was using whatever pressure she could to spray water onto the floor.

"Cherice, stop it right now. I mean it! What's wrong with you?" the woman demanded, not expecting an answer. "Why can't you be good just once? I swear I'd mail you to Timbuktu if I could afford the postage."

Cherice giggled and sprayed water, flooding the Laundromat, until her mother walked up to her and, without a word, slapped her across the face, leaving three distinct stripes. After a moment, the little girl started crying and her mother balled up her hands and ground them under her own eyes in mockery.

"Wah, wah, wah," she teased, through clenched teeth. "Don't be such a baby. It was just a tap. I told you to stop and I meant stop. But just like always you wouldn't listen. No TV for you tonight and you're going to bed half an hour early."

She noticed me watching as I walked through, and threw me a sneer.

"What are you looking at, Pretty Boy?" she demanded from the dark hole of her mouth. "Haven't you ever seen discipline before? I'm her mother, so mind your own business. Go on. Get out of here!"

I wanted to be the kind of person who would try to protect the little girl, but I wasn't.

I wanted to say to the woman, "Hey, Lady, just leave that kid alone," but I didn't.

I even wanted to be the kind of person who would go find a pay phone and call some authorities to come and rescue the kids, but I'm wasn't.

Instead, I was the kind of person who did not need to be told twice to leave any room.

I quickly walked out the back door and into the alley in a state of shock. I was stunned. More even than the assault on the little girl, I was surprised to have been called "Pretty Boy." I couldn't remember a time when anyone had commented positively on my appearance. Even though the lady hadn't meant anything nice by it, I decided to take the insult as a compliment.

Taking the package of crackers out, I walked down the alley to visit Mister, whose glass cage still sat in the doorway.

I leaned over to examine the mouse, who hadn't changed a lot.

"Hey, Mister. How's life treating you? I brought along some food for you."

I crushed the crackers, then took the lid off the cage and poured them in. The mouse ran to the food and ate. I touched him for the first time, and was surprised at how fine his hair was.

"Don't go getting yourself sick by eating too fast, Mister," I said. "Take your time. I don't want a mouse's bellyache on my conscience. That's about the last thing I need.

"Tomorrow, Mister, I'm going to the fair. I'll check around in the barns and see if any of your cousins are there. I'll give them your regards. Tell them you were asking after them and all.

"Much as I'd like to stay and visit with you, I've gotta get going, Mister. I've got this poem I've got to hide somewhere in town and then write about the person who finds it. Kind of a crazy story, I know, and hard for you, as a mouse, to understand."

I petted Mister one last time and put the lid back on the aquarium, checking to make sure it was snug and then looked at the water bottle. It was only about three-quarters full, but I wasn't going back into that Laundromat. I figured the mouse would be fine for a while.

I walked out the other end of the alley, and saw a bakery I'd never noticed even though it was just a few blocks from the apartment. Its pastel sign read "Yummy-Yum Bake Shop." While I didn't much care for the name, I could taste the good smells through the glass doors.

I walked in. Five people stood in line in front of me, but being stranded in a paradise of good smells was pretty good deal.

The first person, somebody's mom it looked like, was picking up a birthday cake and was unhappy about her lavender frosting. She complained about the ratio of red to purple in a proper lavender and got mad at the guy behind the counter when he said lavender was really just a grown-up pink. I couldn't get worked up about the color of a birthday cake myself, since I'd only had birthday cakes those years my birthday had fallen when we'd been living with my grandparents.

A couple stood behind the lady, a man and woman in their early twenties. They'd buy bagels not cake or cookies, I thought. They seemed like the type to eat crunchy foods and raw vegetables and to avoid meat. They had matching pierced lower lips and nose piercings.

I wondered how people with pierced lips ate soup without having it dribble out or when people with pierced noses got head colds, why wasn't snot forced out like a hose with a leak in it?

The couple looked happy, even with the man having flames tattooed onto his neck. They looked at each other and smiled. Someday, I hoped to have a girl, almost any girl, look into my eyes the way this beholed woman looked into the man's.

Right in front of me was a man in his late thirties, with his two- or three-year-old daughter, the man's hands completely covering the little girl's. The man wore khakis, a blue blazer, and a tie-less white shirt, which set off his dark Mediterranean coloring.

If I had to guess, he was either a computer programmer or a teacher of some kind; whatever he did, it was clear that he adored his little girl, who looked like a miniature version of her father in coloring and facial structure.

Still, despite the resemblance, she was all girl from her patent leather shoes to her flowered dress to the pink ribbon in her hair.

"Daddy?" the little girl asked, in a mouse-like squeak.

"Yes, Pumpkin?"

"Can I get a cookie for Becca?"

I guessed that was a sister.

"Of course, Mary-Berry."

"And one for Mommy?"

"Sure, Sweetie."

"And can we go to the cemetery?"

I laughed at the idea of joining them at the cemetery, looking together for an open grave.

"We're kind of in a rush, Mary."

"Please?" the little girl asked.

"Maybe just for a minute."

"Yay!" said Mary, and hugged her father's waist in joy.

"I love you, Sweetie," he said, kissing the top of her head.

I'd heard of a town on Lake Winnipesaukee that in mid-January rolled an old jalopy out onto the ice about fifty yards into a lagoon. The American Legion sold tickets at ten dollars apiece to guess the date and time the car would fall through the ice. Some years they sold up to a thousand tickets. The winner got a third of the proceeds and the Legion the rest. Choosing the moment a car would break through was a mystical ability it seemed to me.

Standing behind Mary and her father, I tapped into that subterranean power. The ice broke, the car dropped and I knew exactly where to place the poem. Without waiting to order anything, I left the bakery, hid the poem, then went home to write the story. Saturday morning and six o'clock came early. I had been dreaming about a mouse at the fair plucked up by a giant machine and turned into a thoroughbred horse that won the big race. Somehow I had bet a thousand dollars on the mouse and now we had enough money to buy a house.

Pops disrupted the dream by roughly shaking me to wake me up.

"Come on, Clayton. It's time to get up."

"I will. I've got to take a shower," I said.

"There's no time. Our ride will be here any minute. Time to get dressed."

"Okay. Okay."

I threw on a slightly stained t-shirt, my good pair of jeans, and my sneakers. Then, because of the chill, I put on a hooded Red Sox sweatshirt. I walked into the kitchen, where Pops handed me a fried egg cooked over such high heat that it was rubbery and starting to turn black. I picked the egg out of the pan with my fingers, and gulped it down in three bites as we walked down the outside steps.

"What time you get in, Pops?"

"Around one. The driver last night had to drop another guy off first."

When we reached the sidewalk, Pops lit a cigarette and scanned the street, looking for the Blue Blazer coming for us. I put my hands in the stomach pouch of my sweatshirt and rubbed them together.

Waiting with Pops was always uncomfortable; he was not a conversationalist and he treated pleasantries as if they were parts of an interrogation. I had learned that standing silently was the best policy.

After a few minutes, the Blazer pulled in. The driver had on a plaid green hunting cap that fought with his plaid red hunting jacket. He had the thousand-mile stare of the drinker pulled from his bed before the night before has been absorbed.

"Clevinger?"

"That's us."

16

"Get in."

Without another word, Pops climbed into the passenger's seat and I sat in the back. Pops pulled out his wallet, and handed a five-dollar bill to the driver.

"Thanks," said the driver.

"Thank *you*."

Pops kept out his wallet and thumbed through the bills inside. He pulled out a twenty and held it over his shoulder without a word. I was amazed. Except for household expenses, Pops never gave me money.

"Take it," said Pops gruffly, without turning his head.

"Are you sure we can afford it?" I was the responsible one when it came to money.

"I said take it," Pops said. "This is the last year you'll be going to a fair as a mark. Starting next year, you'll be old enough to work. Maybe that'll change our luck. Anyway, I'm making pretty good money here. Hundred-fifty a day. Figure you can give some of it back."

"Thanks. Thanks a lot," I said, folding the bill and putting it in my shirt pocket.

"Don't mention it."

Pops cracked his window and turned to the driver.

"Mind if I smoke?"

"No problem," said the driver, pulling out his own pack and lighting a cigarette.

The driver turned on the radio to a country station and turned up the volume, signaling the end of conversation for the forty-five-minute ride. I didn't like music, but it was nice to have time to think about this windfall and how to spend it. With the money I'd saved from doing the laundry, I had twenty-five dollars, a fortune compared to the zero dollars I thought I would have just a couple of days before. I spent the money in my head, not including food, because Pops said only suckers bought food at fairs.

When we pulled into the huge parking lot, we were told to park as far away from the fair as possible. No mark should walk the mile to the fairgrounds and have the walk back weighing on him all day. Pops had explained that the mark should be kept as comfortable and worry-free as possible until all the money had been sucked out of his wallet.

The Essex Fair, while not the largest New Hampshire fair, did have the distinction of offering free parking. In Sandwich, for instance, homeowners could make some nice money renting out their front and side yards to cars at six dollars a pop. The Essex Fairgrounds, though, was set on a huge tract of land in the middle of nowhere.

Later in the day the fair would be filled with smells, sights and sounds, but now it seemed deserted . Except for fair workers making their way in twos and threes to their jobs, there was no movement. The huge rides, like the Gravitron and the Ferris wheel and the Tilt-A-whirl hovered over the landscape, like dinosaurs above the silent tents and food carts.

As we got to the front gate, Pops spoke.

"Fair opens at ten. I've got to go see the boss and get my list of stuff to do. I'll meet you for my lunch at noon right here. I've already found a sausage vendor who knows Michigan Slim and he's been hooking me up right along."

"Okay, Pops."

"And Clayton?"

"Yes?"

"Don't spend that money all in one place."

"Sure, Pops."

Pops squeezed my shoulder in farewell and walked away with the driver, off to be a carny once again.

For the next couple hours, I wandered the fairgrounds, learning the layout and watching the midway bepeople itself. The sun had warmed the day, and I took off my sweatshirt and tied it around my waistband, wishing I'd left it home.

I saw Pops on a tractor smoothing out the sand for the oxen pull at noon. Watching him, in control of a machine and doing work he enjoyed, I thought that maybe I was a parasite on Pops, keeping him from his true life, that of the carny. If I weren't around, Pops could go back on the road, drink when he wanted to and see the world. Watching Pops on the tractor, it appeared he was swaggering instead of slouching.

I wanted to save my money until the afternoon and evening, so watched other people's spending. A skinny old lady with both Republican and Democratic stickers covering her shirt stood in line to buy two fried Twinkies and a fried Snicker's bar. She washed this down with a Diet Coke, and then bought a sausage with onions and peppers.

I sat through a cooking demonstration for Homeonic Waterless Cookware, having a chance to taste chicken, corn and broccoli cooked without water or oil. The lady doing the demonstration wanted to show that fat was bad, so she put a gob of bacon grease on the back of her hand.

"Unless I catch on fire, my body will never get warm enough," she said, "to melt this fat. You can watch for the rest of the session and that fat will still be there. If it's not warm enough on the outside of my body to melt it, do you think it's warm enough on the inside? Nope. That fat will stay just like it is, clogging up your bloodstream forever."

The food was good, and free, but when the lady got to he sales pitch, I had to laugh at the idea of paying thirteen hundred dollars for pots and pans. Heck, if we had that kind of money, we'd buy a car not cookware.

As I walked away, I thought about the fat on the back of the lady's hand and that if she had put a piece of celery there, it wouldn't go anywhere either.

After that, I sat through tryouts for a battle of the bands at the head of the midway, where groups had three minutes to show they could play at all. I heard a cover of a Nirvana song by The Cold Sores, then a cover of "Sweet Home, Alabama" by Pus Theory before being driven away by a jazzy version of "Don't It Make My Brown Eyes Blue" by a band called Ecticity.

In the crowd, I saw some faces I knew from Mastricola, not friends, but people I could acknowledge and be acknowledged by. I was not the completely invisible boy.

For a while, I walked through three or four tents that amounted to a flea market, with all kinds of stuff, from faucet handles to can openers to nail polish. The clothing tent had the widest variety of t-shirts and shorts and baseball caps I'd ever seen.

At noon, I met Pops, who had four sausages in crusty bread in his hands, and a bottle of water for each of us in the oversized pockets of his overalls. I followed Pops into the picnicking section, where we sat at a table with a price tag of seventy-five dollars. Each year, the fair had brand new picnic tables for its guests, with each of them sold off by the end of the four-day run. A box of light bulbs sat at

the other end of the table.

"Having a good time?" Pops asked, his one jab at a conversation starter.

"Yep. I listened to some pretty bad bands and checked out all the rides," I responded. "I'm trying to decide how to spend my money."

I wondered about the light bulbs, but knew Pops didn't share my interest in the trivia of the world. Any time that I had brought home a shiny stone from my journey through life, Pops would look at it, declare it worthless and toss it aside.

When I was younger, I would try to ask Pops questions about things.

"How does your mind decide what to remember and what to forget?" I might ask, which would be met by an indifferent shrug from Pops, followed up by "Who knows?"

That was one of the things I missed most about living with Cookie; even if she couldn't have cared less about what I said, she always faked interest and made me feel important. She gave me the gift of normal, not one of Pops' strengths.

Before I was halfway through my first sausage Pops had finished both of his. He lit a cigarette, huffing the smoke down, not appearing to enjoy it, and then stood up.

"Gotta get back to work," he said. "I'll meet you at six same place for dinner."

"See you then, Pops."

I finished my sausages, and walked to look at the rides. from the Paratrooper to the Himalaya to the Screamer. I divided rides into little kid rides, cool rides and girlfriend rides. Ponies tethered in circles and little boat rides fell into the first category, most of the midway fell into the second and the haunted house and the Tunnel of Love comprised the third. I swore I would not ride a girlfriend ride until I had one at my side.

I stopped at the fiercest looking ride, the Zipper. Freshly painted for this season, the Zipper looked like a brand new medieval torture device. Each rider was herded into a grim metal cage attached to a large wheel. When the operator put the ride into motion, it would spin and rotate so that riders were spun at crazy angles.

While I considered buying tickets or saving my money for later, I watched the crowd by the Typhoon, a section of two rows of stadium seats, each with metal half circle that went over the rider's head and onto his stomach, holding him in place. Once everyone was locked in, the stadium section moved slowly back on forth at the end of a long arm, gaining height with each swing, until finally going over the top. This process was repeated in reverse as the ride slowed down, run by a Hispanic ride operator wearing a New York Yankees shirt.

A familiar face stood third in line. Familiar but not comforting. Blaster wore designer jeans and a polo shirt. I quickly slid back into the crowd, not wanting any contact with him. Just the thought of him took some of the good feeling out of the day. Not all of it, maybe, but some.

I stood by the Thousand and One Nachts ride and watched Blaster climb on the Typhoon. Unless he really searched the crowd for me, I could watch him without being seen. He chose a seat in the front row, between two middle-school girls.

The ride started slowly, then gained speed. As it reached the top, the girl to Blaster's right leaned forward and vomited onto the floor, large chunks of undigested food bouncing off the platform and onto the ride operator. He stopped the ride, much to Blaster's anger. Although I couldn't hear what he said to the poor girl who had thrown up, clearly, he was chewing her out for having the ride cut short. While she wiped drool from her mouth, Blaster yelled at her. She broke into tears, which made him laugh before walking angrily away.

Once the ride had been unloaded, the operator went off for buckets of water. The ride would stay closed until the water dried, and the crowd's tide had moved most witnesses away. I stayed where I was and watched Blaster go to a food concession to order and eat a blooming onion and a smoked turkey leg, followed by some fried dough in a cloud of confectioner's sugar.

I left to avoid Blaster and ended up standing outside a pen with a huge sign: "World Champion Mutton Bustin'." Inside a pen a dozen kids, all six and younger, lined up to last six seconds on a sheep's back. Like bull riders, the kids tried everything to win a ribbon.

I watched for a while, leaving when two men in front of me placed bets on which preschooler would stay on the sheep's back. Betting twenty dollars to pick a good sheep-riding five-year-old made me sick to my stomach.

I went into one of the small permanent structures thrown down on the fairgrounds as randomly as a child's blocks. I found baked

goods in this one, each with a small piece taken out, as though some culinary geologist were taking core samples. Looking at a pineapple pumpkin cake, I saw the judges had removed pieces to taste.

I went back to the midway, still not sure if I should buy ride tickets or not. The Typhoon had started again, so I walked over to watch. Blaster stood in line. I stood behind a tall, fat Hispanic man running a French-fry stand next to the Typhoon. I hid and listened to Blaster argue with the operator.

"Last time, some girl puked and my ride got cut short. That's not fair. You should let me ride free this time," Blaster whined.

"No entiendo lo que usted está diciendo," the operator replied.

"You're in America, now. Speak American," said Blaster angrily.

"¿Qué mena habla a americano?," asked the bewildered operator. "No entiendo."

"What did he just say?" I whispered to the vendor in front of him.

"He said he doesn't know what it means to speak American," the man replied.

"Stop talking gobbledygook," demanded Blaster. "Just let me on the ride. I'll give you the tickets. I don't care."

Blaster pulled out tickets and climbed on the ride and locked himself into his seat.

"Gracias sir. Mayo su madre se acuesta con un potro y hace a muchos hermanos y hermanas para usted," said the operator, with a mocking tone that drew laughs from the French fry vendor.

"What did he say that time?" asked I.

"He thanked the boy, then said he wanted the boy's mother to lie down with a pony and produce many brothers and sisters for him."

I laughed. Unfortunately, the man standing in front of me stepped aside, revealing me to Blaster, who scowled.

"Hey, Clevinger. You can run but you can't hide. I'll find you and get you either today or at school."

Before he could say any more, the ride started and I watched him go back and forth and back and forth and then, as it started to go up to the top, I watched Blaster's face melt in on itself, turning an ugly shade. He puked up the turkey, onion and fried dough eaten twenty minutes before. Through some fluke of timing, Blaster's vomit didn't go onto the floor. Instead, his lap filled with undigested food and stomach acid.

For the second time, the operator stopped the ride early, so other customers could escape Blaster's stench and filth. As he stood up, chunks fell to the floor, and the ride operator said, in unaccented English, "Excuse me, Sir, but there's no eating or drinking allowed on rides. Would you please pick up your lunch and take it with you."

Blaster, too embarrassed and nauseated to respond, walked off the ride in silence, head down.

Right then I got an idea that was either incredibly smart or dangerously stupid. If a fly doesn't want to be swatted, it lands on the handle of the swatter. Instead of sinking into the crowd to avoid him, I walked right up to Blaster.

"I've got a spare sweatshirt," I said, unwrapping it from my waist. "You can cover yourself up until you get a chance to clean off. Then no one will know what happened."

While a bully's first thought in a moment of need is to lash out and hurt somebody who was weaker still, Blaster didn't have much choice here. I was offering him a way to avoid embarrassment, even if accepting a gift from me was humiliating. Confused, he reached out for the sweatshirt.

Before I released it, I looked into his face.

"Just lay off me, okay?" my voice stayed steely and firm, although inside I was terrified.

"Ok. Fine, Clevinger," said Blaster, taking the shirt and tying it around his waist. He walked off toward a men's room where he could clean up.

I was happy to solve the Blaster situation. In celebration, and against Pops' teachings, I bought a vanilla soft-serve ice cream, then strolled the midway for the ten minutes it took to eat it.

As I finished the cone, I felt a hand on my shoulder. Blaster stood there, now wearing shorts and a t-shirt bought at the flea-market tent.

"Listen, Clevinger," Blaster said, a tone of gruff embarrassment in his voice, "your sweatshirt was pretty much ruined, so I threw it away. Even if it hadn't been ruined, I figured you wouldn't want to carry my puke around for the rest of the day. My stomach's still doing flip-flops, so I'm not going to be going on any more rides today and I figured this could pay you back for your shirt."

Blaster held out a fistful of ride tickets, easily fifty tickets, probably more.

"I just bought a bunch of tickets, and now I won't be using them."

"Thanks, Blaster," said I. "Even?"

"Even. And one more thing, Clevinger."

"Yeah."

"Take it for what it's worth, but if I were you, I'd stay away from Chen."

"Chen? Who's Chen?" I asked.

"Sebastian? Sebastian Rutherford? That kid you were with the other day? The squirrelly little kid who calls himself Chen," said Blaster to help clarify.

I realized Shiny had never told me his last name.

"His name is Shiny," I said. "Why are you calling him Chen? And how do you even know him? He just moved here over the summer from Florida."

"Don't worry about how I know him," said Blaster. "Just take what I'm saying and do whatever you want with it. That kid has serious problems."

Blaster walked away, leaving me confused about Shiny, but also with more tickets than I could ever have bought on my own. I decided to wait to see Shiny before making any decisions about anything.

Later that afternoon, as I rode the Ferris wheel to the top and looked over the fairgrounds, I thought Rota Fortuna was creaking away and getting some work done.

17

A s planned, I met Pops for sausages and we sat same picnic table we had lunched on earlier.

"How was the afternoon?" asked Pops. "Having a good time here?"

"Yeah. It's been a real good time. I ran into this kid, Blaster, from my homeroom and we hung out for a while, rode some rides and stuff. He had so many tickets he didn't know what to do with them, so he gave them to me."

"That's real nice. I've always said you were a people person," Pops said, showing a lack of insight. He threw the last bite of sausage in his mouth. Before he swallowed it he had already lit his cigarette.

"Now I might have some big news later. Good news," said Pops uncharacteristically. To Pops, news was hardly ever big or exciting or even pleasant. "Could be our luck's finally changing."

"What's the news?" I asked.

"You just wait until we get home. You just wait," Pops cackled himself into a coughing fit, only soothed when he took a drink of water.

"It's something that could blow a person's mind."

Pops, for the first time in my memory, giggled.

"But I got to be getting back to work now. Let's meet up at midnight, okay?"

"Sure, Pops."

I was a little concerned about Pops' big news, but figured I could hold out for a few more hours. The rest of the evening went by quickly, with my money running out by ten. The local teenagers started drinking once the sun went down, and provided free entertainment until I met Pops.

He carried a heavily weighted cloth bag the size of an extra-large lunch sack. Before I could ask him about it, he put his fingers to his lips.

"Shhhhh," he sounded. "Don't ask about the news until we get home. It's a secret."

Pops was almost giddy when our driver got to the entrance. The three of us walked silently to the car and climbed in.

"Good day for you?" the driver asked.

"Yep," said Pops. "You?"

"Can't complain," and with that the driver turned the radio on.

Pops lit a cigarette, and I just waited to get home. When we got there, Pops arranged to be picked up the next morning, and we walked up the steps.

Halfway up, I said, "Pops, what's the big news?"

"Wait until we're in private," Pops said, as if our apartment offered much more privacy than being ten feet above Main Street in Oxford at one in the morning.

Once I was inside, Pops had me sit down at the kitchen table. Then he dropped the bag on the table with a loud thud and the tinkling of metal on metal.

"So what's in the bag, Pops?"

"Peace of mind, Clayton, peace of mind in a piece of metal."

"What does that mean?" I asked.

"It means when I'm not here to protect you, like tomorrow when I'm at the fair, you'll be able to defend yourself."

"Against what?"

"Prowlers, thieves, murderers, burglar, robbers and crazy people in general," said Pops. "Take a look at this baby. She's a beauty."

He poured out a shining stainless steel revolver and five bullets. Pops stood each one up on its end. I saw five little silos of death standing on the table.

"It's a Taurus .38 special," said Pops. "Small, but it packs a lot of bang. Tear right through a man's belly. It's called The Protector. Got it for only four-hundred bucks from this carny, Hector, who was down on his luck."

Pops was crazy. We could barely make ends meet but he had spent four-hundred dollars on a gun to protect us from the absolutely nobody who had been inside our apartment in the two months we'd lived there.

"It's a five shooter instead of a six shooter," said Pops, "and it fits into your pocket just like it were a couple packs of cigarettes. Nobody could spot it unless you were being frisked."

Pops lit a smoke and smiled at me, a smile that said, "your old man finally came through, didn't he?"

Lifting the revolver, he pointed it at objects in the room and dry-fired. Well, I thought, if that coffee percolator ever turns mean, Pops will protect us from it.

"Pops, don't you need a permit to carry that thing?"

"Only if you're gonna conceal it. I checked before I bought it."

I figured "checking" meant asking an anxious seller who'd say the gun could be used as a baby's pacifier if that would close the sale.

"And the only way they'll know it's concealed is if you pull it out," said Pops, as if people who followed weapons laws just hadn't thought things through well enough.

"Now, wherever I am, I'll know that you're safe," said Pops. "It's like buying an insurance policy, only it's all paid for and I don't have to give anybody monthly premiums.

"Follow me," said Pops, with a conspiratorial tone.

In the bedroom, he opened the bottom drawer of the bureau. The drawer had a bunch of sweaters Pops had taken from Laundromats. He never wore them, but he liked to have sweaters "just in case." He lifted them and dropped the bullets one-by-one, making five separate taps of noise, then gently placed the revolver down, covering it with the sweaters. He closed the drawer and stood up.

"That'll be our secret hiding place," he announced, as if we were both members of an exclusive club. "Don't tell anybody else."

"Don't worry, Pops. I won't."

Although Pops had gone two months without drinking, I pictured him drunk and sad and weepy, with the revolver pointed toward his head. I could almost hear Van Morrison in the background as Pops put a single bullet in the gun playing a nice solitary game of Russian Roulette.

I thought of Pops drunk and happy, shooting out a window at a stranger, a big smile on his face, as if he were at an arcade winning lots of prizes. He'd wave at his victim and call him "Buddy."

Finally, I thought about Pops drunk and paranoid, carrying the revolver in his pocket for the dangerous trip to the liquor store, firing blindly at the first person who asked him directions.

I remembered something Miss Buonardi had said in.

I needed to find some way to get that damn gun down off the wall.

18

"Good morning, Ladies and Gentlemen," Miss Buonardi began. "I trust that your weekends were refreshing and pleasant. May I have a volunteer to spin the Rota Fortuna?"

As though she were a preschool teacher offering caramels, a waving sea of hands met Miss Buonardi's request. She asked Kelly, a shy-looking girl in a pink Aeropostale sweatshirt, to do the honors. Kelly seemed excited to spin the wheel, as though she had been chosen to sit on-stage during a concert. She spun the wheel with gusto and it moved for thirty seconds before settling on the number one-hundred-three.

"Ah, excellent job, Kelly. We have here a poem by Percy Bysshe Shelley, perhaps the greatest poet of his generation, which is saying something, since he lived at the same time as Wordsworth, Keats, and Byron, who were no slouches themselves. As a poet, he was excellent.

"Of course, as a man," she continued, "he was dishonest, controlling and a monster who allowed his children to die at early ages because of neglect. Even Lord Byron, who defended Shelley to the end of his own life, was not immune to the lies and machinations of Shelley. In fact, Shelly may be single most evil men in literary history. Yes, Kathleen?"

"How can that be, Miss Buonardi?

"How can what be, Kathleen?"

"How can he be a great poet and an evil man? That's really confusing."

"Let me try to explain the best I can, Kathleen. It is confusing, I agree, so let me start with a quotation from D.H. Lawrence, an English poet and writer. He said, 'Never trust the teller. Trust the tale.' Again. 'Never trust the teller. Trust the tale.' What he meant, I think, was that we should take the story as itself, not as an extension of the author.

"Let me try to give you a different example. Let's imagine a carpenter who makes fine dining room tables, simply beautiful pieces. Everyone in the countryside wants one of these tables made by, oh, let's call him Norbert Newbody."

At this, some in the class laughed.

"Now let us say that Norbert Newbody, in addition to making exquisite tables, has a hobby of hunting squirrels with his bare hands and popping off their heads. Before the beginning of each carpen-

terial day, he sits on his front lawn with a bag of peanuts and feeds the squirrels until he finds just the right victim then kills it. Once he's killed his daily squirrel, he washes his hands and makes these heirloom tables.

"My question for you, all of you, is 'What difference would Norbert Newbody's hobby of slaughtering squirrels make in your perception of the value of his tables?'"

Shocked silence from the class greeted Miss Buonardi, for they were not used to thinking in a classroom. After a moment, Kathleen raised her hand.

"Yes, Kathleen."

"That's even more confusing, Miss Buonardi, not less."

"Good," said Miss Buonardi, another comment greeted by laughter from some of the students and a hurt look from Kathleen. "No, I'm serious, Kathleen. Real thinking often takes a path through confusion. In fact, that will be your assignment for tonight, to answer the question raised by the behavior of Norbert Newbody."

"Moments ago, I mentioned George Gordon, known also as Lord Byron, one of my favorite poets, a man both extraordinarily underrated and overrated, not an easy task to accomplish. Yes, Kathleen?"

"That doesn't make any sense either. Don't you have to be either underrated or overrated?"

"Good question, Kathleen. Let me explain. Imagine you are a baker who has discovered how to make the perfect apple turnover, the best apple turnover anyone has ever tasted, a Platonic apple turnover, if you will.

"People really like your turnovers, but no baker ever made her reputation on simple tarts, so everyone around you encourages you to make wedding cakes instead. The cakes you make are huge, ornate even gaudy things, with flowers and a fleur de lis that would make Joan of Arc proud. The cake itself tastes of generic vanilla and its frosting has no character, no richness of butter, just the sticky-sweet of confectioner's sugar.

"Now, Kathleen, imagine that people you respect tell you your wedding cakes, which are virtually inedible, are the most beautiful and delicious wedding cakes ever made, and you are crowned the best wedding cake baker ever. From then on, you turn your back on apple tarts for the more serious business of wedding cakes.

"That's just how it was for poor Byron. His wedding cakes were the sweeping romantic sagas he wrote, with dark characters and damsels in distress. Trying to read them today, Byron's long 'serious' poetry strikes me as having no core, no purpose. As Gertrude Stein remarked of Oakland, 'When you get there, there's no there there.'

"Byron's turnovers?" she continued. "He was one of the funniest poets ever, and when he wrote satire he was a comic genius. Unfortunately, two hundred years ago, like today, funny people didn't get to sit at the grown-ups' table. So he was overrated as a serious poet and vastly underrated for what he actually did, make people laugh.

"What's ironic is that a fat short man with a club foot should have created the so-called Byronic hero. In fact, many have tried to make Byron himself the archetype. The Byronic hero is tall, dark, handsome and melancholy. You can think of Jim Morrison or Trent Reznor of Nine Inch Nails or, even, of Heathcliff in *Wuthering Heights*."

"Does anyone know what an archetype is?" Miss Buonardi asked brightly.

"Like Noah's Ark?" asked Jim unsurely.

"Very creative, Jim, but not quite on the mark. An archetype is an original model on which other similar items are based. To return to Shelley for an example, his wife, Mary Wollstonecraft Shelley, who was no great virtue either as a human being, wrote *Frankenstein*, creating an archetype for monster stories.

"But for now enough literary gossip. Let me read the poem for you."

Miss Buonardi read "Ozymandias," the Italian sonnet that tells of a legless statue in the desert with the inscription on the base,

> **"** My name is Ozymandias, king of kings:
> Look on my works, ye mighty, and despair. **"**

Miss Buonardi asked for volunteers to read their homework.

"I can read mine," volunteered Kathleen Keesey.

"That would be fine, Kathleen."

Kathleen cleared her throat and read:

"I left my copy of the poem by A. E. Housman in my mail box on Friday afternoon and I predict it will be found by my mailman, Mr. Cepaitis, on Saturday morning when he delivers the mail. I think he will look it over and see that it doesn't have any postage. Then he

will knock on our door to give it back to us. Then he will notice that it doesn't have any address on it either. I predict I will answer the door and Mr. Cepaitis will give the poem back to me. Then I will tell him it was a poem, not a letter, which is why it doesn't have postage or address and that my teacher told me to put it there. We will have a good laugh, then he will give me the mail."

"That certainly captured the letter, if not the spirit of the assignment, Kathleen. Thank you. Anybody else care to read their story?"

"I will," volunteered Jim with pasty skin and squeaky voice.

"On the Sabbath morn I put a literary creation within my begetter's gazette, placing it in the sporting section, which he unceasingly peruses primordially because he has an affinity for such amusements, especially the Red Sox and the Patriots. Subsequent to his pursuit of java, he reclined on the davenport and initiated his scrutiny of that particular section, like he always does. After he inspected the initial leaf, he forwarded his attention to the second page, and the poem was relinquished.

"'What the heck!' he articulated with gestures of annoyance.

"Then I told him about our assignment."

"I assume," said Miss Buonardi gently, "that you used a thesaurus?"

"Yeah. My mom said that's what she always did in school."

"Well, Jim, I appreciate the effort, but I'd really like to hear what you have to say and in your voice. Thank you, though, Miss Buonardi said gently.

"Is there anyone else who would like to read?"

Miss Buonardi could see that I was itching to raise my hand, but fighting off the itch.

"Clayton?" she asked. "Would you mind reading your piece?"

"I guess I could," I said.

"Once there was a little girl named Mary," I read, trying to make my voice as clear and strong as possible. "She was sometimes called by her full name, Meredith Anne. She was sometimes called Mary Berry. She was sometimes called, when her daddy was feeling silly, Meredith Andrew. But she was mainly just Mary.

"Mary was two and a half. Like most two and a half year olds, Mary had a lot of favorite things. She loved books. She loved her blankie. She loved her doll, although her doll's name changed from day to day. Sometimes Mary's doll was Anna. Sometimes she was

Hannah. Sometimes she was Julie and sometimes she was Spelunkdomino. She was Spelunkdomino when Mary was feeling silly, which was quite often.

"Yes, Mary had a lot of favorite things in the world, but her favoritest thing was her family, her Mommy and her Daddy and her big sister, Becca. Becca was sometimes known as Rebecca and sometimes as Rebecca Marie and sometimes as Becca Boo and sometimes as Poopy-Head. She was known as Poopy-Head when Mary was tired and fussy, which, thankfully, was not very often.

"Miss Buonardi. Miss Buonardi," called out Kathleen, whose hand had been waving since the third sentence. "You said we were supposed to write about the poem. He hasn't even mentioned the poem. That's not what you said to do."

"I believe what I asked you to do was to write a scene about the person who might find your poem. Let's give Clayton a chance, shall we."

"But you said—"

"Kathleen, why don't we listen for now, then we can talk."

"Okay, Miss Buonardi," said Kathleen, in a tone that indicated it was not okay at all.

I was kind of shaken by the interruption, but I continued.

"Mommy and Becca both had blue eyes and very light skin, while Mary and Daddy had brown eyes and dark skin. Eyes and skin color are not <u>very</u> important things, but Mary did feel especially close to Daddy because they looked alike. When Mary and Daddy went on a date to get donuts, the man at the coffee shop would say, "I can sure tell who your daddy is," and this made Mary feel warm and happy inside.

"Each day when Daddy came home from work, he would take one of the girls for a walk. One day Becca. One day Mary. One day Becca. One day Mary. One day Becca. One day Mary.

"When Daddy and Mary walked, they would walk through the neighborhood, seeing Mrs. Bliss in her garden, who would always say, "She looks just like you, Keith. She's so beautiful."

"Daddy would always say, "I don't think I'm that beautiful, but <u>she</u> sure is." Then he would laugh a gentle laugh that made Mary feel comfy.

"After seeing Mrs. Bliss, Mary and Daddy would walk to the cemetery and play hide and seek behind the gravestones or visit the se-

cret forts they had in the shrubs. Whatever they did, they had fun, for Mary loved being with Daddy, because he always made her laugh and always had a new game to play.

"One day, Daddy and Mary invented the Tail Game. Out of the blue, Daddy said, "I've got your tail," and he held up his fist as if he had a tiger's tail in it. Mary reached back to her bottom and said, "Please, Sir, let go of my tail." When Daddy let go, Mary said, "I've got *your* tail," and yanked on Daddy's imaginary tail. Then Daddy said, "Please, Madam, let go of my tail."

"Back and forth they went, pulling each other's tails until they both fell down laughing.

"Another day, Daddy and Mary invented the Game Game. They were running around in the cemetery, when Daddy stopped and said, "Excuse me, Madame, but what kind of game are we playing?"

"A chase game," shrieked Mary and ran off, with Daddy chasing her.

"Daddy said again, "Excuse me, Madame, but what kind of game are we playing?"

"A tickle game," screamed Mary, as Daddy caught her up and tickled her.

"Again, Daddy said, "Excuse me, Madame, but what kind of game are we playing?"

"A hug game," laughed Mary, so Daddy hugged her and rolled her on the ground. This game went on as long as Mary could think of new things for Daddy to do.

"Miss Buonardi," called out Kathleen again. "You said to give him a chance, but he still hasn't even mentioned the poem. He didn't do it right."

"Kathleen, are you enjoying Clayton's story?"

"I guess," the girl admitted. "But it's not what it's supposed to be."

"Kathleen, if you are enjoying the story, then Clayton is accomplishing at least one of the tasks set out for him. I think we can listen to his tale without judging it for right now. Do you agree?" Miss Buonardi asked in a tone that made it clear that Kathleen would, indeed, agree.

"Yes, Miss Buonardi."

"Okay, then. Clayton would you continue? I myself am enchanted."

"It's almost done," I said to Kathleen in a sort of apology.

"That's too bad," said Miss Buonardi. "I'm really enjoying listening. This is exactly what I was talking about earlier, Clayton. The story is written with a voice, not just with words."

"Thanks," I said, then continued reading.

"Because Mary and Daddy walked in the late afternoon, they often had a visitor watching them from above. Before the sun had fully set, a white disk appeared in the sky. The moon. Mary had lots of questions about the moon. What was it? Who lived there? Why did it change its shape from day to day and week to week? Daddy told her that some people thought the moon was the eye of God, and that it was always watching us, even when we couldn't see it in the sky. Then Daddy told her that he would give her the moon, and from then on it had been Mary's Moon.

"On one particular day, after Mary and Daddy had visited with Mrs. Bliss and walked to the cemetery, Daddy looked at Mary and said, "I'm in the mood for a cookie. May I share that mood with you?"

"Then Daddy reached down toward his stomach, as if he were tearing off a piece of his mood, got down on his knees and offered it to Mary.

"Why, yes," she replied. "I would love to share a mood with you. And a cookie."

"And a cookie," Daddy agreed, and instead of turning right to go home at the end of the street, they went left to go downtown and to the bakery.

"When they walked into the bakery, both Mary and Daddy felt like they were in heaven. Everything smelled so good that Mary had a hard time choosing, but finally she asked for two chocolate chip cookies, one for her and one for Becca. Daddy got a peanut butter cookie and they left the bakery.

"Bite for a bite?" asked Mary.

"Bite for a bite," said Daddy, then he held his cookie to Mary's mouth while she held hers to his. They each took big bites, then rubbed their bellies.

"MMMMMMM," they both said at the same time, then giggled.

"Let's walk home a different way," said Mary.

"Let's," said Daddy, taking her by the hand, and leading her down an alley they had never noticed. Although some alleys are not very

nice, and not very clean and not very well-lit, this was not that kind an alley. The brick walls had been painted with pictures of children playing, and each of the doorways had a light over it, although, of course, they were not turned on yet.

"Look, Daddy!" shouted Mary.

"Where?" asked Daddy.

Mary pointed at a trash can.

On top of the can was a glass box.

Inside the box was a piece of paper, but not just any piece of paper. It was moving.

Mary and Daddy walked to the box and Daddy reached in and pulled out the paper.

"It's a poem," he said.

"No, it's not, Daddy. It's a mouse!"

Mary was exactly right. Inside the glass box, was a little brown mouse, eating a cracker.

"He's so cute. Can we keep him?"

Daddy looked up the alley. Daddy looked down the ally. Nobody was there.

"I would say that a mouse in the trash is a mouse who needs a home," said Daddy.

Mary hugged Daddy and made up a song, which she sang all the way home.

"A mouse, a mouse will live at our house," Mary sang.

And Mary was right.

Mary and Daddy walked home with Mary's Moon looking down at them and Mary's Mouse looking up at them.

"Bravo, Clayton!" said Miss Buonardi, walking over to stand next to me and clasping her hands in front of her.

"Thanks."

Kathleen's hand went up before I had a chance to sit down.

"Yes, Kathleen?"

"Did that really happen?"

I was confused by the question.

"What do you mean?" I asked. "It's a story."

"I know, but is there really a mouse?"

"Yes," I replied

"And is he really in a cage in an alley?"

"Well, yeah," I said.

"And is there really a little girl named Mary?" demanded Kathleen.

"Yes. I stood in line at a bakery behind her and her father," I answered.

Kathleen continued, getting angrier with each moment.

"And did she end up taking the mouse home with her to live?"

"No. I made that part up," I said.

"So, are you going to rescue the poor mouse or just leave it there?"

"I'm not sure what I'm going to do about that mouse," I said. "I like that mouse. But this is just something I made up. It's a story."

"I think I'd call it a lie," the girl said with finality.

"That's a little harsh, don't you think?" said Miss Buonardi, placing her hand gently on my shoulder.

"But what about the mouse?" asked Kathleen, a friend of animals everywhere.

"I'll try to think of something, I guess," I said unsurely. "I did move it out of the trash."

Miss Buonardi cleared her throat

"Clayton, why don't you have a seat?"

"Now," Miss Buonardi continued. "Let's look at the notion that a story and a lie are the same thing. They certainly have a lot of similarities, don't they? What are their goals? Or to make it more personal, what is a liar trying to accomplish and how does she do it? What is a writer trying to accomplish and how does *she* do it? A lie, at least most times, is designed so that it will be believed. A good story, likewise, tries to be believable.

"It seems to me that it is considerably easier to lie to someone who doesn't know your baseline behavior, how you typically behave. That is, it's a lot easier to lie to a stranger on a subway train than to your big sister. Likewise, it's easier to lie successfully to your sister on the telephone than it is to lie to her in her bedroom.

"The writer is distanced from the reader by the written word. Once you write for a larger audience than simply your English teacher, your words have to be taken on their own, not compared to your behavior or your history.

"In Clayton's piece, for example, I suspect part of the reason you think of it as a lie, Kathleen, might be that Clayton's written voice doesn't jibe with the young man you see in front of you. It's a voice that appears to be speaking to Mary herself rather than to you or

me. Clayton's piece could easily be a bedtime story told by Daddy to Mary. If you had picked up that story in the form of a children's book, Kathleen, would it have felt like a lie?"

"Maybe not," said Kathleen. "I'm not sure."

"Let's continue exploring," said Miss Buonardi. "A successful lie uses more details than an unsuccessful lie. For example, say Mr. Platine wanted to see my lesson plans, and I hadn't done them. Which lie would be more believable? 'They are around here somewhere, but I can't quite put my finger on them' or 'When I was doing them at home last night, somehow my computer was infected by a virus called Sirius Seven. This virus wormed its way into every word processing document I've made for the past three weeks. They were all trashed. My nephew, Stephen, is home from Stanford and he's coming over this evening to see what can be salvaged.'"

"I think we'd all agree the lie with more details is more believable," Miss Buonardi said, walking to her desk and picking up a black notebook. "And, for the record, here are my lesson plans, and I don't intend to lie to Mr. Platine or anyone else, for that matter."

The class laughed.

"But good writers use a lot of details, so that we know their characters well. It has been said that little minds look for the extraordinary while great minds are fascinated by the commonplace. When I think of my favorite writers, George Elliott, for instance, it is not that she created a fantastic world, but that she created the very world she lived in that is so fantastic."

Kathleen's arm waved.

"Miss Buonardi, you said his name was George."

"*Her* pen name was George. Her real name was Mary Ann Evans, but she felt she needed a man's name to be taken seriously. She is one of those gifted writers who doesn't just make you think, but also makes you wonder. But that's another topic for another time. Let's get back to the idea of details, what gets put in and what gets left out.

"When Clayton tells us that Mary has dark skin and brown eyes, but doesn't tell us what she's wearing, or tells us that her older sister's name is Becca, but never mentions her mother's name, he's made decisions that one set of facts matters more than another.

"This notion of 'mattering' is in itself an interesting phenomenon, for most writers can't tell you why one fact or word or character 'matters,' but if each thing didn't matter to the writer, she wouldn't have put it in."

Here, Miss Buonardi paused for a moment, time enough for Kathleen to raise her hand with another question.

"But Miss Buonardi, isn't that why a liar chooses details, because it will make it more believable?"

"You may be right, Kathleen, but I think the liar chooses facts because they will convince her audience, while the good writer chooses facts to satisfy herself, knowing that if she is satisfied, the audience may very well be pleased as well.

"The writer sitting alone in what Virginia Woolf called 'a room of one's own,' is probably not thinking of her future readers; rather, she is trying to win a game with herself, trying to find the right words and the right sentences and the right paragraphs. She sits alone and stares at paper or, today, a computer monitor, and is completely removed from what she writes about, unless she is writing about writing, which would probably not make a great subject for the average reader.

"Even non-fiction writers—essayists, journalists, historians, for instance—all make decisions that matter in the use of details, what they leave in and what they leave out. For instance, Franklin Roosevelt, our country's president during the Great Depression and World War II, was wheelchair-bound because of polio, yet no journalist at the time mentioned it. Imagine leaving out that little fact. Of course, it's also important to remember that the truth is more than just a collection of facts.

"Finally, a convincing liar can usually convince herself that she's telling the truth, or at least a version of it. Likewise, the writer has to believe that what she writes deserves to be written.

"Kathleen, Ernest Hemingway took your position when he said, 'All writers are liars,' and I think we've seen that such a case can be made. But I also think that the great writers, the ones who matter, are trying to help us see the truth through the series of lies they tell us."

"So, Clayton, was there some higher truth you were trying to show us in your piece?"

"Uh, not really," I said. "I was just telling a story."

19

At lunchtime, I got my sandwiches, and went for the second day of my sentence with Wunderlich and the other inmates of Group. When I got to the room, the faces were pretty much the same as Friday, and once again Wunderlich sat at the head of the table.

"Hey, Fellas," chirped the little man. "Everybody have a great weekend?"

Silence.

"Anybody do anything exciting?"

Deafening silence.

"I myself went to a concert Friday night."

Dental drill to the ear silence.

"Saw somebody you guys probably know. A man who many people think is Da Bomb, Billy Joel."

"Wunderlich, can I ask you a question," said Christopher, knocking back a capful of Chocolate milk. "And get an honest answer."

"Hit it, home boy, what's percolating? What's popping?" Wunderlich asked. "Tell you anything you want to know. Except of course, for disrespecting, because I, as you young folks like to say, ain't down with that. Ask away."

"You're a middle-aged man, but you wear the same cologne as us. Today, you walk in here trying to sound like a rapper. It's as though you read some stupid newspaper article with one of those gray boxes that gives parents definitions for the slang their kids speak," said Christopher, arms resting high on his belly.

"Actually," said Wunderlich, "I visited a web site put up by a Christian hip-hop band. I figured it would be good if you could see that I understand your language, not just your feelings. But you didn't ask your question."

"A Christian rapper?" asked Christopher with a snort of contempt. "What do Christians possibly have to rap about? --Wait, I don't even want to know. My question is this: are you so bad at being a grown man that you'd rather be a ridiculous teenage wannabe?"

For a moment, Wunderlich looked as though he had been punched in the stomach; slowly, though, he absorbed the blow and that big old self-assured by self-delusion smile came onto his face.

"I get it, Big Guy," the psychologist said, beaming brightly into the fat boy;' face. "You think I'm invading your hood, and you think

it's wack for me to be all up in your crib. Well, before you go dropping plates in this mother, let me tell you"

Here, his voice became very crisp and professional

"I am a man who can walk in two worlds. Because you've asked me to, I will return to speaking in my own language rather than that of the streets. It appears to make you nervous to hear a grown man who's still, as we used to say, with it. You view me as a threat."

"No," said Christopher, leaning back in his chair and closing his eyes. "I see you as a dork and not much else. And with that, I'm going to get a little shut-eye. Sorry, for those of you who don't speak English, I'm gonna cop some Zs."

Christopher was clearly hoping to continue the game of the Friday before, but Wunderlich appeared to recognize that that was a contest he would always lose.

"Well, I bet some of you guys are kind of jealous, huh? I got to see the Piano Man himself, Billy Joel, in concert. He sang all his old hits and even a few new songs. Man, that guy is a true entertainer. Right up there with Neil Diamond."

Without opening his eyes, Christopher said, "Isn't he that fat guy that used to be married to a model and isn't he just a drunk? And, Wunderlich, how pathetic are you that you look up to the little monkey?"

"For your information, Christopher, while Billy Joel may have struggled with substance abuse issues, he is still a vibrant, dynamic entertainer, celebrity and artist. And please call me Peter."

"I'll compromise and call you Peter Licker, okay, Wunderlich?" said Christopher, eyes still shut. "So let me get this straight. Billy Joel smashes a car and he's got 'substance abuse issues.' My uncle smashes a car when he's drunk and he got a year in prison and three years probation. That's like the old thing about tragedy is when I stub my toe. Comedy is when you fall off a roof and get run over by a car. It's crazy. And so are you."

"I'm not trying to minimize the dangers of driving while intoxicated," defended Wunderlich. "I just think we need to have a little empathy for the man. He is a genius."

"Sure he is, Wunderlich, and when he overdoses and dies, it will be a tragedy. Any celebrity who dies from drugs is always on the verge of turning his life around."

Here Christopher sat forward and opened his eyes, looking directly at the psychologist.

"You're such a fool, you don't even know you're a fool. You're going to have to work hard just to move up into the category of pathetic."

The giant boy stared a hole in the little man's face.

"Wunderlich," he slowly said, "You're a fraud and a fake. You don't understand what you're saying. Worst of all, you don't understand yourself and how you come across to us."

I was shocked at the fat boy's assessment of Peter Wunderlich, not because it was inaccurate, but because it was so true, but the kind of truth that didn't often get uttered. Even more startling was the psychologist's response.

Wunderlich smiled. And smiled.

And smiled some more.

Finally, he spoke.

"Well, Christopher, that's what we used to call 'rapping' in the old days, speaking the truth to each other. Now would anybody else like to share?"Complete and utter silence

"Then let me get into the meat and butter of group.

Last Friday, Christopher brought up the Platonic chair, Plato's idea of a perfect chair.

"Today, I'd like for us to learn a little bit more about a dude who had a lot to teach us. Plato is most famous for coming up with the story of the cave. He had people imagine a cave and inside some men are chained up to a wall. All they can see is the back wall of the cave. They can't see anything outside the cave and can't even see each other very well, because the cave doesn't allow a lot of light. The only thing they can see is the shadows of whatever is moving outside the cave. Of course, the prisoners eventually thought that the shadows were real and all of life was flat and cloudy.

"Then Plato asked his crew to picture what would happen if one of the men escaped and checked out the real world. Could he possibly explain to other men what the real world was like? Would his buddies believe him or would they think he was crazy and try to kill him?

"I don't want to simplify such a complex and subtle thinker, but I think we can see that the real message that Plato is trying to tell us is the same as that spoken at the end of my very favorite movie.

"'There's no place like home,' 'there's no place like home.' Plato

wants us to be satisfied with the way things are, obey the rules and not try to stir things up. Living in the cave is better than escaping and being killed."

20

My brain folded in on itself, and I spent the remaining eleven minutes of group trying to count as high as he could in his head.

I didn't have a chance to talk with Shiny about Blaster's comments until Tuesday morning.

"Guess what? Guess what?" Shiny said when I saw him.

"What?" I said.

"Oh, you already knew," said Shiny, a mask of disappointment covering his face.

"Knew what?" I said, once again confused by Shiny.

"Well, I said 'Guess what' and you did, which kind of spoiled the surprise," explained Shiny.

"Shiny?" I asked. "Can I ask you a question? And will you answer me honestly"

"Of course," said Shiny brightly. "The only thing I like better than answering questions is questioning answers."

"You know Blaster?"

"Blaster? Like Blaster of Paris?" Shiny giggled as if he had made some very witty retort. "What's Blaster?"

"*Who's* Blaster? I'm serious. That kid Blaster that we saw last week on the bike. His real name is Josh Brazelton, but everyone calls him Blaster."

"I told you before. I've never seen that boy before in my whole wide life," said Shiny with certainty. "I would swear on a stack of Bibles that he's a stranger to me.

"Well, he called you Chen instead of Shiny. I saw him at the fair on Saturday," I said. "He told me I should steer clear of you."

"Clearly, he's crazy," said Shiny. "Don't forget, he's physically attacked you. He probably suffers from an extreme case of pseudologia fantastica."

"What's that?" I asked.

"It's a symptom of one or another kind of mental illness. People with pseudologia fantastica, or P.F. tell stories just for the sake of telling stories. They make up intricate bizarre alternate universes. It's sad, actually."

"But he knew your name was Sebastian the first time he saw you. When I talked with him Saturday, he said you were dangerous and disturbed."

"P.F., for sure," said Shiny, shaking his head sadly. "People with

it just spin these fantastic yarns based on nothing. I mean, here is a boy who assaulted you on the street saying that *I'm* dangerous and disturbed. Look at me. Do I *look* dangerous?"

I looked at the tussle-haired blond with braces and had to shake my head that anyone could think Shiny was a menace.

"See what I mean?" said Shiny. "Your little friend made a lucky guess about my name and now he will go on telling you lies as long as you're willing to believe him. As your real friend, I'd advise you to have nothing to do with him. As your assailant, he advised you to stay away from me. Who are you going to choose?"

"You," I said, still feeling doubtful, but Shiny's use of the word friend did a lot to wipe away my uncertainty.

"When we lived in Palatka, Mommy had a friend who was afflicted with P.F. That's how come I know so much about it," said Shiny. "She used to call him Sneaker Man."

"Sneaker Man?" I asked.

"Yup, because he was a P.F. Liar," said Shiny, giggling. "His name was Dominick Delaney, and he had one of the worst cases of P.F. in all of Florida. You couldn't believe a word he said.

"For instance, Sneaker Man had a lot of theories that he tied together. He believed that fish fall differently from us."

"Fall differently?" I asked, confused. "What does that mean?"

"Well, Sneaker's man's theory was that fish die and go belly up, then float to the surface, that's their way of falling, instead of falling down the way we do. He would say things that kind of made sense, but you couldn't really be sure."

"Like what?" I asked.

"Like 'we used to think that if we knew about one, then we also knew about two because one and one are two. I say, we've got a lot to learn about 'and.'"

"What does that mean?" I asked.

"Who knows?" responded Shiny. "Also, he was an amateur physicist who had created a machine in his basement that didn't use any energy but gave out free electricity."

"You mean like a perpetual motion machine?" I asked. "I thought that was impossible."

"It was, until Sneaker Man came along", said Shiny. "He came up with the technology to make energy free, but he wanted people to think he was a clerk at Seven-Eleven. Imagine that, making a breakthrough discovery that could change life as we know it, but he told people he worked in a convenience store. It breaks my heart to think of it."

"If he was such a liar, how do you know he really had a perpetual motion machine?" I asked, attempting to apply logic.

"Sneaker Man told me himself and then he showed it to me" said Shiny.

"So, you saw a perpetual motion machine with your own eyes?" I asked.

"Yup," said Shiny. "Although it didn't look like much, just a bicycle on a stand. It wasn't even much of a bicycle at that."

"The perpetual motion machine was made out of a bicycle?" I asked.

"Yep. The bicycle, though, wasn't the breakthrough part. It was just a red Schwinn from like thirty years ago. It had a banana seat and high-rise handlebars. Sneaker Man told me it had been his as a child, but I assumed that he was lying. He had a baseball card attached with a clothespin to the back wheel, so when it spun it made a thwackety-thwack sound. I think it was a player from the Dodgers, but I'm not sure."

"So how did this thing work?" I asked.

"We'll be here all day if I have to explain to you how a bicycle works. You see, it has chains and gears and pedals and you have to pump—"

"I *know* how a bicycle works," I responded. "I meant the perpetual motion part."

"Oh, that," said Shiny. "Well, I told you he had suspended a bicycle wheel so that the front wheel was on the ground and the back wheel was raised. Then he took a gravity shield and placed it so that the front half of the back wheel didn't get any gravity.

"Of course, this meant that the back half was always being pulled down by gravity, so the wheel kept on spinning. He attached a generator to the tire, one that was designed to run a bike light, except he had unhooked the light. He used the bicycle to charge batteries that he found discarded on the street."

"I'm confused," I said. "Where did he get the gravity shield? I've never heard of such a thing."

"I think he bought the parts for it at the Radio Shack on Broverton Avenue," said Shiny, appearing to search his memory, "but I'm

not sure."

"Shiny, I don't think you can buy a gravity shield at Radio Shack."

"I said he bought the *parts*; he had to put the shield together himself," said Shiny. "All I know is that he said it worked.

"Anyway, he had these bushel baskets of batteries that he'd filled with free electricity. He'd walk around the neighborhood offering people super-charged batteries for a dollar apiece.

"That's how he got in trouble," continued Shiny.

"How?"

"Well, I said he told everyone he worked at Seven-Eleven. Seems people got suspicious about him because of the cheapness of his batteries. They figured he must have stolen them from Seven-Eleven.

"When the police investigated him, of course they found out he didn't even work there. Never had. The manager had never even heard of him. That's when he confessed to stealing the batteries from Seven-Eleven."

"But he hadn't stolen them, you said."

"I know. That's why he confessed."

"Why?" I asked.

"On account of because he had pseudologia fantastica, just like your friend Blaster," explained Shiny patiently. "I'd steer clear of this guy, Clayton. Mommy, bless her dear little heart, gave me three rules to live by and I try to follow them.

"First, if you want to get a dirty skillet really and truly clean, put it on a burner on high heat. Then you pour in enough kosher salt to cover the bottom all over. Then you take a towel and scrub the hot salt in. It will clean out even the dirtiest pan.

"Second, remember that all disabled people are courageous. There's no such thing as a crippled coward.

"Third, don't trust a man who wears a mask."

"Which of them has to do with Blaster?" I asked.

"The last one, obviously," said Shiny. "Using a name like Blaster instead of a perfectly good name like Josh is the same thing as wearing a mask in my book."

"But your name is Sebastian and you call yourself Shiny," I said.

"Exactly!" said Shiny. "I have a nickname. Your friend Josh, if that is his real name, has an *alias*. Doesn't that disturb you just a little?"

"I guess," I said. "So, nobody ever called you Chen before?"

"Never is a long time," replied Shiny. "It goes back to the beginning of the universe and who's to say that some shepherd in Mesopotamia didn't call me Chen. I will say that nobody I know calls me Chen, on account of because my name is Shiny."

"And you just moved here from Florida?" I continued, wanting more clarity.

"I don't think I'd use the *just*, when it was actually a pretty traumatic time for me. I told you I was in foster care before I came here. Well, the foster family was named Foster—that's probably how they got into the business—and they were real nice. I was real broken up when I moved to New Hampshire."

❋ ❋ ❋

The rest of the week passed without incident. I developed the habit of stopping by to see Shiny either on my way to school or on my way home or both. The squirrel-faced kid might be strange, but he was a good talker, and I wasn't used to people wanting to be with me.

On Friday afternoon, I found Shiny standing outside waiting for me.

"Hey," I said.

"Hay is for horses, better for cows, chickens would eat it but they don't know how," responded Shiny, "That's a poem for you, on account of because you like poetry."

"Thanks, I guess," I said.

"What are you doing tonight?" asked Shiny.

"Well, Pops is working the Sandwich Fair, so I don't guess he'll be home before one or so. I guess I'm pretty much free for the evening."

"I didn't ask about the *evening*," said Shiny. "I asked about the night."

"What do you mean?"

"I mean if your father gets home at one, he'll be asleep by one-thirty, right?"

"I guess."

"Then we'll meet up right here on my porch at two."

"What for?"

"That's what I want to know," said Shiny, "and we won't know until we get there."

"But what will we do?" I asked.

"Have you ever been out on the streets of a small New Hampshire town at two in the morning?" asked Shiny.

"No," I admitted.

"Me neither," said Shiny. "Maybe that's when they water the elephants."

"Water the elephants? What elephants?" I asked

"The elephants that come out at two in the morning," explained Shiny. "They're usually near water, so that's where we should go. Down by the river."

"Shiny, there aren't any elephants here."

"We'll never know unless we go."

"I guess," I said.

"Just meet me here and we'll see whatever there is to see."

"I guess that'd be okay," I said doubtfully.

That evening, I sat in the living room, reading from Reading Gaol.

> " In Reading Gaol by Reading town
> There is a pit of shame,
> And in it lies a wretched man
> Eaten by teeth of flame,
> In a burning winding-sheet he lies,
> And his grave has got no name. "

I memorized great chunks of it while I waited for Pops. At a little before one, Pops came in, surprised to see me still awake.

"What are you doing up so late?" he asked.

"Good book," was my response.

"I'm hitting the sack," said Pops. "G'night."

"Night," I said.

At 1:30, I went into the bedroom and softly called out to Pops. No response. I walked over and stood over and looked down. Pops' face, which during the day carried hints of his demons, looked peaceful and younger, as if he were the child and I were the father checking on him. I leaned over and kissed his forehead, pulled the covers up over Pops' shoulders, then softly walked out of the room.

Putting on my jacket, I tiptoed out of the apartment and down the stairs, making no noise.

Getting to Shiny's porch, I stood, softly blowing on my hands, worried that maybe Shiny wouldn't show. The lights were off in his aunt's trailer. He might have fallen asleep. He might have been teasing me when he said he'd meet me. I worried these thoughts like a dog searches a bone for a last shred of meat.

After a few minutes, though, I could hear approaching footsteps, not from the trailer but from behind me. I watched the shrubs and saw Shiny come out, a big grin on his face.

"Sorry I'm late," he said. "I told Aunt Margaret I was sleeping at your house. Figured since you don't have a phone, she couldn't check it out. So, I've been having some adventures of my own. I had to take a little detour on account of because of these."

Shiny held a small package in his hand, but I couldn't make out what it contained in the dark.

"These what?"

"Firecrackers! I've got three left. Two houses down there were some little kids having a sleepover. I tied four fuses together and lit them. BANG! BANG! BANG! BANG! Those kids probably need to change their underwear. I hid in the bushes and watched them run into their house, screaming like babies. It was hilarious."

"I bet," I said. "What do you want to do?"

"I don't know. What is there to do in Oxford, New Hampshire at two on a Saturday morning?"

"The Laundromat's the only place that's open now. You have any dirty clothes?" I said. "If we have enough money, we could walk over to Manchester and go to the all-night pizza place. I've got four bucks. How about you?"

"I've got five. That's enough for pizza and a couple of sodas."

* * *

While I walked stiffly, trying to be as tall as possible, Shiny hunched and shrunk down to fourth-grade size. Step after step we walked silently, until Shiny finally spoke up.

"So, I know you live with your father. Is your mother dead or something?"

"Or something," I replied.

"What does that mean?"

"Well, I don't really know whether she's dead or not," I said. "I

haven't seen her since I was six. Before that, I hadn't seen her since I was three. It's been just me and Pops for a long time."

"What happened to her, though?" asked Shiny.

"You know, Shiny, when I've stayed with my grandparents, they have a backyard that looks into a wood. Every now and then, I'd see a fox, either first thing in the morning or when the sun was going down. There was no way to predict when that fox would make an appearance, and I never really tried to look for her. She'd just be there and then be gone.

"One time I was talking with Pops about that fox, and I said wouldn't it be great if we could see the fox all the time, instead of just now and then. He got this real serious look on his face and said, 'Clayton, there are only two ways you could see that fox all the time. First, if we killed it, and second, if it were comfortable enough to be here all the time, which would mean it was probably going to kill us. Either it dies or we do. There's no hunting allowed in town so we can't shoot it. Anyway, we don't have a rifle. You need to just be happy with the times you can see it and be thankful that you don't see it enough to have it become your predator.'

"That's kind of how it is with my mother. I expect that staying in one place, and being seen all the time would mean either that she was dead or that she was going to kill us. Now, I just think about her now and then and let it go. You can't miss what you never had is what I say."

"Oh," said Shiny. "Sorry I asked."

"Shiny, it's no problem talking about it, there's just not much to say. I don't know the lady, so I can't really be mad that she left. I don't love her, so I can't really be sad. I just kind of let it be."

As we walked in silence, I thought that maybe I'd sounded too harsh. Whenever I thought of Lucinda, all I could do *was* think; no feelings were attached to her memory, for she had left few memories indeed.

Shiny got out his firecrackers and a pack of matches.

"You wanna use these?" he asked brightly, apparently hoping to change the mood.

"Sure," I said, as we walked past a churchyard. "Waddya wanna blow up?"

"Something cool," said Shiny.

"We'll be on the lookout," I said.

By now, it was close to three and we were only halfway to Manchester.

"You wanna turn around?" asked Shiny. "I'm getting kind of tired."

"No, let's keep going," I said. "If we try, we can be there in twenty minutes. Just think how good the pizza will taste when we finally get it."

"I suppose," said Shiny. "So how do you like Oxford so far?"

"It's a place," I said. "I've lived in a lot of places. They kind of blend together after awhile."

"I know what you mean, but living in New Hampshire is sure different from Florida. I mean, when Mommy and I were together, neither of us ever had more than a windbreaker to keep us warm. Here, you got to have about six sweaters just to go out in December. Also, the people are different."

"Different how?" I asked.

"Well, in Florida, people come in all varieties. There's black people and Cuban people and Dominican people and about a thousand others. Here in New Hampshire, there are just white people. It's like a Mr. Potatohead convention. It gets kind of boring to stare at the same pasty faces all the time. I like a little spice."

"Well," I said. "I lived in Boston for a long time, and there's lots of different kinds of people there."

"What kind is your dad?" Shiny asked.

"What do you mean?"

"You said he's a drinker. There's lots of kinds of drinkers. I could make up a chart of drinking types just like I could a chart of butterflies. In fact, one of the schools I went to in Florida was a charter school that did just that."

"Did what? And what's a charter school?"

"A charter school is a school where you make a lot of charts and a company pays for them. The school I went to was sponsored by H & R Block, the tax people, so we studied things having to do with taxes, any kind of taxes."

"Taxes?" I asked uncertainly.

"Yup, for math we did tax worksheets. For science we did taxidermy, which if you don't know what it is is taking dead animals' guts out and replacing them with stuffing. For social studies, we studied the history and impact of taxes. And for English we studied taxono-

mies, which if you didn't know, is ways of organizing information."

"Shiny, what does this have to do with Pops and his drinking?"

"I'm getting to that," Shiny responded. "Just be patient. You see with any taxonomy you can divide things up a whole lot of different ways. Like my big project was on butterflies. First, I made a scientific taxonomy dividing butterflies up into a bunch of families like the swallowtails, the gossamer-wings, the metalmarks and a bunch of others. Then I took each family and broke it down into different kinds of butterflies that go in it. That's one way of doing taxonomy, but you can do it lots of different ways.

"For another project, I divided up all the butterflies in the world into four categories: butterflies I've seen and am glad I saw, butterflies I haven't seen but wish to see, butterflies I've seen and want to forget and butterflies I haven't seen and do not care to see. Once I'd assigned a butterfly to one of those categories, I had to make up a chart with a bunch of subcategories. So the 'butterflies I haven't seen and do not care to see had subcategories like: butterflies I am afraid of, butterflies which are so small that I couldn't see them even if I could see them, butterflies that have been so beautiful in my dreams that seeing them in real life would be a disappointment and butterflies that look so much like butterflies I've already seen that there is no point in seeing them.

"I spent most of the semester making charts of butterflies, and if we hadn't moved I'd probably still be making them.

"You wanted to know what this had to do with your father's drinking. I'll tell you. I asked you what type of drinker your father was, and you couldn't tell me. Well, just like you can put butterflies into categories, you can divide up drinkers.

"Some guys drink every night until they pass out, then they get up in the morning to start all over again. Other guys get pie-faced every Friday and Saturday but don't drink at all during the week. Still others have a favorite breakfast wine and lunchtime beer and after-dinner whiskey. There's probably as many types of drinkers as there are butterflies.

"So, what kind of drinker is your father?"

"Well, it's not like he drinks every day."

"That's called 'intermittent' or 'periodic,'" Shiny said like a scientist. "And when he's drinking, does he keep on drinking?"

"Between a couple days and a couple weeks, I guess."

"That's 'binge,'" said Shiny. "And what does he like to drink?"

"He likes brandy," said Clayton, "but when he's drinking he's not real particular. Anything that has alcohol can go in his mouth."

"So, he's a Periodic Binge Omnibiber. That last word means he'll drink anything. If you'd just told me that, I would have known."

"Known what?"

"What kind of drinker he was."

As we crossed the bridge into Manchester, we speeded up. John's Pizza, famous for being open twenty-four hours, not for its pizza, was only a few minutes away. Soon, we went into the pizzeria, and stood at the bar to place our order with the clerk, an older man with a cauliflower ear. I had to force myself not to stare at the left side of his head as we ordered a small pepperoni pizza and a couple of cokes.

We sat at the table farthest from the counter, and waited for our order. After paying for the food and drinks, we had one dollar and some change left.

"Did you get a look at that guy's ear?" whispered Shiny. "How do you think he got it?"

"I bet he lost a bet and had to put whirring blender blades up to his head," I suggested. "Or he's an old semiprofessional football player who suffered a concussion on the field. His head swelled up and the doctor's did that to him tearing his helmet off to save his life. Whatever happened to him, that kind of stuff freaks me out."

"It doesn't bother me so much," said Shiny, "because I once had a teacher who had a face that looked like a bag of melted caramels. Miss Finch I called her, on account of because that was her name."

"What happened to her?" I asked. "Was she in a fire or something?"

"Nope. Miss Finch was an art teacher at one of my schools, and she was an artist on the outside of school," explained Shiny. "I guess she was a pretty good artist. I mean she could draw a cow better than anyone I've ever seen and that's hard to do. Anyway, when she had just gotten out of college, she started selling lots of her paintings. The thing was, she was pretty, too, so the men who bought her paintings all wanted to date her.

"One day, she looked in a mirror, and realized that her paintings might not be that good after all. It might just be her looks. There and then, she came up with a plan."

"A plan?" I asked.

"Yup. She went into her kitchen and opened up the cabinet under the sink, and got out a bottle of crystal Drano and some rubber gloves."

"Drano? What was she going to do with Drano?" I asked.

"I don't know if you knew that some women have mud baths to make themselves prettier, but Miss Finch mixed the Drano with a little bit of water and spread it on her face to make herself a lot uglier. She wanted to uglify herself to find how good an artist she was. Of course, the Drano mud started eating away at her face just like her flesh was a hairball clogging a drain, so she started screaming before she'd even gotten it all on. Even when she was calling for an ambulance, though, she kept on pushing the mud so that it would cover all of her face."

"That's awful!" I said.

"That's not even the awfullest part," said Shiny, "on account of because after she got out of the hospital, people were buying her paintings because they felt sorry for how bad she looked, so she never really got to find out how good an artist she was.

"There's an old saying," Shiny continued, "that you can't turn a butterfly back into a caterpillar. I think that's doubly true when it comes to Drano mud baths. By the time she was my teacher, she had pretty much stopped worrying about whether she was pretty or ugly, on account of because she didn't have any choice."

The pizza came and we blotted it with napkins to get some of the hot grease off.

"You and your mother sure know some strange people," I remarked. "I'm not saying that's a bad thing, just that my Pops and I hardly meet anyone, period, much less people with melted faces."

"Why's that?" asked Shiny.

"Why's what?"

"Why is it that you and your father don't meet people?"

"It's kind of personal," I said, not wanting to talk more about Pops' drinking, and the fact that when he was sober, he was pretty meek and shy, but when he was drunk he was loud, obnoxious and unlikable. Neither condition was part of any Dale Carnegie course on meeting people.

"We're friends, right?" asked Shiny.

I couldn't remember ever having been asked this question in my life. While there had been some guys I'd hung out with for a while, the notion of friendship had been left unsaid.

"I guess we are," I said.

"You guess?" demanded Shiny. "You guess? It's almost three in the morning. We've both snuck out of our houses to go get pizza and if we get caught we'll both be in plenty of trouble when we get home and you're telling me you 'guess' we're friends."

"Okay. Okay," I said, laughing. "We're friends. I take back the 'I guess.'"

"So, if we're friends," said Shiny, "then what's so personal about you guys not meeting people? Your dad's a drunk. Big deal. Lots of people have drunks for fathers or mothers or even little sisters. That doesn't explain why you and your father don't meet people, does it?"

"I guess not," I said, confused but relieved and not sure why.

"I think part of the reason you don't meet people," said Shiny, "is that you're not very outgoing. I mean, here we are friends, and I've practically got to pull information out of you. Open up. Be yourself. If you can't get that skeleton of your father out of the closet, then at least teach it to dance. Let people get to know the real Clayton Clevinger."

21

Walking into the outskirts of Oxford at a little before five, I mentioned I was thirsty.

"Well," said Shiny, "I guess it's your lucky day. We've got one dollar bill, and the Laundromat's open."

We hurried down Main Street. Down at the other end, we saw the town's only police cruiser, parked outside Smitty's grocery. Its lights were out.

"Probably a cop catching a little sleep," I guessed. "There's not a lot of crime here, so I guess I can't blame him."

"Well," said Shiny. "Mommy always taught me to be respectful toward police officers, because you never know when you're going to have to deal with them. She, for instance, had only gotten one ticket in her life before the whole problem with Stella. It wasn't a driving ticket, either. It was football-related."

"How the heck do you get a ticket because of football?" asked I. "Did she go wild at a game or rally or something?

"Mommy would never go to a football game," said Shiny, as if "football game" were synonymous with "ritual killing." "She doesn't like crowds. Especially loud crowds. Most especially large crowds with cheerleaders."

"Cheerleaders?" I asked. "What's wrong with cheerleaders?"

"What's wrong with cheerleaders?" repeated Shiny. "I'll tell you what's wrong with them. You see, back when Mommy was seven, she went to her first and last football game with an uncle from Mississippi. It was just the local high school football team, but to Mommy it was the most glamorous place she'd ever been, from the marching bands to the players themselves to, especially, the cheerleaders. From the kickoff on, they, fascinated Mommy with the way they moved, like dancers and athletes together. She loved their costumes, the frilly white skirt and the maroon megaphones on their white sweaters. Most especially, she was drawn by the fact they were able to keep smiling for an hour at a time.

"To Mommy, smiling that long is about the same as a lizard's ability to keep from blinking. It was both fascinating and scary. This one cheerleader in particular, drew Mommy's attention, because she was even able to put lipstick on while maintaining her smile and not even getting any on her white teeth.

"Anyway, at half-time the cheerleaders went out to the middle of the field to put on their performance. Mommy's uncle asked her to

go to the concession stand with him, but she really wanted to watch the show, so she let him go. Mommy watched the cheerleaders do their act, building pyramids and throwing each other around.

"After a while, her uncle came back. He had brought her a bottle of grape soda and a hot dog. He had a beer and a hot dog. He sat down next to her and they watched the finale, with each cheerleader jumping into the air and doing a split. Well, the one that Mommy had been focusing on the most must have been the captain, because she got to go last, the climax of the climax.

"As this cheerleader ran into the center of the field Mommy asked her uncle to open her grape soda. He was just putting the bottle up to his jaw to pry off the cap when the cheerleader went into the air. As she floated down and her skirt was lifted, everyone saw she had gotten her period from the damp red stain on her white cotton panties.

"Unfortunately, the shock of seeing all that was enough to cause Mommy's uncle to inhale the bottle cap, which lodged in his throat. While everyone else in the stands was either showing they were out-raged or laughing uproariously, Mommy's uncle was turning blue. By the time things settled down, he was fully and completely dead. Mommy did say the funeral was nice, and that the cheerleading team sent a sweet floral arrangement, although they had to decline the invitation to cheer for Mommy's uncle at the grave site.

"So she got arrested as a little girl at a football game?" I asked, trying to make sense of the story.

"No," said Shiny. "That's why Mommy doesn't go to football games, out of respect for her uncle."

"Then how did she get arrested because of football?" I asked. "I'm confused."

"Oh, that," said Shiny. "No that happened years later, when Mommy was working for a while at a sports bar in Palatka. It was just a little place, but it was always packed with men on their way home from work, if they had work. Men would come in and bet on anything, under the table of course.

"Mommy says that gambling is one of the worst sicknesses there is, because alcoholics always eventually run out of alcohol but there's no end to what people can gamble on. Mommy liked to tell about one customer who would bet on balls and strikes in a baseball game as it was being played on TV. Mommy also told about another one who loved to bet on how many peanuts there were in a bowl. Most especially, though, Mommy told stories about Walker.

"Walker was a man who had spent most of his twenties in jail. It seems that he had a problem with pennies. He liked them a lot, so he would go from convenience store to convenience store, looking into the 'leave a penny/take a penny' cups and emptying them into his pocket. It was his belief that the money in those cups belonged to no one and that he was as welcome to take seventeen as the next man was to take three. Well, there was one convenience store clerk who . . ."

"Shiny, no offense, but is this really part of the story of how your mom got arrested?" I asked.

"Well, not exactly," said Shiny. "But it's an interesting story any way and it does help you *understand* the other story."

"Maybe some other time then," I said.

"Fine. Getting back to Mommy and Walker and gambling. Walker loved to bet on flipping coins. In fact, when he had free time, which was often, he would while away the hours flipping the same quarter and recording how it landed. He had whole notebooks divided into two columns, one said 'heads,' the other 'tails.' Each column was filled with tick-marks, and Walker believed that he was on to something.

"According to Walker, flipping a coin was *not* an even chance. In fact, it was almost a sucker's game. Walker claimed to have flipped the same quarter exactly 100,000 times. Mommy said that once Walker got a few drinks in him, he would start holding court. It's a pretty boring subject, though, so people shied away from him as a rule. Of course, Mommy was his waitress so she couldn't get away. She had a professional duty to him, so she became his sole court member.

"'With one-hundred-thousand flips, you would expect to have fifty thousand heads and fifty thousand tails, or at least that's what they want you to believe,' said Walker. 'In actuality, though, my records show that I got seven-hundred-fifty-seven more heads than tails.'

"'If I had bet on heads at just one-thousand dollars a flip, I'd be a rich man today,' Walker would complain. 'And I've got the numbers to prove it.'

"Here, Walker would point down at a beat-up briefcase he always carried with him, which contained the notebooks in question.

"Now, Mommy is a nice person who doesn't believe in shooting people's dreams and leaving them to die in the gutter, so she didn't even have clue how much she would upset Walker with her question."

"Getting arrested, Shiny," I murmured. "How did your mother get a ticket and why?"

"I'm getting to it," said Shiny, sounding hurt. "Don't you want to know the question?"

"Sure," I sighed.

"Mommy asked Walker why he had used the same coin for all those tosses. He said it was so he would get a reliable outcome. If he'd used different coins all the time, he wouldn't have been able to trust the results.

"'But haven't you changed the question?' Mommy asked, 'so that you've only proven that one coin in the entire world is off, not that they all are?'"

"Mommy said Walker stared at her for a full minute," continued Shiny, "then laid his head down on the bar and looked like he was gong to cry. She wanted to make him feel better, so she said, 'Anyway, where would you ever find the crazy fool who would bet you a thousand dollars on flips of the coin? Why I wouldn't bet matchsticks on it.'"

"Walker looked at Mommy with the eyes of a madman and he said through clenched teeth, 'You've shown me my life has been wasted and you wouldn't even bet matchsticks with me? What kind of monster are you?'"

"'Well, maybe I'd bet matchsticks,' said Mommy, 'but not for keeps.'"

"'Call it in the air,' said Walker as he flipped his now unlucky coin."

"Tails," said Mommy, and it was.

"Tails," and it was.

"Tails."

"Heads."

"Tails."

"Heads."

"Heads."

Every one of them right.

Walker stared at her.

"'You can't do that,' he said. 'The odds are one-hundred-twenty-eight to one against doing that.'

"Mommy didn't know what to say, so she asked him if he wanted another drink. Instead, he demanded she tell him her trick. Of course, Mommy didn't have a trick. She was just being lucky, I guess.

"Walker said he wanted her to keep going so he could figure out what she was up to. Mommy told him she didn't mind playing with him a little while longer, but that she had other customers to take care of. Then she went on to pick the right side seventeen more times in a row. Walker shoved his coin into his pocket, and stomped out of the bar.

"Within about ten minutes, he was back, and he'd brought a police officer with him.

"'There she is, officer,' he said angrily, although Mommy hadn't really done anything to him. 'Write her up. I know the law in this town and she's not following it.'

"'I can't write her up until she does something,' the policeman said with embarrassment.

"'Call it in the air,' demanded Walker.

"'Heads,' said Mommy and of course and it was.

"'There's your evidence, Officer. She's in violation of the statute we talked about.'

"'I guess you're technically right,' said the officer, looking down at his feet, 'but wouldn't you like to find a different way to handle this?'

"'Write her up,' Walker said. So the policeman did and gave Mommy the ticket.

"For what?" I demanded.

"Mommy got a twenty-five dollar ticket for telling fortunes without a license. Later, though, the policeman came back and told Mommy he'd take care of things for her."

"Shiny, you told me your mother got a football-related ticket," I complained. "Where does the football come in."

"Oh, yeah. That," said Shiny. "Sports bars make about eighty percent of their money because of football. If it weren't for football, the bar wouldn't have been there and so Mommy wouldn't have worked there and she never would have gotten a ticket."

The Sudsomat was right before them.

"And you," said Shiny, "must be getting thirsty.

22

A t five o'clock in the morning, we walked into the Sudsomat. I needed to get home soon, since Pops would be getting up to work the fair. I pulled the last dollar out of my wallet and walked over to a washing machine to smooth the bill out before putting it into the soda machine. Five times I smoothed it up and down, then we walked to the back of the laundry for our drink.

"Coke?" I asked. At Shiny's nod, I inserted the money into the machine, and pressed the button. Nothing happened. No Coke. No change. No nothing.

"Aw, that stinks," I said. "The machine ripped us off," I said.

"Let's get it back," said Shiny.

"We can't get the money back. The machine ate it."

"No," Shiny said, "I mean let's get the machine back. Get some revenge on it for stealing our money."

Shiny pulled out the last three ladyfingers and carefully twisted their fuses together, then slid them into the dollar slot. The firecrackers were right beneath the electric eye when Shiny lit them.

BANG! BANG! BANG!

The laundry filled with noise, and I looked at the damage three small firecrackers could do placed in an enclosed area. The plastic parts of the dollar slot were blown off, and something glass must have broken, because there were shards on the ground. The smell of gunpowder filled the air.

"That'll teach that Coke machine," said Shiny. "It'll never steal from us again."

We were facing the machine, when we heard a siren. We ran out the back door as the front door of the Laundromat was being kicked in.

"Halt. Halt or I'll shoot!" said the voice of the formerly sleeping policeman.

A million thoughts raced through my mind in the split second that I had to make a decision. The cop must have thought he'd heard gunshots. Pops would find out I'd snuck out. Shiny and I could get shot. What if a ricocheting bullet hit Mister Mouse?

Before I had a chance to really think, I came up with an instinct-inspired plan.

"Follow me," I said, and ran down the alley to the left, cutting in to the deep doorway that housed Mister Mouse.

As soon as we were hidden, we heard the cop rushing out the back door, then heard his footsteps as he ran down one of the other alleys. I peeked out from the doorway and saw the cop disappear.

In the moment before we left our hiding spot, I was overcome by etiquette.

"Shiny, this is Mister Mouse. Mister Mouse this is Shiny. My two best friends in the world. Mister, we'll try to come back later."

We ran down the long alley the cop hadn't taken, coming out a half block from my apartment. Scanning the street, I was happy the cop had not circled around. We ran to my stairs.

"Where are you going?" asked Shiny.

"I live here," I said and we climbed the stairs as quietly as we could. At the top, before I opened the door, we could hear Pops' snoring in the bedroom through the living room window.

As I reached out to open the door, I heard Shiny laugh.

"That door has got to be for sure the ugliest green I've ever seen."

"C'mon in," I said. "We'll go into the kitchen and have a seat for a while. Pops will be getting up soon, so you can't stay long."

"Don't you get it?" asked Shiny.

"Get what?"

"It's not late any more. It's now early," Shiny explained. "If I showed up at your house at two in the morning, your father would think it was suspicious that I was out so late. If he gets up at six and finds me here, you just explain I'm an early riser and then it's a mark of character."

"Mommy always taught me," Shiny continued, "that 'on the other hand' always has an on the other hand. She also taught me that anybody who says they like opera is lying and that frogs don't taste as good as they look. But mainly she taught me the other hand rule, because it doesn't really matter what you say or do, it's that you can convince people."

"I never really thought of it like that," I said, admiringly. We sat at the table, like desperados waiting on a train.

I shrugged.

"I'd offer you something to eat, but there's not a lot in the house. Applesauce, chicken and a block of cheese the size of your head."

"What kind of cheese?" asked Shiny.

"Government," I said, trying to hide my embarrassment.

"I love government cheese," said Shiny, clapping his hands together in delight. "Why didn't you say so?"

"I didn't know that anybody liked that orange stuff," said I. "If you'll eat that, you'll eat anything."

"I don't know about that," said Shiny. "I mean, I'll try a lot of different foods, but I'm no Lindy Lu."

"Lindy who?" I asked as I got out a plate and knife for the cheese.

"No, Lindy Lu. You weren't listening."

"No, I mean, who's Lindy Lu?" I asked, cutting off hunks of cheese.

"She was a friend of Mommy's when we lived in Hilliard and she really would eat anything."

"She would eat any food in the world?" I asked.

"Nope. She would eat any <u>thing</u> in the world. I'm sure you've heard of pagophagia, right?"

"No, I don't think so," I said. "What does that mean?"

"It means having an obsession with eating ice," Shiny explained. "What about xylophagia, do you know what that is?"

"No," I confessed.

"An obsession for wooden toothpick eating," Shiny said. "Coniophagia is a lust for eating dust from Venetian blinds. Geophagia is the need to eat clay or dirt, and it's pretty common in pregnant women. If you eat anything strange, they've got a phagia for it. If you have an obsession to eat snot it's called mucophagia. Sharp objects? Acuphagia. Stones? Lithophagia. Raw potatoes? Geomelophagia."

I found that this talk of eating things that were not food had turned my stomach so that even eating things that <u>were</u> food didn't sound so good. I put down my cheese.

"Now each of those different phagias could get annoying pretty soon," Shiny said, "but they are nothing compared to the disease poor Lindy Lu had."

"What was that," I asked.

"Omniphagia," replied Shiny. "The obsessive desire to eat all of God's creation."

Shiny paused to let this sink in.

"You know the feeling you get when you see and smell a slice of pizza on the table in front of you?"

"Yes," I said. "Of course."

"Well," said Shiny, "That's the feeling that poor Lindy Lu got

when she looked at a television remote control or a fork or a candle. Everything in the universe got her hungry and looked good enough to eat. With one exception."

"What was that?" I asked.

"Anchovies," replied Shiny. "Nobody really likes *them*. They just pretend to. Anyway, getting back to poor Lindy Lu. We take our appetites for granted. When we're hungry, we eat some cheese or a sandwich or some clam chowder and our hunger goes away.

"Imagine what it was like for Lindy Lu. She would get hungry, and everything in the room looked like food. Poor Lindy Lu would pick up a sponge and eat it as if it were a piece of bread. Of course, that didn't do anything to satisfy her hunger, so she might pick up a box of thumb tacks and eat them the way you or I would a box of raisins."

"Shiny, I don't want to be gross or anything, but doesn't everything you put in your mouth have to come out at some point?"

"Of course it does," Shiny agreed. "Luckily for Lindy Lu, she was the first person in Florida to have a surgical zipper."

"A zipper?"

"Yup, her stomach was cut open like it was a piece of cloth, and they sewed a foot-long zipper into her, just like they were making a jacket. Now a lot of stuff she ate would come out the normal way, but every few days she would lie down on her back, unzip her stomach, and take out whatever was stuck there. I watched her do it a few times and it was like watching a nature show about the stuff they find inside sharks."

"Of course, now that she's in jail," Shiny said, "I expect that the authorities are probably able to control what goes in, so she may not have to unzip as often."

"Why is she in jail?" I asked, not sure if I could believe the story, but not wanting to offend Shiny.

"Because of her omniphagia."

"They can't put someone in jail because of a disease," I said.

"No, they can't," agreed Shiny. "But they can put you in jail for the things you *do* because of your disease. As soon as Lindy Lu walked into Belmark's Coins and Jewelry on Aster Avenue in Hilliard, that hunger of hers got her in trouble. Before she could help herself she had swallowed eighty-three thousand dollars worth of coins and jewelry—"

Shiny's story was interrupted.

Pops, dressed only in boxer shorts and a ZZ Top t-shirt, weaved into the kitchen, his revolver waving around wildly, looking for something, anything to shoot. The gun pointed first at the refrigerator, then at me, then at the sink, and finally drew a bead on Shiny. I saw the gun growing and growing until it seemed to have taken over the kitchen.

"Pops," I barked, holding both hands out in front of me. "Put that thing down before you kill someone."

"Sorry," said Pops, appearing to wake as from a dream. "I was just waking up and checking on the time and I heard a voice in the kitchen and I thought it was a prowler. I didn't even put bullets in the gun. See?"

Pops pulled at the trigger, which gave off a tiny "click."

"Pops," I said, "If you walk into a room with a gun, anybody in the room with any kind of weapon is going to use it against you. If it had been a burglar, he would have shot you first."

"I know. I know," said Pops. "I'm sorry. Guess I just wanted a chance to use my new toy."

Pops absently reached up and scratched his beard with the gun barrel.

"So who's your new friend, Clayton?" Pops asked. "And why are you boys up so early?"

"My name's Shiny, Mr. Clevinger, and Clayton and I are going to go hike up Blue Jay Mountain and look for birds. I'm kind of an ornithologist, and Clayton said he'd like to learn about birds himself."

"That sounds real good, son, Pops said. "You boys have a good time. Enjoy your cheese, too."

With that, Pops walked, gun still in hand, back into the bedroom. We heard him shut the bottom drawer after putting the revolver back into the bureau under the sweaters.

"Clayton, can you make me some coffee?" Pops called through the open doorway,

"Sure, Pops," I responded.

I went to the cupboard and got out the generic coffee that Pops bought, with its black letters on white paper.

"Do you drink coffee?" I asked Shiny.

"Nope. Never," Shiny said. "Mommy knew two different men who died from coffee, so I stay away."

"How do you die from coffee?" I asked.

"Well, the first man wanted a cup of coffee very badly each morning when he got out of bed. He was addicted to the stuff," said Shiny, looking up when Pops, dressed, entered the room. "No offense to coffee drinkers, but it is an addiction. Anyway, this man, Alberto was his name, and he had a tattoo of a snake across his face, but that doesn't enter into the story. Alberto really loved his coffee. He ground his beans in a little grinder within one minute of when the water would hit it.

"Poor Alberto got out of bed one morning and heard jackhammers outside his house. When he went to make his coffee, he found the water had been turned off because of the construction.

"Now, if he weren't addicted, he would have gotten angry that he couldn't take a shower. But he *was* addicted, so what he did was sit down at the kitchen table with his newspaper and pour himself a bowl of coffee beans. He started snacking on them, the way you or I might a bowl of cashews, except, of course, he didn't chew them, just swallowed them down.

"The first bowl of coffee was fine, but he wasn't satisfied, because he wasn't addicted to *coffee*, he was addicted to the caffeine inside it, and he was not getting the caffeine he wanted on account of because it was still trapped in the beans.

"So he got up and he brought the whole bag over to the table and started eating them by the handful, until he'd eaten a whole pound of coffee. Well, what he was really doing was planting a time bomb in his very own belly, because as his old digestive juices starting breaking down the coffee beans, they were absorbing away the caffeine like nobody's business.

"Within half an hour," Shiny said, "that caffeine started kicking in like an adrenaline syringe to the heart and Alberto was so jacked up he couldn't stand it. His heart was racing like it was going to burst and he could not stand still. He actually started running into walls, just because he had so much energy.

"It didn't take him long to recognize that he was in real trouble, so he ran five blocks to a hospital, but by the time he got there, he was just babbling and jumping around and shaking.

"The doctors and nurses didn't know what to do with him, so they took him to an exam room and let him throw himself against the walls there while they thought about the problem.

"Needless to say, he had a heart attack and died within fifteen minutes. Now you would think that would be that, but even though he was dead, Alberto was still very much awake on account of because he had so much caffeine in him.

"Now, it's bad to be dead" said Shiny, "but to be a wide-awake corpse is really creepy."

I looked at Pops, who just shrugged and grabbed a cup of coffee and got ready to go outside and wait for his ride.

"See you tonight," he said, while putting on his coat. "if you're still up. Sorry about the gun. I just overreacted, I guess. Good luck with the birds."

He left.

"Shiny, you said your mother knew two men who had been killed by coffee. Who was the second?"

"Oh, that was when we lived in Thonotosassa. Mommy was working at the Piggly Wiggly there and she knew a guy who worked on the loading dock. His name was Phillip, and he loved Archie comic books. He was crazy about Jughead, and hoped to meet him some day.

"How do you meet a comic book character?"

"I don't know," Shiny said, "on account of because he died before he had the chance."

"From coffee?"

"Yup. A whole crate of Chock Full of Nuts fell right on his head."

"Shiny, you tell me these crazy stores and I have a hard time believing them," I said.

"That is a problem," said Shiny.

"I know," said I. "And I don't know what to do about it."

"Well, I think you might need to see a faith healer," responded Shiny.

"A faith healer?" I asked. "What does that have to do with you telling me stories I can't believe? I thought faith healers cured people of diseases or made them walk again."

"No, that's *doctors*," Shiny answered. "But they can't help you with this. That's why you need to see a faith healer, so he can heal your faith and you can believe me again. Doctors can't do that.

"But," I said, "are the things you're telling me real or what?"

"Of course, they're real," protested Shiny. "If they weren't real, I wouldn't tell them to you and if I didn't tell them to you, they

wouldn't be real. Can I have some more cheese?"

"Sure," I said, confused but not sure what to do about it.

Maybe this is what friendship is really like and I should just get used to it.

23

"What was that stuff you were telling my father about bird watching?" I asked. "Do you really know anything about birds?"

"Well, in Florida, every private school with any self-respect has a mascot and you have to learn certain facts about your school's mascot. Moving as much as we did, I got a lot of fact cards about a lot of different birds.

"For instance, when I was in second grade at The Academy of Knowledge, their mascot was the fish crow, which can swim under-water for up to three minutes, on account of because it has very large lungs. Its predators are alligators and raccoons, and other birds don't much like it.

"Then, later on that year, I went to The School on the Hill with the Red Door. That place wasn't bad, but the director wasn't that creative when it came to naming things. His boat, a little fifteen footer, was named 'Boat' and his son was named 'Boy,' just like in Tarzan.

"Anyway, the mascot there was a black-bellied whistling duck, which is a very annoying bird if you ask me. Instead of quack-ing, it whistles, on account of because that's its name. It's what's called a mimic and it copies the songs it hears. Well, Florida is filled with transplanted New Yorkers and back about twenty years ago, two men who really liked Broadway songs put speakers outside and taught a band of ducks some tunes. These days, as ducks have inter-married and moved on to join other flocks, you can be walking by a swamp and hear some stupid duck whistling 'Surrey with the Fringe on Top' or 'Life is a Cabaret' or 'I'm Gonna Wash that Man Right Out of My Hair.'"

"So, yeah, I know a little bit about birds," said Shiny, "but only Florida birds, not New Hampshire mountain birds. And private schools up here don't seem to care for mascots as much as they should, so it might be my birding days are over for now."

"Oh," I said, a common response to Shiny's explanations. "It's getting on toward seven o'clock. What time do you need to get home?"

"Any time's fine," Shiny said. "Aunt Margaret can't worry, re-member?"

"Well, I don't know about you, but I know I'm really, really tired," I said, stifling a yawn. "I need to get some sleep. If you want you

can sleep on the couch, and I'll go into the bedroom"

"Sounds good."

I went into the bedroom and lay down on the unmade bed, pulling a stained sheet over myself. For the first time in a while, the alphabet visited me as I lay there, trying to relax myself into sleep.

My old nursemaid T hugged me and hummed a lullaby into my ear, then the whole alphabet played a game of Red Rover until one side consisted of seven players, who then lined up in order. I-T-S-O-V-E-R. I tried to figure out what it meant, but before I could, I'd fallen into a dreamless sleep.

* * *

I was awakened just before noon by a huge thumping sound from the living room.

"Hey," came Shiny's sleepy voice. "You're sitting on me. Get off."

"Wha? Sorry, Buddy," Pops said. "Didn't see you there. You're so little hardly noticed you."

So, Pops was back in familiar territory.

He was drunk.

He was obnoxious.

He was Pops.

"Wanna hear s'music? Like music? I got tapes. Lots of tapes. Waddya want listen to. Foreigner? Motley Crue? Aerosmith?"

Before I had even climbed out of bed, I heard Deep Purple's "Smoke on the Water" from Pops' cassette player. Thankfully, the nineteen-seventies era box couldn't go too loud.

As I walked into the room, I saw Pops weaving back and forth, like the final moments of a kid's punching bag after a punch has been thrown. Pops loudly sang along with Deep Purple. He was out of tune and out of time but not out of enthusiasm.

"Hey, Clayton," said Pops, lopsided embarrassed smile on his face, his glasses sitting crookedly. "Sorry 'bout all this. One thing led to another and here I am drunk again. Sorry. How you doing?"

Pops held a brown paper bag containing, undoubtedly, a berry brandy of some kind.

"Fine, Pops," said I, "I'm doing just fine."

I was glad I had told Shiny about Pops and his drinking. Shiny sat transfixed on the couch, staring at Pops, as if he were a zoo animal.

"Sorry, Clayton. Really sorry. Really really sorry. Really really really sorry." Pops laughed, thinking he was being witty, and tried to light a cigarette, not able to get the lighter near the end of his smoke, the flame weaving back and forth in front of his face, flushed with alcohol.

"Not even my fault, though," Pops continued. "The driver guy, Bill, he's in the program with me, it's all his fault. Not mine. See, he and I stopped at a convenience store and I got a coffee and a donut. That's all. It was him that picked up a twelve-pack, just on a lark, neither of us planning on drinking anything until we got off work. Maybe not even then.

"It was about eight o'clock," said Pops, "and that twelve-pack was sitting there on the seat, practically calling our names out loud. We had a little time to kill, so we pulled off into a rest area.

"Bill looked at me and I looked at him. Then we both agreed that one beer wouldn't hurt. Now one part of me knew it was stupid, but that little man on my shoulder was so convincing I didn't know what to do. He just kept telling me to have one beer. So I did what he told me. Course that first beer tasted so good we thought it would be a shame not to follow it with another. And when we'd had two, I remembered that odd numbers are lucky, so we had to have at least one more.

"Pretty quickly, that twelve-pack was gone. Just disappeared. So we drove back to the convenience store and picked up another. By the time we'd finished that one, we would have been late for work. We were probly too drunk to show up anyway, so we stopped and picked up a bottle apricot brandy and bottle of sloe gin. Just drove around. Finished the sloe gin, then Bill dropped me off."

"Not my fault," he muttered. "Bill's one who bought the beer. Not me."

Slumping down on the sofa next to Shiny, Pops laid his head back and, as was often the case, closed his eyes and went to sleep, the blessed unconsciousness of the drunk.

"He'll be passed out for a while," I explained. "I'll walk home with you. I just want to go get that gun, just in case he does wake up. Be right back."

I walked through the kitchen to the bedroom. I opened the bottom drawer and reached down through the sweaters to find the re-

volver. I searched with my hands and found all five bullets, which I placed in my right pants pocket.

I picked up the gun, impressed with its heft. For its miniature size, it was really heavy. I tried shoving the barrel into my waist band, like some liquor store robber, but felt sure the gun would slide down into my underwear and make walking nearly impossible or, worse, go through my boxers and land on the street.

I found the gun fit snugly in my jacket pocket. It then struck me that if Shiny and I had somehow been identified for the Laundromat incident, I wouldn't want to explain carrying a revolver.

Sober, Pops was no great detective; drunk, he had little energy for searches. I took the gun and ammo from my pockets and lifted the stained mattress. Putting them on the floor as far under as I could, I dropped the mattress to cover them.

I grabbed a blanket from the bed and returned to the living room. Lifting Pops' feet, I pivoted his body on his buttocks so that his head fell gently onto the couch and his legs splayed over the armrest. I picked up the blanket, folded it over on itself and covered the unconscious Pops, tucking it under him.

"Welcome to the land of the living dead," I said without emotion.

"Wow," said Shiny just as flatly. For once he was speechless.

I walked into the kitchen, cut off a fist-sized piece of cheese and nestled it into the pocket where the revolver had been two minutes before. Then I filled a plastic bottle with water and shoved it in my other jacket pocket.

"I'd like to give Mister some breakfast, if you don't mind," I said when I got back to the living room. "I kind of promised him."

Shiny said nothing.

We left the apartment and began walking to Shiny's aunt's trailer. Shiny said nothing when we walked down Mister's alley.

I bent down and lifted the lid off Mister's cage and gently placed the cheese inside. Then I removed the water bottle and filled it.

"There you go, Mister. Sorry I didn't have anything for you earlier. I'll try to do better."

Mister nibbled at the cheese, stopping occasionally to look around.

"He's awful cute," said Shiny, almost maternally, reaching down to pet Mister's head. "And he kind of saved us this morning. If you didn't know about this place, that cop would have gotten us."

"I know."

"Why don't you bring him home," Shiny asked, "instead of keeping him in an alley?"

"Pops doesn't like pets and he'd probably just let him go."

Shiny appeared to think about this for a moment.

"So your father's a binge drinker, huh? How long does a binge last?"

"Seems like forever," I said, "but it might be two days or two weeks. He'll just stay drunk until he gets sober, then he'll stay sober until he gets drunk. It's a vicious cycle rolling down the hill.

"I don't want to sound all philosophical or anything," I continued, "but I think people are wrong when they talk about time being like a line. Time is really just a series of now-points and when the now-point I'm in is when Pops is drinking, that particular point is real deep, more like a well I've fallen into."

"I'm sorry," said Shiny.

"It's not your fault."

"I know. I'm still sorry," said Shiny. "I might have a solution for one of your problems, though. Mr. Mouse could come live with me."

"I thought your aunt had a dozen cats," I said. "Wouldn't he drive them and they drive him crazy?"

"She does. But he could live out in the shed, at least until the weather gets cold. That would give us time to think of something else."

I stood up and looked down at Shiny. So this is what friendship feels like, I thought. I reached out and took Shiny's bony little hand.

"Thanks," I said, trying not to sound emotional. "Thanks a lot."

"It's nothing, really."

I picked up the cage and we walked to Shiny's house, again in silence. When we got to the driveway, Shiny stopped and looked at me.

"If that's what drinking does, I'm not ever going to drink. Ever."

"Me neither," I said, and we walked Mister Mouse to his new temporary home, clearing a shelf of paint cans to make room for his cage. Just as we finished, Shiny's aunt joined us.

I looked more closely at her than I had the day I'd first met her. It was clear that she and Shiny were related, because she was as bird skinny as he was and their faces looked similar. Her light brown hair, flecked here and there with gray, was drawn back with a ribbon. Al-

though her face showed her fifty or so years, her wrinkles were more like laugh lines. Pronoia seemed to have agreed with her looks.

"Morning, Clayton. Morning, Sweetie," she said. "What are you boys up to?"

"Morning, Mom," said Shiny with a just discernible oral under-lining of the second word. "Clayton's going to keep his mouse here for a while."

"Why here, instead of inside in your room?"

"On account of because this mouse can't get too warm. This mouse is an Arctic mouse. Clayton got him from an Arctic mouse breeder in Northwest Alaska and he's going to grow to be about two feet long. See, there's not many mouse hunters in that part of Alaska and no natural mouse predators, so the species had a chance to grow to the size that God originally intended.

"By the end of the month," Shiny continued, "Clayton's going to fly this mouse to Prince Edward Island in Canada and release him into the wild. There's another kid who's growing a female mouse, and they're hoping these mice will reproduce and thrive and spread across Eastern Canada."

"Oh, Sebastian. You and your stories," said Aunt Margaret, and then ruffled his hair. "Come on in when you're done. I've got some soup I just made. Clayton, would you like to join us for lunch?"

"No, Ma'am. I need to get going."

I looked down at my shoes.

"That's a shame. Well, some other time. We'd love to have you."

With that, Aunt Margaret left.

"Shiny," I said, "why'd you tell her that crazy story instead of the truth?"

"Well, Aunt Margaret really likes those cats, and I didn't want her to think badly of them, keeping me from getting a mouse."

"Oh," was all I could say.

"Here's my phone number, in case you want to call me or find out about Mister Mouse," said Shiny, scribbling onto a scrap of paper with a pencil stub he'd found in the shed. I took the small piece of paper, folded it twice and put it into my wallet.

I walked back to the apartment, preparing to be nursemaid to a drunk. I thought of a stanza from Reading Gaol.

" Yet each man kills the thing he loves,
By each let this be heard,
Some do it with a bitter look,
Some with a flattering word,
The coward does it with a kiss,
The brave man with a sword! "

"Gallant looks forward to the opportunity to serve his father in his moment of need, hoping that, perhaps, he can help the dear man regain dignity and sobriety sooner rather than later."

"Goofus tries to estimate the best places to put holes in his father, and whether he will need an alibi or not, whether he could possibly be convicted by any jury in the world."

24

Pops stayed drunk for the rest of the weekend, sobering up enough Saturday night to wander out to the liquor store and get enough supply to keep him drunk overnight. He did tone down his drinking by Sunday night, so that while he was hung over Monday, he was still able to go to work, which I took as a good sign. Monday night, Pops went off to his regular AA meeting and came home at eight-thirty, newly convinced of his need for sobriety.

"Clayton," Pops said, "you've got to remember that change is a process, not an event. I just need to keep the plug in the jug and expect miracles. This too shall pass."

Whenever Pops made a new stab at staying sober, his language changed for the first few days, and AA slogans were about all that came from his mouth. Drunk and newly sober, Pops was a talker; if he was silent, it meant he was deep in sobriety. Boring as Pops was when he was getting sober, it was way better than the boredom of when he drank. I felt as though we had dodged a bullet, although a bullet from a weapon that was sure to fire again.

Over the next few weeks, I found life falling into a comfortable rhythm.

Daily, I stopped by Shiny's house, or shed, actually, to see Mister Mouse and drop off a treat or two. Most days Shiny was there, filled with fantastic stories, which I let him tell. I had decided that while Shiny told some stretchers, it was best just to let him go on. Shiny was amusing and liked me, so there was no cause for giving offense. Besides, we were friends.

Pops continued to go to meetings, toning down his preaching over time and finally falling into a peaceful pattern.

* * *

Over Columbus Day weekend, while I was visiting alone with Gramper and Cookie, Pops went on another bender. Based on the empty bottles in the trash, the cigarette butts ground out on the wooden floor and the knocked-over furniture that greeted me, it had been quite a spree. I found Pops on the couch, snoring loudly and reeking of booze.

When Pops came to, at around ten that night, he slowly sat up, his boots banging hard on the wooden floor. With slits for eyes, Pops had dried white spittle in a line leading down his right cheek and into his ear.

"Hey, Clayton," he muttered. "Been sleeping. How's your grandparents?"

"Good, Pops. They're doing real good," I responded. "How're you doing, though?"

Pops continued to stare down at the coffee table, then reached out to light a cigarette. Coughing on the smoke, he poured himself into the back of the couch.

"Had a little slip is all," he said, not looking at me. "Gonna have to change things back to the way they've been going, not the way I took them this weekend.

"By the way," he continued, "I thought I heard a prowler outside this morning. When I looked for our gun, it wasn't in the drawer. You know anything about that?"

"Sure, Pops," I replied, glad that Pops hadn't found the revolver. "I put it under the mattress a while ago. Sorry I didn't tell you."

"Not a problem," Pops said. "I just wanted to make sure it hadn't been stolen is all. For now, what I've got to focus on is stopping this slip before it becomes a slide. It's the first drink that gets you, not the tenth, because without a first you can't have a tenth."

* * *

To his credit, Pops did sober up again. The weeks passed quickly and on Veterans Day weekend, we helped Gramper and Cookie move out of their house and into their new apartment at a complex called Redden Gardens in Plattsfield, next to Mastricola.

It was a nice two-bedroom place on the third floor, with a balcony on which Cookie planned to grow flowers come the spring. Redden Gardens had elevators and an indoor pool and a health club. To me, who had stayed in crummy walk-ups all my life, Redden Gardens was like heaven. I used free weights in the health club. Later, as I swam laps, I thought Gramper and Cookies' invitation to live with them, but I had thrown in my lot with Pops and I wasn't going to take it back. Still, life seemed good in that pool, and even Pops enjoyed the place, although he complained about not fitting in with all the rich people there.

Of course, to Pops rich meant people who paid their bills, or even had bills to pay. Other than rent, Pops had not been extended credit in his life, nor had he ever bothered to ask for it.

* * *

Finally, Thanksgiving break began at noon on Wednesday. The afternoon was given over to parent teacher conferences, but I knew Pops wouldn't go.

I'd only had to make it through four hours, and now I would have four-and-a-half days with Gramper and Cookie; luckily, ninety minutes of the time had been spent in Miss Buonardi's class, where I was a favorite. I stopped by Shiny's shed to say goodbye to Mister Mouse, having saved some cheese from a sandwich.

"Hey, Mister," I said, petting the downy fur on the mouse's head. "I'll miss you. Thanksgiving's tomorrow so I'll be gone a few days, visiting my grandparents. Shiny'll take care of you."

I was amazed how much I loved the little mouse, especially since the animal, other than eating whatever scraps of food he was given, paid almost no attention to me. Still, it was a friendly enough lack of attention and I was used to it.

Shiny wasn't outside, and I always felt squeamish around his aunt, so I walked back to the apartment. I would call Shiny daily to check up on Mister Mouse.

Cookie and Gramper were coming at four. Pops had a chance to get some overtime this afternoon, and then he was getting his umpteenth thirty-day medallion at his regular Wednesday night AA meeting, and had arranged to have one of the guys in the group drive him over after the meeting.

In the bedroom, I packed up a plastic shopping bag with under-wear, toothbrush and comb, along with the khakis and blue shirt Gramper and Cookie had gotten me for graduation, which I had not worn since. I planned to dress nicely for Thanksgiving dinner, like one of those boys in a Sears advertisement. I had hoped to be a good example for Pops.

I only had five stanzas left to go in memorizing "Reading Gaol," so I grabbed the book, planning on finishing up over the weekend, then wrapping it up nicely and giving it to Shiny as a friendship gift.

25

Before I had waited two minutes, the old Buick cruised up, Gramper honking and Cookie waving. I got in the back seat.

"Well, if it isn't the handsomest fifteen-year-old boy I've ever seen," said Cookie, turning her body halfway around to look at me. "I'd swear you've grown even in the last two weeks. So your father's going to come over later?"

"Yep, after tonight's meeting," I said. "How's the new place? Getting all settled in?"

"Well, I'll tell you," said Cookie. "It's very nice, and a lot easier to keep up than the house was. There are a lot of these Indians and Pakistanis in the complex, and they're very nice, keep to themselves, but they're friendly enough. In fact, one woman is going to teach me how to cook curry and I'm going to teach her how to make potato salad.

"And this move has opened us up to some other changes as well," Cookie continued, reaching into her purse. "We're buying a computer for Christmas, and we just bought this."

She pulled a small white cell phone out of her bag and handed it back for me to admire.

"Cool!" I said. Computers and cell phones were things to be dreamed of, not held.

"So, Clayton," asked Gramper, "how are your studies? How is school going?"

"We just got our first report cards and I'm getting all Bs except for an A in English."

"Good, very good," the old man murmured supportively. "Clayton, you should know that it turns out your grandmother and I made a good deal of money when we sold the house, and we'd like nothing better than to spend some of it on college for you."

"Maybe I *will* go to college," I said. "We'll see. But you should meet my English teacher, Miss Buonardi. She's about the best teacher I ever had in my life. She just makes the stuff we read come alive. And she must know more about more things than anybody I ever met.

"And my best friend, Shiny, you should hear the stories he tells. I can't wait for you to meet him. I bet he'll be a famous author someday."

"That's real nice, Clayton," said Cookie. "Glad to see you're get-

ting along."

The rest of the ride to the apartment was very comfortable, with me agreeing mashed potatoes were better with garlic and with the peels left on, and that apple pie without the cheese was like a kiss without the squeeze.

We had a quiet dinner and played gin rummy until ten or so, a talk show out of Boston murmuring on the radio in the background.

"Pops would have liked this. He really likes cards," I said. "He should be here soon."

My grandparents exchanged looks that said more than words could have.

"Yes, well," said Cookie, "he could have been here. I know, though, that the holidays are difficult for your father, any holidays."

"Really, Cookie, he's trying to change. He really is," I defended. "He's been going to his meetings just about every day. He'll be here."

"All I know is what my mother used to tell me, 'If you keep on doing what you've been doing, you'll keep on getting what you've been getting.' I expect you know what I mean, Clayton."

I had a familiar gummed-up feeling inside, as I was yet again putting myself in position to defend the indefensible.

Pops ought to quit drinking. Period.

Pops ought to grow up at the age of forty-two. Period.

Still, I had to admit that simply saying period wouldn't change things.

* * *

I got up at six the next morning, and quickly went to look at the couch, hoping against hope that somehow Pops' ride had just been delayed, but the sofa was empty and untouched. I could try to call Val's Beautette to check on Pops, but it was pretty unlikely even the most dedicated hairdresser worked on Thanksgiving. Anyway, I couldn't really imagine asking Val to go upstairs and find out Pops' sobriety.

I decided worrying wasn't going to make Pops any safer or soberer, so I chose not to rent out any more space in my head to it.

Thanksgiving was my favorite holiday, perhaps because its expectations were so clear and so low. Christmas and birthdays were a life-long disappointment, and every other holiday, with the possible exception of Groundhog and Arbor Day, were simply excuses for Pops to drink.

For Thanksgiving, though, even if he was in the middle of a binge, Pops usually held off on drinking until after dinner. Also, there were no presents for me to not receive. Pops was usually satisfied with checking on the turkey and stealing bites of the side dishes at least until dinner.

Cookie, being both mother and grandmother to me, had created a Thanksgiving family traditions, and I actually looked forward to some of them.

Back when I was a toddler, she had purchased a thick white linen tablecloth and a permanent black marker. Before dinner could be served, each person present had to write down three things for which he or she was thankful, and make a prediction for the upcoming year. Until I entered school, Cookie had written for me, so now each year I could look back and read my history.

When I was two for instance, I was thankful for snow, which had come early that year, Cookie's chestnut stuffing and pecan pie. I predicted that a lot more snow would fall that year, and that I'd get a sled. It did, but I didn't.

Lucinda Watkins had been there for that Thanksgiving, although of course I had no memory of her. As the marker was permanent, Cookie had left what Lucinda had written, or scrawled, actually, as she did not have Pops' fine sense of etiquette about raising a glass of brandy on Thanksgiving morning.

"I am thankful for good music, good food and good times and I predict that over the coming year, things will work themselves out."

I turned three the following August, and by mid-September, Lucinda had worked her way out of our lives by walking out of the door. At the following Thanksgiving, my prediction was that Lucinda would probably come back by Christmas.

At my fourth Thanksgiving, I was thankful for my family, turkey and that Lucinda was gone.

When Pops had mentioned back at the beginning of the school year that Lucinda Watkins might be coming for a visit, I couldn't figure out why she would bother. It had been seven years since we'd seen her, and I figured we could go another seven.

At about noon, Cookie got out the magic markers for writing on

the tablecloth.

"Shouldn't we wait a little longer for Pops?" I asked hopefully. "It's kind of a tradition that we write our Thanksgiving prophecies as a family. He could be on his way right now."

"Well, yes," said Cookie, "he could be, but I doubt it. And it is a tradition, just as calling when you're not going to be someplace on time is a tradition."

I couldn't counter that argument. I wrote that I was thankful for my family, my friendship with Shiny, and Mister Mouse, which gave me a chance to tell them about my pet, swearing them not to tell Pops that I was feeding the animal government cheese, among other choice foods.

After we wrote on the tablecloth, I helped Cookie unpack the Haviland china she had inherited from her grandmother. Kept boxed all year, except for Thanksgiving and Christmas, the china wasn't too badly chipped or damaged. Seeing the gold piping on the plates made me feel special, knowing I would inherit the service, and serve Thanksgiving dinners to my own kids on it some day.

Pops was not there at two, when the turkey had finished cooking. Gramper and Cookie sat at opposite ends of the table, I sat and looked at my plate. The linking generation's chair sat empty, bringing more attention to Pops' absence than his presence ever deserved.

"Gravy's real good, Cookie," I said, once the meal had been served.

"People talk as though gravy's hard to make," said Cookie. "When really all it takes is patience. You'd think it was rocket science to pour off about half the fat, then put the turkey pan over the stovetop burners and gently add and brown flour. You just have to wait until the flour's good and brown before you add some chicken stock steeped with mushrooms, and not those white ones, nice brown mushrooms with a little half and half. That's all there is to it."

I was comforted both by the gravy and by the gravy talk, a speech that Cookie delivered every Thanksgiving when her gravy was complimented. Soon, there would be a friendly debate about the merits of chestnut versus oyster stuffing, with Gramper holding out for the chestnut and me arguing about the texture of the oyster.

Still, my gut ached when I thought about Pops and whether he was all right. This was the first holiday meal I had ever eaten without him.

"Cookie, aren't you concerned about Pops?" I asked.

"Clayton, I long ago stopped worrying about David. They say that God protects fools and drunks, and, for better or worse, your father is a bit of both," she said. "When your father first took off with the carnival, I wrote him off as dead, figured I'd never see him again. I've always thought a person does what he is and he becomes what he does. Your father has become exactly what he has done.

"Clayton," she continued, "listen to and hear my words. The surest way to find unhappiness in this world is to exchange what you really want in life for the sake of what you want right now. Every right now of your father's life that he has chosen to drink, he has traded off what he really wants. At this point, I'm not sure there really is anything he wants, besides his next drink.

"They say that the liver replaces itself with new cells every seven months. The heart replaces its cells every five years and the stomach lining has to completely replace itself every four minutes. The whole body has replaced itself every seven years, which is how long your father was gone with the carnival before he returned with that Lucinda woman. Therefore, he was actually a completely new person, and a person who didn't bear much resemblance to the baby I had held in my arms twenty something years before.

"That person has been replaced by you, Clayton, so, no, I'm not really worried about your father. He died to me a long time ago, only to be resurrected in you. Life is like a taxi, and the meter has been running on your father, even though he never bothered to tell the driver where he wants to go."

"Still, he is my Pops," I said doggedly. "And he seems to be doing better. He's really trying to change. He really is. Until yesterday he hadn't had a drink in more than a month."

"Yes," said Gramper, "well, when it comes to drinking and your father, if you don't want to be lied to about it, don't ask him about it. Lying is a basic part of alcoholism, just as virtue is a basic part of sainthood. They say that if all you've got is a hammer, everything looks like a nail. Well, if the only tool you've got is a bottle, everything is an excuse to drink.

"And, you're right," Gramper continued. "He is a 'Pops,' when he should be a father. With all his talk about 'luck,' he docsn't understand it at all. He's never seen the truth—the harder you work, the more luck you seem to find.

"But enough about that," Gramper concluded gravely. "Clayton, have you thought more about coming to live with us? We'd really like to have you, and I know it would be in your best interest."

"Yeah, I've thought about it, Gramper," I said, "and I just wouldn't feel right about deserting Pops. I know you and Cookie think I should walk out, and there's a part of me that wants a normal life. Somehow, though, I can't leave him, no matter what.

"Could you please pass the oyster stuffing?" I asked, hoping to change the subject.

"Well, you keep on thinking," said Cookie, handing over the stuffing. "The offer's always there."

I served myself gobs of the rich sweet stuffing, used the back of my spoon to make a reservoir, and then filled it with gravy.

"After dinner," I asked softly, "and after we clean up and put everything away, do you suppose I could use the phone and call my friend, Shiny, and have him just go check out the apartment and make sure everything's okay with Pops if he's there?"

"Of course," said Gramper. "Course you can."

"I'll be right back," said Cookie, leaving the table and returning in seconds.

"Clayton," she said haltingly. "Please take this. I was going to give it to you at the end of the weekend, but I guess now is as good a time as any."

She handed me a box about half the size of a Kleenex box, delicately wrapped in pastel blue paper.

"Thanks," I said, tearing at the paper. Inside, I found a cell phone. "Thanks a lot!"

"It's just like ours," said Gramper proudly. "We trust you to be responsible in its use. We just didn't feel right not being able to get in touch with you or you with us. I know your father doesn't manage life well, so it might be best if you didn't tell him about this. You are the responsible one."

"Thanks again," I said, pushing the power button on his new phone and hearing the jingle that showed it was powering up.

"Now don't use up your minutes calling your friend," said Gramper. "Save them for calling us. We've already programmed in our number to speed dial. Just hold down the number 'one' and we'll be on the other end."

Pops still had not been heard from at three, when the last piece of pie had been consumed. I had one piece of pumpkin, just to keep from hurting Cookie's feelings, and two pieces each of the pecan and the apple, the latter with a slab of sharp cheddar cheese.

I helped Cookie with the dishes, hand drying each piece of the China and returning it to its nest, where it would sit for the next four weeks. After Christmas dinner, the dishes would have eleven more months before being called into service again.

At five, I went into my grandparents' bedroom to use the phone there with a little privacy. Reaching into my pants pocket, I got out my black leather wallet and unfolded Shiny's number, then sat down on the double bed to make the call.

"Hello," a woman's voice. Shiny's aunt.

"Hello, Ma'am, this is Clayton. Is Shiny there?"

"You mean Sebastian? No, Dear, he's gone out. May I take a message for him?"

"I guess. Can you ask him to go and check on my apartment, just to make sure everything's okay? Then have him give me a call at my grandparents' house," I gave her the number.

"Thanks a lot, Ma'am."

"No problem, Dear."

I placed the receiver gently back onto the phone, and sat staring at the wall for a good two minutes. While I wasn't even close to asleep, my old friends the letters paid me a quick visit, organized into a message of some sort, although I couldn't understand it:

F A L L I N G I N P L A C E
O R
F A L L I N G T O P I E C E S

26

I returned to the kitchen and sat at the table.

"Did you reach your friend?" Gramper asked.

"Not exactly. He lives with his aunt and I got her instead. I left a message."

Gramper sat down at the table across from me and reached out his hands to gently cover mine.

"Clayton, can I tell you a story?"

"Sure, Gramper. What's it about?"

"Just listen and then you tell me what it's about," said Gramper. "It seems that a long, long time ago, a very rich man went to a wizard and asked him to write down words that could encourage the prosperity and happiness of his family for years to come. On a large piece of leather, the wizard wrote down six words."

"What were they?" I asked.

"'Father dies. Son dies. Grandson dies.'"

"Huh?" I said.

"That's just what the rich man said," replied Gramper, "although he was a bit angrier and said, 'I told you to write down something that would bring happiness and prosperity to my family and you write this depressing message. What's wrong with you?'"

"The wizard looked at the rich man and said, 'If your son dies before you, that would bring terrible grief to your family. If your grandson should die before your son, that too would be unbearable. If, instead, your family disappears in the order I have listed, you will be living in the natural course of life. That, indeed, is true happiness and prosperity.'"

"I don't get it," I said, puzzled. "I mean, I understand the story, but why are you telling it to me?"

"Because, your life is not being lived in the natural course."

"What do you mean?" asked I. "Nobody's died or anything."

"No," agreed Gramper, "but you are now worried about your father. The normal course is for a father to worry about a son, not the reverse. You deserve, at your age, to be the one worried about, the one taken care of, the one making mistakes to learn from. That's why your grandmother and I want you to live here, so that you can return to the normal course of life."

"I appreciate it," I said. "I really do. It's just that I feel like I need to be where I'm needed, and that's with Pops. Once he licks this drinking thing then things will get better. They have to."

"Clayton, I have waited twenty-five years for this 'drinking thing' to be cured, but I think your father doesn't have an identity outside of alcohol. A great painter defines himself by his art. A great carpenter defines himself by the houses he makes. Whether he's drunk or trying to get sober, your father has spent his entire adult life defining himself in terms of booze. It may be that he's become nothing more than a way of measuring alcohol."

"Much as it pains me to say it," said Gramper, "your father may be an alcohol zombie, careening through life with no purpose other than to drink or not drink. Like the zombies in movies, he cares not a whit for anyone else. He's just waiting to fall into an open grave. While many men see drinking as a pause from thinking, I believe your father may see thinking as a pause from drinking."

"That's kind of morbid, Gramper."

"I know, Clayton, but it's also accurate, as you of all people can best attest. Just keep our offer in mind. That's all I'm asking."

"I will," I said. "I promise."

The telephone rang and Gramper rose to answer it.

"Hello," he said. "Hold on. He's right here."

Gramper handed the phone to me.

It was Shiny, of course.

"I went and checked on your father and you might want to come back here as soon as you can."

"Why?" I asked. "What's wrong?"

"I don't know if anything's wrong, but your dad and your mom are drinking a pretty lot."

"*She's* there?"

"Who? Who's there?" asked Gramper from behind me.

"Some lady who's helping take care of Pops," I said, feeling guilty about lying, but not wanting to talk about Lucinda.

"I'll say she's some lady," said Shiny into his ear. "She's kind of crazy, but a lot of fun. She's even got your dad dancing with her. They asked me to come back after I called you."

"Can you kind of keep an eye on things, until I get there? Please?" I asked.

"Sure. I'll keep an eye out. I'll even keep an ear on things," replied Shiny. "But I'm not going to use my nose, on account of because they both kind of smell."

"That's great. I'll be there in an hour or so."

I hung up the phone to find both Cookie and Gramper staring at me.

"Pops needs me," I lied. "He's feeling awful sick. I know I'd planned to stay the weekend, but please can you take me to him? Please?"

"Clayton," said Cookie calmly, "for your sake, of course we will, but don't you think rushing home because he's drunk—"

"He's sick," I responded.

"Sick, then," she continued. "Doesn't that just teach him that when he messes up you will always be there to help pick up the pieces?"

"I don't know what it teaches," I said. "I just know that he needs me now."

"As we were discussing earlier," said Gramper, "the normal course of life is that a father rushes home to take care of his sick child. Not vice-versa. Regardless, get your things and we'll drive you to Oxford."

The ride to Oxford was taken in silence, me feeling the loving disapproval of my grandparents. When we pulled up in front of twenty-seven-and-a-half Main Street, Cookie turned around and looked at me.

"Clayton," she said, "just because you're born some place doesn't mean you have to die there. Your father has chosen death on the installment plan, one drink after another. You don't have to watch him."

"I know, Cookie," I said. "I know."

I leaned forward to kiss Cookie's cheek, then got out of the car and walked forward to the driver's side, leaning in to hug Gramper around the neck.

"I love you guys so much," I said, a few tears falling despite myself.

"And we love you," said Cookie.

I walked to the staircase. As I climbed the steps, I oddly had the feeling of going down rather than up. Halfway up, I heard music and loud conversation. Although it was downright cold outside, now that the sun had gone down, the windows were open. From the steps, I could hear the "Flashdance" soundtrack playing a number by some band called Cycle V doing "Seduce Me Tonight." I had misheard the song when I was little as "So Juicy Tonight" and assumed it was a song about getting drunk.

I braced myself and opened the door.

Pops sat sprawled on the sofa, a glass of some thick green liqueur in his hand. His eyes had the electric glaze that I knew signaled this drink would not be Pops' last.

"Hey, Buddy. How's the old camper?" Pops asked.

Shiny sat next to Pops, a drink in front of him.

"You ought to try this stuff, Clayton," Shiny said. "It's pretty good once you get used to it. C'mon drink up. Be a man."

"Shiny, your aunt will kill you," I said.

"My aunt?" asked Shiny. "Oh, you mean my mom."

Shiny took a long drink.

"You really believed that stuff I said?" he asked. "What's wrong with you?"

"I didn't believe everything," I said, "but I believed what you told me about your mother."

"Well, it was all a load of crap," he said. "Just stuff I made up."

"Stella the dog?" I asked. "The schools? Perpetual motion?"

"Crap, crap and more crap," he said. "the private school I go to is for so-called emotionally disturbed kids. I can't believe you bought that stuff. You are so naïve."

"Shiny," I said, crying. "Please leave. Just get out."

"Maybe it'd be best," said Pops. "Give Clayton a chance to sort things out. Spend time with his mother."

Shiny stood up to leave.

"I'll see you around, then," he said.

"No," I said. "You won't."

When he left, I turned to Pops.

"I thought you were working overtime, then getting a ride over. What happened?"

"Well, I got to work a few minutes late," said Pops, "and the boss man, Jason, decided to act like a pissant. Got all in my face. Called me lazy. Called me a thief, just for taking chicken home. Like everyone else there doesn't do it. Just my luck to have a punk boss."

"Well, Clayton, a man can only take so much, and then he reaches a tipping point. I told Jason he can take that job and shove it, just like the old Johnny Paycheck song. Made me feel good. Then I came home to quite a surprise."

I heard the toilet flush, then movement in the kitchen. An aging, overweight woman who looked as if she'd been rode hard and put up wet came into the room. Her graying hair was teased straight up and her nose showed the bright red glow of broken blood vessels.

"Mommy," I thought. "How nice. A fresh slice of hell for me."

"Hi, Sweetie!" Lucinda Watkins said, smiling ghoulishly. "How was your Thanksgiving dinner?"

"Why are you here?" I asked, feeling fight or flight instincts battling within me.

"Is that any way to greet your mother?" Lucinda Watkins asked, appearing genuinely hurt. "After all, it's been a long time. Come here and give your old mom a kiss."

I didn't move. I stared at the woman who had borne me.

"Go give your mother a kiss," Pops ordered and took a long sip of the green potion. "Sorry 'bout the change in our Thanksgiving plans, Clayton."

I didn't move, so Lucinda Watkins came to me and kissed me on the head.

"Thinking that she's my mother just because she had me," I said, "is like thinking you're a pianist just because you own a piano. Saying doesn't make it so. It was easy enough for her to *become* a mother, but she never really learned to be one."

"David and I decided it would be nice to have just a private Thanksgiving this year, the two of us," said Lucinda, appearing to ignore my comments. "And now I've got my son here to finish up the day."

I felt revulsion at that word coming out of this woman's mouth.

"We are *not* a family," I said surely. "The last time I saw you was when I was too little to protect myself. You hit me and then you ran away. It may be your womb that carried me for nine months, but I've been pretty much free of you since then. I don't have any desire to change that now."

"Now Clayton," said Pops, sitting sluggishly forward. "There's no need to be so rude to your mother. And this is the first time I've heard about any hitting. What are you talking about?"

"David, he's just trying to get you mad," lied Lucinda. "Oughtta get'm drunk. Loosen'm up little, the little priss."

"Hey," I heard Pops' voice, maybe coming to his rescue. "That's my boy you're talking 'bout."

Here Pops paused to take a slurping sip of booze.

"Oh NOOOOO he's not," Lucinda cried, delivering the phrase

as if the two of them had been playing around with it for a while. She laughed hard, joined by Pops.

"That's right," said Pops. "I forgot that part."

"He made the whole story up. Just like the stories he made up about you. After all, you can't trust a boy who throws away letters between adults"

Lucinda took three steps toward Pops and placed her hand gently on his shoulder.

"The last time she came to visit, Pops," I said, "when she left she also left a note for you on the counter. It had a lot of mean and hurtful things and lies in it, and I knew you were upset about her leaving, so I kind of threw the note away."

"You're little sneak," hissed Lucinda. "How dare you destroy private correspondence. And now you falsely accuse me of hurting you. As if we can believe a word of what a liar like you says."

"I don't lie," I said in a firm voice.

"Like hell you don't," spat Lucinda. "You're a liar and a sneak and, just like I said seven years ago, your father should have given you up to the state, if even they would have taken you!"

"Lucinda. Clayton," said Pops, trying to discover a drunken order in the conversation. "Nobody's giving anyone away. Let's just act like a family, can't we?"

"Pops, I know you're drinking," I said, "but have you gone crazy, too? She's walked out twice before and, just because she shows up here with a bottle of booze, you're trying to act like she's human. Let's just forget about her and go off with Gramper and Cookie. You can stop drinking right now and keep going to meetings. Get sobered up and stay sobered up."

"Huh!" said Lucinda. "Like those stupid meetings ever did anyone any good. I've been through the whole AA racket, court-ordered and on my own. Bunch of religious creeps, if you ask me. Drinking is nothing more than a pastime, a hobby, and if goody-two-shoes like you would just leave your father alone about it, maybe he wouldn't drink so much.

"And as for your precious 'Gramper' and 'Cookie,' they're judgmental old hypocrites who never gave me a chance," Lucinda continued angrily. "When they looked at me and your father, they saw two pieces of trash, smelly trash at that. I think if I'd just aborted you in the womb and stayed a carny with your dad, we could have had a nice life for ourselves."

"Instead," she continued, "I interrupted my career in entertainment for you, for those important first three years of your life."

"That's a funny thing," I said, my voice remaining calm and firm. "We had a career day at school last spring, but I must have missed the table for drunken carnival sluts."

Lucinda walked the three steps from Pops' shoulder in a flash and, once again, raised her hand and slapped me hard across the face.

"I tried to be nice to you," she spat out, "but it didn't work. Somehow, you've turned yourself into a monster. The only thing you understand is pain and punishment."

"Simply seeing you here is enough of that for me," I said, and turned and left the room.

In the bedroom, I lifted the mattress and pulled out the revolver and the five bullets.

"Goofus loads the gun with all the bullets and storms into the living room, where he fires five quick shots into the carnival tramp's midsection, then watches her bleed to death as quickly as humanly possible. He then puts the still smoking gun on the coffee table, and says to his father, 'I'm out of here, Pops. Just can't take it any more.'"

"Gallant wants to protect his father and his poor, misguided mother from what they might do to themselves or each other. He carefully packs the gun and ammunition in the plastic bag, glad to be able to help."

Once I had shoved the revolver and ammo into my pocket, I walked back into the living room and picked my bag.

"Pops, I'm going out. Are you going to stay here with that creature?"

Pops looked me in the belt buckle and shrugged his shoulders, holding his hands out as if to say, "what choice do I have?"

"Okay," I said sadly. "Maybe I'll see you later."

"Well, it better be with a better attitude," snarled Lucinda. "There's going to be some changes made now that I'm here, even if it's just for a visit."

"That's all it better be," I said, and left them.

Walking down the stairs, I could hear Pops and Lucinda laughing loudly, maybe at me, maybe at something else, definitely at something not funny.

Standing there at the bottom of the stairs and at the bottom of

Rota Fortuna, I remembered something Cookie had said.

"If you keep on doing what you've been doing, you'll keep on getting what you've been getting."

She had been talking about Pops and his drinking, but I used the same logic on myself. All my life I had denied myself the right to be a normal, regular kid to stay with Pops, believing Pops sober was the real Pops.

Now, the ice broke in my mind and I watched the car sink to the bottom of the lake

Pops was who he was, but I didn't need to go on being who I had been. I could recreate myself, or, more accurately, I could become who I wanted to be simply by changing what I did.

Unsure of myself, but at the same time completely certain about what I would do, I walked back up the stairs. At the top, I pulled out the revolver and the bullets. Quietly lifting the wooden top of the mailbox, I placed the bullets inside, and closed the lid. I took the revolver and slid the trigger finger guard down the length of the flag-pole. It was a nice picture, I thought, as I turned and walked down the steps away from Pops, away from Lucinda and away from Shiny.

When I got away from the apartment, I reached into my pocket and got out my phone. Holding down the 'one' button, I listened as the connection was made with my grandparents.

"Hi, Sweetie," Cookie's voice answered.

"I'm ready to come home, Cookie."

"But we just dropped you off."

"No," said I. "Not here. My real home."

"We'll be there in ten minutes."

I gave them directions to where I would be.

As promised, ten minutes later, Gramper and Cookie pulled up, and I climbed into the back seat, a glass box on my lap.

"Once Rota Fortuna takes you to the bottom," I thought, "there's no place left but up."

It was dark and the moon had appeared itself in the sky. It smiled down on me as Mister Mouse looked up at me.

AFTERWARD

The air was a little cool for a June night, but that helped carry the smell of the lilacs, my favorite smell in the world. I know lilac bushes are ugly most of the year, but from mid-May until mid-June, they're beautiful. Cookie kept cuttings from them throughout the apartment because they carried the promise of summer. She said it was good luck to step on fallen lilac petals, because "grace is the smell the lilac leaves on the shoe that crushes it."

I looked in the mirror and adjusted my floral-print tie, which Gramper had shown me how to tie that afternoon. I was happy with the way I looked. Freshly shaved, with a razor I had been given at Christmas, I also had a two-day old haircut. I looked at an image of a happy boy, which made me happy.

Cookie and Gramper were already dressed and waiting in the living room. Still, I lingered, unbuttoning my shirt to put on more deodorant, spraying more cologne than I needed, experimenting with a part on the right instead of the left.

"Clayton," Cookie called, "We've really got to get going if we're going to walk. It's such a nice night, I don't want to have to take the car."

"Coming, Cookie."

I entered the living room and Gramper let out a long, low whistle.

"You clean up real nice, Clayton," he said, walking over to inspect my tie job. "I don't know that I've ever seen a handsomer boy. Except me at your age, of course."

"Of course, Gramper. Of course."

"Now you two handsome men stand together and I'll get a picture of you. I'll send it in to Gentleman's Quarterly and you'll both be famous."

I smiled.

"Not bad photographs," she said.

"How could they be with subjects like us?" said Gramper.

I had received another nice email from Miss Buonardi, or Eleanor, now that she wasn't my teacher. She had been very positive about a piece I'd sent her, saying "it reads like a tale told over a campfire."

Walking the three-quarters of a mile to Plattsfield High School, I was sandwiched by Gramper on one side and Cookie, holding my hand, on the other. Although her hand was old, Cookie's skin still felt soft and comforting touching me.

As we got closer to the school, we found other families walking to the awards ceremony, second only to graduation as a social function in the small town. Although I was not the most popular student, I had worked on the yearbook for the seven months I'd been in Platts-field and had made friends with the rest of the staff. For the first time in my life, I had a gang that I hung with, that thought I was okay, that liked me.

"Hey, Clay. Waddya ya say?" called out Phil, one of them.

"I haven't seen you since early May," I responded in a call and response game we had made up. "Hey Phil. You feeling ill?"

"Not since the doctor gave me that pill," Phil said.

Phil was wearing a white shirt and a red tie, with a blue blazer, un-buttoned. The sort of boy who always knew the latest jokes, he had been my mentor, encouraging me to write captions for the yearbook pictures, and submit stories to the school newspaper.

"Evening, Mr. and Mrs. Clevinger," he said. "I'm meeting my parents at the ceremony, because my little sister was being a pain about having to wear a dress. I figured I'd skip the fight and get some exercise."

"That's one nice thing about being an only child," I said. "I don't have any brother or sister holding me back. There's just the three of us and we can do as we please."

Since my friends thought my parents were dead, I hadn't men-tioned the April phone call, collect, from Pops in Tulsa. He was drunk and crying. Lucinda had left him again, and he'd signed on for the season with Hutchinson's Carnival. When he said he missed me, I hung up. Luck hadn't skipped a generation in our family, but paternity had.

"So, Phil," said Cookie, "what are your plans for the summer? Doing anything exciting?"

"I've got a job painting houses with my cousin, and I'm plan-ning a week-long canoe trip with him up north in the Connecticut Lakes," he said. "Hey, Clay, do you like canoes?"

"I guess," I said. "I mean, I haven't spent a lot of time on water, but I do like being outdoors and all."

"You should think about joining us. First week in August. It's going to be great."

"I will. I will think about it," I said. I'd never been asked to go away with someone.

Arriving at school, Phil saw his parents and sister and went to join them. Cookie, Gramper and I wandered into the gym, still decorated from the prom held the previous weekend. As the theme had been "Bright Lights, Big City," the gym was decorated to look like New York in the nineteen forties.

"Clay! Over here."

I looked and saw Becky Goldman, who had been in my English class and on the yearbook committee. While we had joked around a few times, I hadn't really gotten to know her well and was pleasantly surprised that she would call out to me. Becky was usually quiet, but she could be funny and had a very pretty smile.

"Let's go over here, guys," I said.

"Becky Goldman, this is my grandfather, Joseph Clevinger and my grandmother, Cookie. Cookie and Gramper, this is Becky."

"It's very nice to meet you, Becky," said Cookie with a smile.

Becky introduced her parents, and then I sat down next to her, with Cookie on my right, and Gramper next to her.

"These things are usually so boring I can't stand them," I leaned over and whispered to Becky, "but sitting next to you makes even this special."

"Why, Clay Clevinger! I didn't know you were such a flirt!"

I had never thought of myself as a flirt.

* * *

"And now," said the principal, "I'd like to present the author of the best short story submitted to the school literary magazine. For a variety of reasons, this award usually goes to a senior. This year, though, the committee was unanimous in its selection of a winner. I would like to ask him to come up and read his short story. Breaking with tradition, this year's winner is a freshman and his name is Clay Clevinger. Clay, would you please come up here?"

I was surprised. I walked up to the front of the auditorium and picked up the manuscript I had submitted the month before. As a freshman, of course, I had not expected to win.

Clearing my throat, I read in a clear, loud voice.

"Joshua Mapleton was a boy for whom the phrase 'used to it' may have been invented. He had long ago accepted the universal truth that if you live with anything long enough, it starts to feel normal."

That will do.

Keith Howard is a writer, educator, nonprofit leader and drunk. Keith has published short stories and essays on topics ranging from baseball to education to adoption to politics. *On Account of Because* is his first published novel. He began his career as a print journalist, writing straight news, features and a humor column, then moved into radio and theater.

For eight years, he directed and acted with the Clearway Improvisational Theater, which performed before more than 100,000 people nationwide. He is comfortable as a public speaker and has numerous appearances to his credit.

From 1988 until 2004, Keith ran alternative high schools, until leaving education to pursue a writing career. He holds a master's degree in educational administration and is certified as a school principal, reading specialist, English teacher and elementary teacher.

In the previous paragraph the phrase "pursue a writing career" is code for "finally started drinking the way he wanted, culminating in homelessness, despair and a taste for stolen dollar-store mouthwash." Keith got off the streets and into recovery in 2007.

From 2012 until 2017, Keith was executive director of Liberty House in Manchester, NH. There he worked with formerly homeless veterans, brought in a significant amount of money and won PR battles with the universe.

Today, Keith lives in a tiny white box in the Great North Woods on the property of 45 North, a retreat center for veterans to which all profits from this book will be donated. He is working on a memoir, a novel and keeping warm.

Keith can be reached at keithhoward@gmail.com

www.ingramcontent.com/pod-product-compliance
Lightning Source LLC
Chambersburg PA
CBHW060312260626
47160CB00007B/2581